KU-063-068

Amelia Mandeville has been creating stories and characters in her head ever since she can remember. When there became too many, she started to write them down. Now twenty-one, Amelia is the debut author of *Every Colour of You*. Besides getting lost in the stories she's written, Amelia spends her time attempting to bake, dyeing her hair and vlogging for the YouTube channel she shares with her sister, Grace – the aptly named The Mandeville Sisters.

CUMBRIA LIBRARIES

3800305076141 0

County Council

Libraries, books and more.........

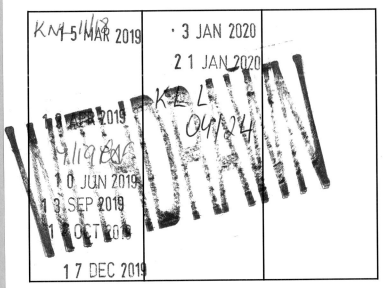

KM 5/1/18 15 MAR 2019 · 3 JAN 2020

2 1 JAN 2020

K L L

04/24

1 APR 2019

9/19

1 0 JUN 2019

1 3 SEP 2019

1 OCT 2019

1 7 DEC 2019

Please return/renew this item by the last date due.
Library items may also be renewed by phone on
030 33 33 1234 (24 hours) or via our website

www.cumbria.gov.uk/libraries

Cumbria Libraries

Interactive Catalogue

Ask for a CLIC password

Amelia Mandeville

every colour of you

sphere

SPHERE

First published in Great Britain in 2018 by Sphere

1 3 5 7 9 10 8 6 4 2

Copyright © Amelia Mandeville 2018

Lyrics on p. 265 from 'Mr Brightside' by The Killers. Lyrics © by Mark August
Stoermer, Brandon Flowers, Ronnie Vannucci Jr and Dave Brent Keuning.
Lyrics on p. 266 from 'Motorcycle Emptiness' by The Manic Street Preachers. Lyrics
© Polow da Don, James Dean Bradfield and Richey Edwards.
Lyrics on p. 268 from 'Where is my Mind?' by Pixies. Lyrics © Charles Thompson.

The moral right of the author has been asserted.

*All characters and events in this publication, other than those
clearly in the public domain, are fictitious and any resemblance
to real persons, living or dead, is purely coincidental.*

All rights reserved.
No part of this publication may be reproduced, stored in a
retrieval system, or transmitted, in any form or by any means, without
the prior permission in writing of the publisher, nor be otherwise circulated
in any form of binding or cover other than that in which it is published
and without a similar condition including this condition
being imposed on the subsequent purchaser.

A CIP catalogue record for this book
is available from the British Library.

Hardback ISBN 978-0-7515-7169-1
Trade Paperback ISBN 978-0-7515-7170-7

Typeset in Sabon by M Rules
Printed and bound in Great Britain by
Clays Ltd, Elcograf S.p.A.

Papers used by Sphere are from well-managed forests
and other responsible sources.

Sphere
An imprint of
Little, Brown Book Group
Carmelite House
50 Victoria Embankment
London EC4Y 0DZ

An Hachette UK Company
www.hachette.co.uk

www.littlebrown.co.uk

This book is for those who need
more colour in their life

And for my lovely mum x

We had a story, short, but not a simple one. I wouldn't be able to stay here and explain it all to you. If you really want to know, you'll have to take time out of your day. You'll have to read it.

Chapter 1

Tristan

I turn towards Lucy. I'm having to look down at her because she's about five foot nothing. Lucy is pretty, so I can only imagine how pretty she looks when she's out of the nurse's uniform. She stops by the door, opens it and stares up at me. 'You got everything?' she says. 'These past few weeks have gone so quickly. It feels like just yesterday we were celebrating your birthday.'

I feel my forehead crease. I wish she wouldn't remind me of my age. It's safe to say that turning twenty-two here was not a personal highlight. How many twenty-two-year-olds are in a situation like mine?

I was allowed out on my birthday. Luke and I went to Winter Wonderland. It's something we used to do every year, with Dad – that's what happens when you have a December birthday. It was okay, if a bit strange. I grew out of it, years ago.

But today, I don't know how I feel about leaving. This time, I won't be coming back. I've had my assessment – Luke and I had a meeting with Dr Lawn a couple of days ago – so it's real, and has been for a couple of days; but somehow it's only just hit me, and now I feel strange. I don't like it.

'We're going to miss you,' Lucy says with another soft smile.

I wonder how many times she has said that to the other mentally unstable dickheads like me. 'Yeah,' I reply. I'm not going to say, 'I'll miss you, too' because, honestly, I won't. She was a good nurse, but that was her job. And now she will be a good nurse to the next guy. She's getting paid for this shit.

'You've done so well, Tristan, we're proud of you,' she says, reaching up and placing a hand on my shoulder. I look at her hand as she holds it there. I'm not proud. I haven't changed. The only way that I'm different now is that I've learned the way to do things, the right things to say, the right way to act. I've got the hang of the game. Yes, I am cheating, but if it means I win, it's okay, isn't it?

And it's not that I've given up; leaving this place doesn't mean I'm going to jump off a bridge. This place might not have fixed me, but I still want to try to change. In fact, I'm *going* to change. I'm going to change for Luke, for Dad, maybe even for the people here, like Lucy, too. But I don't want to be in this place any more. I *can't* be in this place any more.

Lucy's attention is diverted at the sound of an alarm. It's coming from her waistband, where a small plastic device is flashing. Her pager. 'Shit,' she mutters as she looks down at it to see which room is calling for her help. 'Not again.' She looks at the door in front of us that leads towards reception, which she'd just started to open, then back at me, then at her fob, and then at me again. 'I bet that's Russ. Okay, I've got to run, Tristan,' she says, already heading back the way we came, down the corridor to the ward. 'I will be back, I promise. Just stay here.' She motions to the plastic seats lining the wall.

'But I've got to—'

'I'll be right back to sign you out. I promise. I just really need to help with this,' she says, as the door in front of me swings shut again. My freedom being slammed in my face.

There's no point arguing. I nod my head.

So with one more smile, Lucy legs it down the corridor to help restrain whichever poor sod is losing it right now.

I turn back towards the door in front of me, and my stomach jolts as I notice a green light. The door didn't lock this time. Lucy didn't fully close it. And now that the option is there, it's tempting. I can get to the reception by myself, can't I? The decision to send me home has been made and it's not like I need to be chaperoned. I don't need to be looked after.

I look back to the green light again. What does green mean? Surely green means good, as in, *Good idea, Tristan*. No, wait – green means *go*.

Chapter 2

Zoe

Let's play a game. How many differences can we find between a private hospital and an NHS hospital? According to Jerry, the reason he pays for private health care is because of the *major differences*. It's all about the differences, Zoe, he says, they could be life-saving.

Personally, I didn't notice the differences last time I was here. Or the time before that. Or the time before *that*. So concentrate this time, Zoe. Really concentrate!

I walk through the doors. (Revolving doors, might I add. Do they have revolving doors in NHS hospitals? Probably.) I stride through the usual bustle of people in the waiting room and inhale the same sterile smell that always burns my nose. My phone pings; I know without looking it'll be Jerry – eyeroll time – checking I'm okay again. It was all I could do to stop him coming with me.

I glide up to the outpatient's desk, leaning my arms on

the table, before beaming a toothy smile at the receptionist. She doesn't smile back. Reception desk, leaflets, moody
lady – the NHS have these too, you know.

'Yes?' the receptionist says, her lips still pursed tight.

Okay. A smile doesn't hurt anybody, lady.

'I have a reason to be here,' I say. I don't say why, and
I don't say who I'm seeing, nor do I say what my name
is. Let's see if she can work it out from my very vague
sentence. Because maybe the *private* factor is that the
receptionists are mind readers. Now that would be worth
paying extra for.

'And that is?' the lady replies with an exaggerated sigh.

Okay, she's not a mind reader. Slightly disappointed, but
good to get it clarified early.

I form another smile, sickly sweet this time. 'My name
is Zoe Miller, and I'm here to see my—'

'Are you in the system?' She cuts me off as her eyes move
to her computer.

'Erm … yeah, I guess so, but last time I just told them
my name and—'

'I need to check you're on the system first.'

Jesus. She won't let me get a word in edgeways. 'Okay,'
I start, 'but I'm pretty sure I go to floor three. I always do,
and I'm here quite a lot—'

'Madam, as I was saying, I need to check you're on
the system first.' Did she just call me *madam*? She gives
me a wad of paper and a pen. 'In the meantime, fill this
in,' she says.

I look down at the paper, it's some standard new patient form. 'I don't think I need to fill this in. I'm seeing—'

'Madam,' she says, cutting me off again. Since when have I been a madam? 'Take a seat and I'll call you.'

She turns away and I lower my eyebrows in defeat. I'm not one for conflict, so I sigh, turn around, walk towards the waiting area and sit down next to some twitchy bald guy.

I look at the form and start writing my name, but I know it's pointless. So I drop the form on the floor, ungracefully flick off my flip-flops, cross my legs, and then throw a smile at the twitching guy. It's safe to say he has other things on his mind. Bless him.

I glance around. So this is the waiting room of a private hospital, eh? I never pay much attention when I'm here, as I usually glide on upstairs, but I have to say it is a lot quieter, calmer and cleaner than other hospitals I've been to. I shuffle my bum in the seat. Hmmm. The seats are pretty comfortable, too. Okay, private hospital, I'll give you that, you have comfy seats. But still, these aren't life-changing differences, for sure. What is Jerry chatting about? Jerry is my dad, by the way. I call him Jerry because, well, it's his name – and I like to keep things simple in life. I rarely call him 'Dad' because that would just confuse things. So, Jerry it is.

I'm still scanning the waiting room, trying to find the thing that makes it extra special, when, boom. Pow. Whack. I find it.

A coffee machine.

Yes, people, there's a coffee machine in this waiting room – a fancy barista-style one, no less. Move over Starbucks, private health care has got our backs. I'm not entirely sure why I'm getting so excited about this when I don't even drink coffee any more. But still, my past inner-coffee-addict is jumping up and down. *Flat white, please. In fact, let's add an extra shot to that.*

Resisting that dark, velvety espresso-urge inside me, I turn my eyes back to the receptionist, wondering when she is going to call me. I know for a fact that I'm not supposed to be chilling here, and I'm so bored that I have now entered into a staring contest with her. She's staring at her computer, I'm staring at her – which of us will blink first? Well, my friends, only time will tell. And I'll let you in on a secret: I'm amazing at staring competitions. Call me cocky, but I always win. And you know what? It was going pretty well until some guy walked in front of the desk, blocking my line of sight. The unexpected movement distracts me, getting me all flustered, and I blink. Great. Thanks for ruining the game, man. I was only going to win. No big deal.

The guy turns, his eyes narrowed, towards the nurse who led him in, like he's unsure of himself. Or maybe he needs glasses. 'Thanks,' he mumbles. 'I'm sorry ... I just ... I got lost.'

'No problem,' the nurse says with a kind smile, before walking away.

I shuffle on to the seat next to me to get back my view of the receptionist. She is typing away on her computer but once she sees the guy standing in front of her she lifts her head up and smiles. Yes, I said that right, people, she smiles at this random boy. Well, I feel slightly offended now.

'One minute, hon,' she says.

Hon? Seriously? I get madam, and he gets hon. Not fair. The guy looks nervously around the waiting room, his eyes scanning from face to face, door to door. I think he's looking for someone, and the longer he searches, the more panicked he's seeming to get. He quickly turns back to the lady at reception. She's focused on her computer screen, and it looks like he wants to say something, but then he whips his head back to us coffee-lovers in the waiting room. I can practically see his chest pumping underneath his ragged, grey denim jacket. He glances back at the receptionist one last time before hesitantly shuffling away and slumping himself down in one of the chairs opposite me.

I watch him as he continues to survey the room. He's definitely looking for someone, and getting impatient with it as well.

He's an odd-looking one. I'm not saying he's the worst-looking, but he's not typically beautiful either. He has a very distinctive face. I'd say he's probably about my age, maybe older, with dark hair and dark eyes to match his clothes. Hmm, nothing like a bit of colour, hey? He looks like the love child of Green Day and Nirvana. Stick some eyeliner on him and he'll be an American Idiot. Wait. *Is* he wearing eyeliner? I squint at his face. No. I think he just has rather impressive eyelashes, and if that's the case, I'm jealous. Though I'm definitely not jealous of this dude's eye bags; he looks a whole other level of tired. Maybe he's older than I thought, because how can a twenty-year-old have bags like that? He looks like he hasn't been outside in a while either. All in all, he looks a little bit ill. Maybe he's a vampire, because his sweaty white skin seems to be shivering under the white hospital lights.

As I cup my head in my hands and continue to watch him, I exhale a happy sigh. I love people-watching. I can't work out what sort of guy he is. I wouldn't say he's purposely trying to be punk rock, more like his genes have just made him fall into that sort of category. His hair might be dark, but I highly doubt it's dyed.

A plump woman, who reminds me of an overgrown peach, shuffles her way past me, reeking of smoke, and sits herself down to Mr Billie Joe Armstrong Jr. She smiles at him, he tries to smile back, but his mouth gets twisted on his face. It looks painful. He glances around at the spare seats, probably wondering why she chose to sit right next to him. Then the woman looks over at the desk and stands up, placing her handbag on the seat.

'Will you watch my bag for me, dear?' she says to him. He got a *hon* earlier and a *dear* now, lucky boy.

9

Mr Eyeliner forces a short uncomfortable nod, and his eyes stay glued to her as she shuffles her way up to the desk again. He's gripping on to either side of his chair, and his foot is tapping on the floor. This guy needs to calm down, it's only a handbag. Have some herbal tea or something, I'm sure it's on offer here.

Mr Eyeliner slowly and carefully moves his eyes from the woman waiting at the desk towards her bag. Oh, now things are getting interesting. Get the popcorn out. As he glances back to the lady, he swiftly slips his hand in her bag. He rummages for a few seconds before taking out a packet of cigarettes and a lighter. He looks down, analysing them, and must be content with his findings because he shoves them into his pocket. His eyes quickly dart around the room to check that no one saw him.

But, oh.

His eyes catch mine and his face falls.

Yes, dude. I saw what you did there. I caught you red-handed. As he stares at me, I can't help but feel my mouth turn up at the corners. I start smiling. I'm evil, I know, but I continue to smile as the lady sits back down next to him. He doesn't let his eyes leave me.

'Thanks, love,' the lady says, moving the bag back on to her lap. He shuffles in his chair in response, not letting his eyes stray from mine. I stick my tongue out at him. He registers it – his mouth tightens and his eyebrows lowers – but he doesn't seem to know how to react. So I cross my eyes. But again he just exhales and sits up straighter in his chair.

Ooh. Wait till you see my monkey impression, friend. Things are going to get fun here.

Chapter 3

Tristan

I decided I could find my own way to the waiting room, but I ended up getting lost, stopped by a nurse and chaperoned here anyway. There's no sign of Luke. And now there is this girl staring at me. Not just staring, but pulling faces. I don't like it. She saw me steal a woman's fags, and I thought she was going to call me out for it, but then she just started pulling faces. I have a feeling she knows she is making me uncomfortable, but she's still not stopping. Right now, she is jutting her chin out, creating a bizarre shape with her mouth.

Even if it wasn't for the stupid faces she's pulling, I'd have noticed this girl anyway. For starters, she has purple hair. Her hair is actual bright purple. It looks like she's been photoshopped. She has it tied up into a messy bun, and is wearing giant bright pink hoops in her ears. But that doesn't even compare to the rest of her outfit. She's got these blue high-waisted trousers on, pulled in with an overly tight belt around her waist, into which she's tucked a giant multicoloured sweater. It's like she's from the eighties or something. She is sitting cross-legged on the chair with bare feet, her flip-flops discarded nearby on the floor. Do I need to remind you it's February?

The girl is still staring. What is she doing? Does she even have a reason to be here, or does she visit hospital waiting rooms to pull faces at people?

Talking about people, where *is* Luke? Please let today be one of the days that he behaves like an older brother. *Please*. I'm scared he won't show up at all, and then Lucy will find me and ask why I took off. Then she'll say she doesn't think I've changed, and she'll take me to Dr Lawn, and they will tell me I need to stay.

No. I don't want that to happen. I *can't* let that happen.

Breathe, Tristan.

I should ask the receptionist if Luke has shown up, but what if she calls Lucy, or Dr Lawn? What if I get in trouble for leaving? Lucy is probably looking for me already.

I stroke the cigarette packet in my pocket. They let me smoke here, though they weren't keen on it. Only a few times a day in the designated area outside, and sometimes it wasn't even that. Luke always used to get annoyed about me smoking when he visited. He complained about it to them, but he didn't realise he had no control over it. Even if he did send me away, he needs to realise I'm an adult, not a teenager, not a kid.

I look down at my bag, which I thought would have been fuller. It has all my belongings in it, as well as my prescription, letters about the follow-up meetings and some leaflets. I say belongings, but it's hardly even that. I wasn't allowed anything of mine in the ward. The amount of times Luke used to bring me stuff from home and they'd say it broke the rules in some way. So eventually he stopped bringing my things, and brought Nando's takeaways instead, which I didn't complain about. So, basically, what I'm saying is that after a six-month stay my bag is pretty empty, considering. I have nothing to take away from these past six months, nothing to show for it.

It probably didn't help the situation when I lashed out and smashed my room up. They had to restrain me, pinning me to the floor, even harder than they had any other time. Do you know what it feels like to have people pinning you to the ground in order to calm you down? Well, it doesn't calm you down, I'll tell you that.

After that 'episode' I wasn't allowed anything. And it's not like I brought a whole load with me initially. When I first came here, I wasn't planning to stay long. In fact, I wasn't planning to stay full stop.

I stroke the cigarette box in my pocket again. I wonder how many cigarettes you'd have to smoke in one sitting to die.

'Zoe Miller,' the receptionist calls. The girl with purple hair stands up, and I'm not sure what name I was expecting her to have, but something like 'Rainbow' would have made much more sense than Zoe. She nods her head, before dashing towards the lifts. I look back to her seat. Her multicoloured flip-flops are still on the floor.

Chapter 4

Zoe

I pick my flip-flops up on my way out, not without getting some stink eye from the receptionist. She definitely didn't like me. Maybe she's jealous of the hair. Did I tell you that I forgot my flip-flops? I noticed once I got upstairs but I wasn't going to run downstairs and get them. Anyway, I quite like being bare-footed. It's good for you. Not necessarily in a hospital, but outside it is *so* good. You connect more to the earth when you're bare-footed, your skin making contact with the ground, you know? It's the way it's supposed to be. The best thing is walking through dirt, feeling it beneath your toes, smelling it in the air. Ah man, it's just great.

Once I get outside I text Jerry to let him know I'm making my way home, ignoring his five messages from earlier. If you can't tell . . . he worries. Whereas Paul, even if he didn't hear from me again for two weeks, would be as chilled as cucumber. Well maybe not quite. Jerry and Paul are both my dads, but Jerry is definitely the mother-dad, while Paul is the father-dad. Ask my little sister Leia (Jerry was, and still is, a huge *Star Wars* fan) and she will totally agree.

Jerry has a motherly nature – he's over-protective, nosy and highly controlling, but he's also understanding. I think that's a decent description of a mother, right? I don't actually know because I've never had one, so I'm making my best guess here. Paul couldn't be more different from Jerry – he's much more relaxed, as well as quieter, but also very serious when he wants to be.

I'm walking towards the bus stop right outside the hospital but I come to a sudden stop when I see a certain someone already standing there. Yes, it's Mr Eyeliner, the Jesus of Suburbia himself. He's leant up against the brick wall, smoking one of his stolen cigarettes. He's in a world of his own, and hasn't seen me. Unlucky for him. He puts the cigarette in his mouth again. He is sucking on that thing like it's an inhaler, with his other hand tapping against the wooden side of the bus shelter, and he's mut-tering quietly. It's like he's having a silent argument with himself. But hey, I'm not judging. After all, it's not any of my business . . .

I'm about to keep walking when in one smooth move-ment he lifts one of his hands up, clenches it into a fist, and . . . *smack*.

Oh.

Okay.

He just smashed his hand into the wood of the bus shelter. This guy just punched the wall.

He turns around, and his eyes catch mine. Yet again, mystery man, I think, I've caught you in the act of something you probably shouldn't be doing.

I can't work out what he's thinking, but I know he doesn't waste any time in leaving. He frowns, drops his cigarette and walks away. As he quickly shuffles off, the cigarette box falls delicately out of his trouser pocket. Almost as if it's calling out to me. He doesn't notice, of course; he's too worried about leaving.

Once he's rounded the next corner, I glide towards the spot he was standing and peer at the wood. There is a faint smear of red – it's blood. Why would he choose to do that to his own hand? I look down at the cigarette box on the floor and pick it up, feeling a small smile creep on to my face.

I have your cigarette box, mysterious dark-eyed dude, and what are you going to do about it?

Chapter 5

Tristan

I can't believe Luke didn't show up. I can't believe he abandoned me. I can't believe I hit that bus stop.

I will admit I have slight anger issues, but that wasn't why I punched the bus shelter. No, I did it because I wanted it to hurt. Pain makes me feel, and feelings mean I can temporarily escape the numbing sadness that sinks over me. It's a way of relieving the tension, I guess, and it just makes sense – until I actually do it. Then I'm overcome with the biggest feeling of regret that could ever sweep over me.

It's a vicious circle.

The hospital is only a twenty-minute walk from where I live, which feels almost painfully ironic. I've been so near to the outside world yet locked up in my own bubble for the last six months. I take my time walking, going past the garden centre, over the railway bridge and along the row of old people's homes where they sit watching behind their curtains. Seeing all the familiar sights makes me realise that I'm anything but happy to be back. But, then, I don't want to go back to hospital, either. There isn't really anywhere I want to go. I'm so lost.

When I finally get to our front door, I stop. It's been so long, and I'm still the same messed-up person. Except now I'm in a worse position, because everyone will think I've changed. They will all think I'm better, when really I'm not.

So now I need to pretend I am what they think I am.

I knock on the door.

No answer. I knock again.

Still nothing.

I knock once more, aggressively this time, with both fists.

Is Luke not in there? I look around at the cars parked along the road, and realise his isn't one of them. My stomach drops and my heart pounds as I feel my cheeks start to get warm. *You're jumping the gun, Tristan,* I try to tell myself. *You're overthinking this.*

I turn back to the house. The blinds are closed. Since when does Luke bother to close the blinds?

Oh my God. I'm not bloody jumping the gun. He's not here, is he?

What if he was never planning to pick me up? What if he's ditched me and moved away? What about Misha?

The counsellor suggested to Luke that he get me Misha when I moved back home from university last year. So he did what they said and bought a dog, my dog, a golden Labrador retriever who was the runt of the litter. And he's perfect. Luke isn't a dog person and has always found Misha annoying, but I loved him from the start. Unlike Luke, Misha has always been there for me. That's the great thing about dogs – they're there for you no matter what an arse you are in life. They don't care. All dogs want in life is love. We humans should take after them, rather than overcomplicating everything.

When I saw Luke last week he said he was looking after Misha; that he was being a cheeky little bugger but everything was good. I should have known not to trust him.

I'm pacing up and down the pavement with thoughts racing through my head. I'm trying to remember what Dr Lawn told me to do when I felt like this. *Breathing exercises*, she used to say, *practise breathing exercises for your anxiety*. But I can't waste my time on that. I just want to find my brother.

Maybe he's at work. That would explain why his car is gone. But why would he be at work when he knew that I was leaving the hospital today? That he was picking me up at 2 p.m.?

I slump on to the pavement next to our garden wall, which really isn't a wall at all. It seems Luke didn't get it fixed while I've been away, but then again I guess it was my fault the wall was wrecked in the first place. When I said that I have slight anger issues, I might have understated it.

I stare at the mounds of bricks resting on the ground as I try to contain my panting. And then something clicks in that weird head of mine.

Smash.

The brick goes through the living room window easily and the glass collapses around it. I don't feel any guilt about it, in fact I feel a little bit proud. I move closer and use my elbow to shove the remaining shards away. Once I'm satisfied with the size of the hole, I step back and admire my work. I can understand why there are so many burglaries if breaking into a house is this easy. *And* therapeutic. I feel a lot calmer now. I look at the gaping hole one last time, before putting my hoodie over my head and heaving myself up and through. Small shards of glass wrestle with the fabric of my denim jacket and I can feel myself getting tangled in the blinds, but I eventually land inside.

I stand up and quickly survey the living room. I can't help but chuckle. I just broke into my own house. And it *is* my house. I have no idea why Luke isn't around, but he clearly still lives here. I know that because his treadmill is in the corner of the room, a half empty bottle of Jack Daniels is resting on the coffee table, the pull-up bar is mounted in the doorway, and even Misha's bed is still resting in the corner. But where the hell is Misha?

One thing I know about Misha is that he has super powers. His hearing is better than any dog I've ever known. If a single noise is made in the house, he comes running to it straight away. He never barks though – I don't think he's physically capable. Maybe it's that his hearing overbears his ability to bark. Anyway what I'm trying to say is, I just broke in through the window. So why hasn't Misha trotted along to investigate the noise?

His bed is here. If Luke got rid of him, he would have got rid of the bed as well. He always said it made the place smell of piss. So Misha has to be here somewhere. I make my way into the hallway, heading towards the kitchen.

'Misha?'

No answer.

I look around the kitchen, but there's no sign of him. I run towards the back door where his dog tin is. Everything is in there – his food, his poop bags, his treats, his toys. Even his lead is here, so Luke isn't taking him for a walk. But let's be real, when does he ever take him for a walk?

'Where are you? Where the hell are you?'

Silence.

Luke got rid of him. Luke got rid of *my* dog. He promised me.

I lift up the tin and throw it across the room. It crashes on to the floor and slides, taking the coat rack tumbling down with it. I stare at it, as my chest starts thumping. How could he do this to me? How could he do this to Misha?

I can't be in this house any longer. I move swiftly

through the kitchen, into the living room – and now I'm heading towards the door, and that's when I feel a force pulling roughly against me.

In one heavy motion I'm thrown on to the floor, collapsing on to my hands and knees. I suck in a breath of air as fire surges through my right hand. My palm has slid into a shard of broken glass. I'm just about to yell in pain when my knees buckle beneath me, and I'm pinned to the ground. Jesus Christ.

'What the hell are you doing breaking into my house?' a gruff voice says. 'Tell me what you're doing here!' The voice belongs to Luke.

'Luke, wait,' I try to shout. But when I say he's pinning me to the ground, I mean it. He's right on top of me, and he's not a skinny guy. I'm struggling to breathe, let alone speak. I try again. 'Luke, it's me.'

After a pause, I feel the weight of his body lift off me. I manage to turn around to look up at Luke, standing over me in his boxers. It's not a pretty sight. His eyes look bloodshot and tired, and are accompanied by deep bags, which darken as he stares at me.

'Tristan?' he says, rubbing a hand through his hair.

I watch him, my lip twitching nervously.

'Tristan,' Luke says again. His voice has dropped, it's gone soft and pathetic. 'Are ... are you okay?' He offers a hand to help me up. I ignore his offer and clamber up on my own to stand opposite him, staying silent. Luke starts shaking his head. 'I don't understand. What are you—'

24

He pauses. His eyes widen. He brings his hand to his mouth.

'It's Saturday?' he says, like I'm going to answer. 'Shit,' he groans, dragging his hand down his face. 'Shit. Shit. Shit.' Luke kicks the floor before moving his eyes back up to mine. 'I'm sorry, Tristan. I don't know how I forgot, I . . . ' He sighs before finally rubbing his eyes and taking a step closer to me. 'Are you okay?' he says.

I can smell alcohol on him. I turn my head away. 'I'm fine.'

'You sure? I'm sorry that I—'

'I'm fine,' I say again, firmly. I don't want to be having this conversation.

'Okay, good.' Luke sounds as if he's trying to work out a maths problem. 'Good.' A forced smile forms on his face. 'Well, you're home now. This is good. Come here.' He walks forward, wrapping his arms around me. I don't hug him back, I don't do anything. I just stay there in uncomfortable silence. 'I'm proud of you, you know,' he says.

Just like Lucy the nurse, he's proud of me too. Surely *he* can tell I'm not okay. Surely out of everyone, Luke knows the truth? But maybe he's pretending, like I am. Pretending is much easier.

'Is everything okay, babe?'

Luke swiftly lets me go, as we both turn around in the direction of the voice. Standing by the stairs there is a brown-haired girl with smudged make-up, still buttoning up her shirt and wearing baggy shorts. Though on a second look, I realise that they're not shorts, but Luke's boxers. Luke moves towards her, putting his hand around her waist, and brushing her scruffy hair away from her face. 'Yeah, it's all cool. It's totally fine. This is my brother.'

The girl squints at me, maybe her smudged make-up is obstructing her vision. 'So ... it wasn't a burglar?' she asks, looking up at Luke.

'No, it was just my brother ... I've told you about him, remember?'

'Oh, yeah,' she says. 'It's Tyson, right?'

Luke frowns. 'No ... His name's Tristan.' He tries to throw a smile at me. 'Tristan, this is, erm ... ' He turns towards the girl, scratching his head. 'This is ... Jen ... Jenna.'

'Gemma,' she says.

'Gemma, right, yeah. This is Gemma.'

Gemma moves towards me and holds out her hand. 'Nice to meet you, Tristan, I've heard a lot about you.' I look down at her hand, but don't take it. I'm not shaking that. I don't know where it's been.

'Er, babe,' Luke says pulling her hand away and weaving his fingers through hers. He moves himself close and starts muttering words in her ear. I sigh, and move off, slumping myself on the sofa. I can hear the odd phrase if I bother to listen in.

'Yeah, babe, I'll call you later,' Luke says. He follows this with, 'It's more complicated than that.' And then comes the grand finale of, 'I just need some time with him.'

That's the last thing I want from him right now. The panic I felt earlier has now settled into anger. My brother forgot to pick me up from the hospital because he was with some girl whose name he couldn't even remember.

But this shouldn't surprise me. It is Luke we're talking about.

Chapter 6

Zoe

'There's an envelope on your bed,' Jerry calls as soon as I get in the house.

He's stood at the end of the hallway. I beam my excited eyes at him. 'Is it what I think it is?'

Jerry shrugs his shoulders, a slight smile twisted on his lips. I know he knows what it is, which means he must have looked through my post, but I'm not even mad about it. Well, maybe a little, but I've had to come to terms with the fact I can't change Jerry.

Abandoning my bag and coat, I run upstairs into my room and squeal with delight at the brown envelope on my bed. Sure enough, it's already been opened by Jerry – I can tell from his poor attempt to stick it back together. I carefully reopen the seal and take out the contents. I'm holding sixty developed photos in my hand, and each one feels like another piece added to me. They feel so precious in my fingertips; so clean, fresh and new. I'm so proud of them. Is this the way mothers feel when they hold their new babies?

I take so many photos on disposable cameras that I get a new package of pictures about once a month, but it brings me this much joy every time. Maybe I'm going overboard, but hey, it's nice to find happiness in the simpler things in life. That way you can find a lot more to be happy about.

After looking through each one, I head back downstairs in perfect time to see Leia coming in after her day at college. She's in her final year, studying Biology and Chemistry. So yes, basically, she is a lot smarter than me. She closes the door and stares at me, tilting her head appraisingly as she takes in my new hair colour. I smile back, posing for a photo she isn't even taking. 'You like?'

'Yeah,' she replies, dropping her bag on the floor and walking past me into the kitchen. 'When did you do it?'

'This morning, before I went to the hospital,' I say, following her in.

'And how was that?' she asks, head in the fridge.

'It was a hospital, what more can I say?' I hoist myself up on to the counter. 'Want to do yoga with me?'

'Yeah, after I've done some coursework.'

I jut my lip out, pouting. 'I can't later, I took overtime at work tonight.'

'You're working tonight?' Jerry says, peeping in through the doorway, half in the kitchen, half out.

'Yes, my lovely father, I do believe I told you.'

Jerry frowns deeply, creating even more lines and dents in his wrinkled forehead. 'So you're not eating dinner then?'

I shake my head, grabbing an apple from the fruit bowl and slowly biting into it. There is a satisfying crunch.

'You seem to be taking a lot shifts lately. Any reason why?' Jerry asks, seemingly casually.

I take another bite of my apple, smiling at him. 'I'm just not as busy as I was last year, and you know I like to keep myself distracted.'

Jerry runs his hand through his white hair. He can't work out if that was a dig, or if it was totally innocent. I'm not sure either. 'Well, maybe you can keep yourself distracted with your degree? Maybe start planning your dissertation ... Weren't you supposed to have worked out what you were writing it on by now? May will be here before you know it.'

I watch Jerry carefully. 'Just because I'm back at home, doesn't mean you can start telling me to do my uni work. I've had two years of living on my own, remember. And I did that pretty well.'

'Yeah, I know, honey but—'

'Anyway,' I say, jumping off the kitchen counter, 'I'm going to go do some yoga.'

'Do you have time?' Jerry calls, as I run up the stairs.

'Of course I have time,' I shout back over my shoulder.

I didn't have time for yoga.

Usually I would walk to work, but in the end Jerry had to give me a lift so that I wouldn't be late. As usual, he gave me an earful about how 'I can't always rely on him blah blah blah' and that 'I should give myself more time to get to work blah blah blah'. I followed this by politely letting him know that it would make his life a lot easier if I had a car. It would turn a thirty-minute walk into a five-minute drive for me. All that extra time I'd have to give him more daughterly love. He quickly changed the subject after that, because neither of us wanted to get into the same old argument about why he didn't want me driving.

Anyway, I'm at work now, and I ended up being a whole twelve minutes and thirty seconds *early*. I'll only need to wait a couple of minutes before Ree comes in, quickly followed by Anna, who probably shared a lift in together. This is why I took this shift – I knew we were all working today, the three amigos back together.

Ree and Anna both chatted to me on my first day in the summer, and they've taken me under their wings ever since. I had just moved back home for my last year of university, and was feeling a bit lost. I needed friends around me. And I'm grateful to them for recognising that.

Anna is from Leeds and is at Surrey Uni, same as me. She studies English, though, so I had never even seen her before I worked here. Ree works here full time, and they are talking about putting her up for a supervisor position soon. I know she's going to ace it; she'll be the manager here before long. Retail work runs in the family, her sister Alice is working her way up in Pandora just down the high street, and her mum works in the head office of M&S.

Anna and Ree have worked here a while longer than me, so their friendship was good mature cheddar age before I popped into their lives. I totally understand three can be a crowd, but for some reason it seems to work with us. Maybe it's because I don't care that they see each other more, because Ree's house is near Anna's student house, or that they have their inside jokes, or that I end up so busy with work, uni and badminton coaching that I rarely have time to hang out with them. All I care about is that they are friends to me, and I love them both for that.

'Ooh, purple!' Anna says, taking in my hair as I put my apron on, tying it loosely at the back. My apron is a mess compared to theirs. I don't even know how I get it so messy when I'm always on the tills. Anna forms a confident smile as she holds her hand out to Ree, who grudgingly hands her a tenner. They placed bets on my next hair colour again, and Anna guessed correctly for the second time in a row. I tell you, going from green to purple isn't easy.

'You like?' I ask with a proud smile.

Ree nods her head. 'What time you doing today? Until nine?'

'You know it.'

'Sweet, I won't be left on my own for once.'

'Hey, what about me?' Anna chimes in with her highly entertaining northern accent.

'It doesn't count, you work on shelves,' Ree replies, fiddling with her fob.

'Not all the time.'

'But today you are, right?'

'Yeah,' Anna replies, sulking down on the bench, before she quickly straightens and dramatically grabs Ree's arm. 'Did you hear?' she says.

Ree turns to her, eyes widening. 'Oh my God, yeah I did.'

'Apparently he's coming back here. I heard Juliette talking about it this morning.' Anna's eyes are equally wide.

'Have you seen him yet?'

Anna shakes her head.

I pop my head into this rather confusing conversation. 'Saw who?'

'Is he definitely coming back? I didn't even know he was out yet.' Ree carries on without answering my question.

'Yes, girl, Georgia told me so. I didn't know either.'

'I can't believe they are still letting him work here.'

'Hey,' I say, chiming in again. 'You said that about me because of my hair, but five months later I'm still here,' I say with a chuckle. But neither of the girls even register my comical input, they just keep talking. I thought I was being quite funny, and I'm not enjoying this lack of attention. I like attention.

'I wonder if he still looks the same?'

'I don't know why you'd care, you like girls. Not guys.'

'Hey,' Ree replies with a frown. 'Just because I haven't liked a boy before doesn't mean I won't ever like a guy.

33

Anyway, I want to see if he's back so I can let my sister know, she hasn't heard anything from him.'

Anna kisses her teeth. 'Typical. Of course she hasn't.'

'Um, earth to Ree and Anna?' I say, and by now I'm practically sitting on them. 'I want to know who you're talking about!' I'm surprised I have to explain myself. They know I love the gossip. I raise my eyebrows at the girls, until Ree's brain finally clicks. 'Oh, you want to know who we're talking about?' she says.

Well, I did say those exact words. I nod my head eagerly.

'Well, rumour has it that Tristan Grenander is back,' Ree says with an excited smile, before clocking my confused face. 'Oh, yeah. You never met him.'

I lower my eyebrows. Is she going to elaborate?

'Basically Tristan Grenander is a guy who used to work here,' Anna whispers, shuffling forwards. I can tell some gossip is about to come. Exciting.

'Yeah, he'd worked here longer than me, since he was sixteen,' Ree adds on. 'We knew him pretty well, everyone did. He was the kind of guy that people knew around the town. He was nice, I guess, but a bit of a lad.'

'A lad?'

'Yeah, a lad. All the girls loved him. He saw a fair few girls that worked here as well. He was seeing Ree's sister for a while. They had a thing.'

'Yeah, they did,' Ree says, nodding like it's something to be proud of.

'And what ... he moved away?' I ask. I'm still confused.

34

'No ...'

'But you said that he's back.'

'About a year and a half ago his dad died. A week or two after he started his final year at uni,' Anna says, serious now.

Oh. That wasn't what I was expecting.

'I think sometimes death changes a person and, well, it really changed Tristan.'

'So, what – he dropped out of uni?'

'Not at first, he stayed on, he even carried on working here, but he just ... strayed. He stopped seeing people, seeing girls, stopped going out, stopped it all,' Ree says. 'He just separated himself. When he was here, he would do his job, but that was all. He wouldn't speak to anyone, wouldn't smile, wouldn't get in to conversations, he would just do what he had to do and leave.'

'Also,' Ree adds, like she is actually excited about this topic, 'when he worked, his eyes were glassy, almost dead-looking. It was creepy.'

'Yeah ... He just gradually became less and less like himself until he wasn't him any more. And then apparently he started causing trouble, shouted at one of his lecturers, got in a few fights and eventually stopped doing his uni work altogether. And then one time, I guess it was about nine months ago, he was on the tills, and right in the middle of serving a customer he calmly turned off his till, and without saying anything he left. I was on the customer service desk when it happened, he walked right out, and never came back here after that. After that he quit university, and he only had a couple of months left of his final term. He totally cut contact with everyone. No one has heard from him since. He even deleted all his social media.'

I try not to show my shock at this. I know it's ridiculous, but I can't imagine deleting my Instagram, my Pinterest. All my precious mood boards, vanishing into thin air . . . Let's stop before I get emotional.

As bad as it is, I want to find out more. It's like a soap opera. And thankfully for me, Ree is as eager to tell me more as I am to listen. 'My hairdresser dated Tristan's brother for a while.'

'Well, everyone knows Tristan's brother,' Anna chimes in with a slight smile. I wonder what that means. I don't know his brother.

'And apparently his brother was finding it so hard to deal with Tristan, he didn't know what to do,' Ree says.

'Yeah,' Anna adds in. 'And apparently, over summer, he was left with no choice but to shut him away.'

'Shut him away?'

'Yeah, like a mental place.'

'It's called an asylum, Anna.'

'Actually, I think it's called an institution, Ree.'

'Wait,' I say, struggling to absorb all this juicy information. (Crap. That was a heartless adjective to use.) 'Why did they lock him away?'

'Tried to kill himself. And it wasn't the first time either.'

'Oh.' That's all I can make come out of my mouth. Yep.

For someone who loves talking. Just, *Oh*. But what can I say in response to that?

'Apparently, he's been let out, or is getting let out soon and for some reason Juliette decided to give him his job back.'

'I bet it's out of pity.'

'Nah, Juliette totally likes him, she always used to give him the easiest jobs. She can't wait to have him back.'

Ree looks dubious.

'Hey, he's hot,' Anna shrugs. 'And I bet he's even hotter now he's all dark, depressed and mysterious.'

Wait, rewind. What did she just say? 'Anna!' I say, scowling at her.

Anna bites her lip. 'I'm joking! I'm only joking ... It's sad. But trust me, he is hot. Now that he's better, hopefully he'll start dating girls again. Who knows, I might have a chance.'

'Or me,' Ree says. 'He could be the first guy I date.'

While Ree and Anna carry on talking about how hot Tristan Grenander is, my mind starts turning over all the sad things they've just told me.

How does depression work? I really don't know. Do you get cured from it? Is he really better now? I've never known anyone with a mental illness – at least not that I knew about. I mean, it's not like physical illnesses, is it? You can't tell just by looking at someone. 'Do you know if he ever finished uni?'

'No, he didn't. He didn't do his dissertation, or his final

exams, he fucked it up,' Anna says, standing up to head to the tills.

'Oh.' Again, just, *Oh*.

'Yep. But hey, it's his life, not ours,' Ree says, standing up, too. 'Okay. Evening shift, here we go.'

Chapter 7

Tristan

I'm sitting on the sofa, rolling my eyes at Luke as I grudgingly show him the cut on my palm. It took a stubbornly long argument for us to get to this point. I thought my hand was fine, Luke thought otherwise.

He stares intently at the gash on my hand, eyes squinted. Though I downplayed it, it hurts really badly, and I'm struggling not to make a fuss as he prods it. 'Jesus, Tristan, I'm sorry. If I'd known it was you, I wouldn't have pushed you like that.' I don't say anything. 'Why didn't you just call me from the hospital?'

'I don't have a mobile, do I?' I'm trying not to wince as he rubs an antiseptic wipe on my hand – from the pain and the embarrassment.

'Oh yeah, I need to give you that back.'

'That would be good,' I say. Then I can't help adding,

'Most twenty-two-year-olds don't have to request permission from their brother to use their own phone.'

Luke decides to pretend he didn't hear my last sentence. 'So you walked all the way back from the hospital?' he says, keeping his tone light.

'Yeah.'

Luke turns his head towards the broken window, before looking back at me gloomily. When Gemma left and he'd finally checked his phone, he had five missed calls from the hospital, asking if he'd picked me up because they were worried I hadn't been officially signed out. They didn't know where I'd gone – another half an hour and they would have called the police. But, of course, Luke didn't know any of this because he had been too occupied to answer those phone calls. 'You could have just knocked on the door.'

'I did knock on the door,' I almost shout, looking up and glaring at him. 'Don't you think I would have tried that? You must have been too busy to hear.'

Luke looks away, as if I've made him feel awkward, because of course I'm the one who is making this situation difficult. *Right.*

Luke is dressed now. Before Gemma left, she told me she hoped to see me again soon, but she won't. Luke has always had a lot of Gemmas around this house, and they all hope to 'see me again soon' but it never happens. There's something Luke doesn't like about the 'soon' part. Or maybe it's the 'again' part, too. Luke is twenty-seven, and I think it's time he settled down – there's only so long he can keep going to bars, getting drunk and bringing girls home before he finds himself fifty years old and alone.

Where I live, everyone seems to know everyone – and Luke has slept with just about everyone here. The girl from the café, the butcher's daughter, the girl that cut my hair that one time. I don't know how he's not embarrassed. He doesn't even avoid them after he calls it a day – instead, he'll show his face the next night, make everyone laugh about it, make it a night to remember. But that's Luke for you, he can make friends in a second, knows how to get a crowd going and always ensures everyone has a good time.

'So, you really thought I had moved?' Luke asks.

I shrug my shoulders.

'Didn't you notice my car parked on the road?'

'Obviously *not*, Luke.'

'Oh yeah, I have a new one now.'

I didn't know that. Why has he never mentioned that when visiting me?

There is a pause, and I know I'm going to have to get it over with. I look down at the floor. 'So, did you get rid of Misha?' My voice is barely more than a whisper.

'What?' Luke says, and I lift my eyes up to his confused face. 'No – God, no! That's why you were freaking out?'

'Well he's clearly not here . . . and I know you never liked him so I—'

'Hey, I do like him! I chose him, remember. I just find the little bugger annoying sometimes.'

It feels like a weight has lifted off me. 'Well, where is he?' I say, sitting up straighter.

'He's at the vet's.'

My stomach suddenly drops again. 'Why? What happened? What's wrong—'

'Hey, Tristan. Calm down. I promise you he's fine,' Luke says. 'I just got him neutered. He was humping every living thing he could find! And when you went away it seemed like he did it even more.' I can't help but smile. Good dog.

But my smile quickly falls as a hundred more questions enter my head. *Misha is alone at the vet's right now? Will he be in pain? Will he even remember me?*

'When did you do this?' Luke asks, interrupting my own internal questions. His eyes are focused, staring at my bruised, grazed knuckles. Fuck's sake.

'Don't tell me this was from breaking in, because I know it wasn't.' His voice is serious, mimicking the tone Dad used to take. I hate it when he talks to me like this. He knows I find it patronising. I feel my jaw start to tighten.

'Tristan?'

I don't say anything, I don't have to. Luke already knows I punched something, he's more than familiar with the signs. He sighs and starts shaking his head. 'I thought you . . . ' He doesn't finish his sentence. He can't tell me he thought I'd stopped this. Out of everyone he's the one who should know that I haven't changed. That I won't change.

I avoid his gaze, but feel a pressure on my hand, looking down to see Luke now wrapping a bandage around my palm, and quickly pull myself away. 'What are you doing?' I ask with a grimace. My hand feels raw red. It really does hurt.

'You need to cover your cut.'

'Leave it.'

'You have a huge cut on your hand. I can either put a bandage on it or take you to hospital. Your choice.' I chew on my bottom lip before grudgingly shoving my hand towards him. 'Talking about hospital, they said on the phone that you didn't pick up your medicine.'

I stare at Luke. 'No.' He could call them what they are – antidepressants – he just doesn't like to. Calling them medicine is worse. I don't see them as that. They aren't going to cure me from something I can't get cured from. The unfortunate thing about mental illnesses is that popping a few pills doesn't solve anything. It's not the flu. I look at my hand as Luke continues wrapping the bandage around it. I can't do that with my brain. I can't shove a big bandage on my head and make everything better, though I wish I could.

It's hard. I'm in control of my own brain, so I know I'm the one doing this to myself. I just don't understand why I can't stop. That's why the antidepressants don't work. They don't make me feel better, they make me numb. They just make me feel even further away from Tristan than I already am.

Now I'm back at home, I've decided I'm going to stop taking them. I've had enough of the drugs. They drugged

43

me up on all different types while I was in hospital. First it was these things called SSRIs. They said I would hopefully only be on them for four weeks. I remember thinking to myself, *Oh my God. I'm going to be staying in this hospital for a whole month?* How naive was I? The four weeks turned into six, and they decided to up my dosage. But that only made me worse. I became a version of myself who would cry, scream, break down, run towards something sharp. It felt like a whole chunk of my feelings had been taken and mixed up in a blender.

So then they gave me SNRIs. After that it was TCAs – those were the ones that made me feel really crap. The side effects were non-stop – my mouth was permanently dry, my vision blurred, and I was tired all the time. Yes, they made me cry less, but like everything else, they didn't fix me. Not really.

The doctors used to say I shouldn't feel bad about the different drugs they were trying on me – that everyone is different, and every drug has a different effect on each person. That eventually we would find the right one for me. Six weeks turned into a six-month treatment, and in my last meeting with the doctor I was told it will be two years. *Two more years on drugs.* No thanks.

I've been cutting them out of my diet for a while now. Not every day, because it's hard when you're in hospital and being monitored. But slowly, gradually, for the last month or so. Hiding the pills under my tongue, crushing them in my hand, smearing them on my bed sheets, even hiding them in my sleeve and flushing them down the toilet. It might sound bad, but I have a right to be in charge of my own life. I deserve that much.

I think I'm feeling more right already. Not better, but more like who I'm supposed to be. Someone who doesn't like life, but that's fine. I don't have the energy to care any more, and maybe that's good.

I'm not going to tell Luke that I'm stopping the anti-depressants. It would only stress him out. 'I've got the prescription in my bag, I'll pick them up from the pharmacy tomorrow,' I say, as I take back ownership of my hand.

'No, I'll pick them up, that's fine,' Luke says. 'And you're still going to have weekly follow-ups at the hospital, right?'

'Yes,' I reply, though I'm trying to work out a way of cutting the meetings out, too. I don't think I'll be able to do that as easily. It's not like I can crush the counsellors between my palms.

'Do you want me to go to them with you?' Luke asks.

'No.'

'Okay ... But if you do, I'm completely happy to, Tristan. You know that, right?'

I nod my head.

'So ... are you sure you want to go back to work next week?'

Work means going back to being a Customer Assistant in the local supermarket. Such fun. 'Well, Juliette said there were shifts—'

'I know what she said, but do you not want to give it some time?'

I sigh heavily and frown at him, though he's just trying to make conversation. I know I'm being difficult, but every time I look at Luke, I see my older brother who let them shut me away. It's my fault I ended up in that place, but I wish he'd stood up for me, believed I could get through it on my own – instead, he signed the form and left. And then off came my Green Day T-shirt, the festival wristbands, and on came the hospital clothes, the stupid plimsolls, followed shortly by the drugs. All those bloody drugs.

'Everyone's going to be watching me at work, walking around me on eggshells.'

'Hey,' Luke says, clapping his hands together and standing up. 'Let's not get all negative Nancy here. You're back home. We need to celebrate. Let's go out for a meal!' He starts walking to the door as if he expects me to follow.

'Luke?' He turns around with an exaggerated smile. 'Are you driving?' I ask. His red eyes narrow in confusion. Jesus, he really doesn't look healthy, and I can't help but feel guilty. I think I'm ruining him just as much as I've already ruined myself. Luke's eyes follow mine to the nearly empty bottle of Jack Daniels on the table.

He turns back towards me. 'Do I sound drunk to you, Tristan?'

'No, but you look it.'

He rolls his eyes and shuffles uncomfortably. 'I just get

tired a lot these days. I had a drink earlier, hours ago now. Gemma had more than me.'

I watch Luke and feel a stab in my heart. This would be him and Dad every Friday night – when Dad would make him promise to leave his car keys at home; when he would say that Luke didn't always need to get wasted to have a good time, that he was gifted with a personality to socialise sober; when he would try to convince him to stay in with us, instead of going out. But for some reason alcohol is Luke's friend, always has been. And sometimes he needs reminding that friends can stab you in the back. Luke sighs and moves away from the door and flops back on the sofa. 'I'll drive,' I say, standing up.

'Nah, nah, nah,' Luke replies, chucking his phone into my hands. 'Takeaway?' he says with a toothy smile.

I slump down on the sofa too, nodding my head slightly. 'All right, takeaway.'

Chapter 8

Zoe

I've had three days off since my last shift, and during that time I've mainly been coaching badminton, and catching up on uni work. Today I've gone from a boring lecture straight to a boring shift at work, from one to the other all within twenty minutes. I'm impressed with myself.

Before my shift started, I managed to grab Ree on her lunch break in the staffroom for a quick chat, but then she went back on to shelves and so now I'm here. On the podium tills all by myself. To serve the smelly smokers, the people who want free coffee and the old ladies that want a chat because they like to pretend I'm the granddaughter that doesn't speak to them any more. Lucky me.

Sometimes, when I'm standing on the tills, I ask myself why I'm working here. What am I doing? I don't really want to be working here. I don't really want to be living at home. I miss when I'd just started uni and everything and everyone was fun and new. I miss who I was then, too. But I have to remind myself that it's okay – even though I feel a bit lost right now, I'll get there someday. How are you going to find yourself if you don't get a little bit lost along the way?

And you know, it's fine that it's not going to be for a while yet. It's awesome, actually, that I haven't worked out what I'm doing with my life, because now I have more time to be successful. It would suck if my peak was at . . . twenty-five, let's say. I would spend the rest of my life comparing myself to young, successful, twenty-five-year-old me's accomplishments. No thanks. At least this way I have something to look forward to.

I sigh, looking out the giant glass window that makes up one side of the supermarket. The building is right next to the train station and, more importantly, opposite the sports field, so in quiet periods like right now I can look out and watch the games that are being played. It's football now. In the summer it was rounders. Some days it's athletics. On Fridays it's always rugby. I continue watching. It's a bittersweet feeling – beautifully annoying, simply complicated – because I want to be out there, too. I want to be out on the field so much it makes me buzz about my next badminton-coaching session next week. I hope Jack will be there – he was away this week, and he always makes it so much more fun; worthwhile, even. Coaching the badminton club doesn't really fulfil me. The kids are too young, and they're not competitive enough. What I really want is to play. I suppose I just want to do *more*. Watching the football being played out there right now makes a heat glow inside of me. I can't work out if it's frustration or vicarious exhilaration. But it's something.

Tearing my eyes away, I sigh. They never used to make me work on the podiums. It used to be mainly Naomi's job, but since her scoliosis operation she has to stay seated, so I've taken her place. We're supposed to stand when there are customers.

Yay for me, standing alone on the podiums.

I. Just. Love. It. So. Much.

Usually, I spend my shifts chatting to people – because that is something I'm good at – but how do I make my shifts go quickly if I'm stood in silence?

Maybe I should hold a strike against being on the podiums yet again. Yes, I'm going to. A silent strike so I can regain my right to have a partner on the podiums, or not be on the podiums at all. It's not fair to be bored like this. I smile to myself and start scribbling on my notepad. *RIGHTS FOR ZOE! RIGHTS FOR ZOE! RIGHTS FOR ZO—*

Wait.

If I go on a silent strike that doesn't work in my favour, because I enjoy talking. Maybe I could go on a hunger strike ...

'Zoe.'

I jump at the sound of Juliette's voice and quickly crumple my paper, pretending to look pleased to see her. Her curly brown hair that spurts out in all directions is extra curly today. Juliette is tiny, even smaller than me, yet somehow very intimidating. I don't know how old she is, but she's way too young to be managing this place.

'Hi, Julie, it's quiet today.'

'It's *Juliette*. And yes, it can be quiet during the week.'

I smirk, resting my chin on my hands. 'So ... are you taking me off podiums, Julie?'

'No,' she says, her mouth pursed into a tiny tight smile.

'What can I do you the pleasure of then, dear Julie, my lovely manager, who loves me so much?'

'A new associate joined us today,' (the supermarket likes to call all its employees 'associates', probably to make us feel more valued) 'who is returning after some time away. Would you mind if they shadowed you on the till? They'll be working on podiums with you. I just want to get them back into it at their own pace.'

My eyes widen. 'So I'll have someone to talk to? I mean ... work next to?'

Juliette rolls her eyes, and ignores my question. 'I'll bring them over,' she says flatly, as she swishes away. It's only a couple of minutes before she returns, leading some guy towards me.

No way.

Have you guessed?

I'm going to tell you anyway. It's only Mr Eyeliner. You know, the serious guy from the hospital waiting room about a week ago. The guy who stole the cigarettes. The guy who got all weird and punched a bus shelter. I have his box of cigarettes under my bed right now.

His head is lowered as he shuffles his feet along the floor. I notice that his hand is wrapped in a bandage. Was that from the bus shelter? Dude.

They reach my till and Juliette smiles up at him, but he's still looking at the floor. I don't think he's even seen me yet.

'Zoe, this is Tristan.'

Wait. Let's rewind a second, please.

Mr Eyeliner is the Tristan dude?

Suddenly my mind is swamped with everything Ree and Anna told me about him. His dad, his depression, where he's been for the last few months. I stare at him, wondering if he's still depressed – does he look like someone that's depressed? What does that even look like?

'Anyway,' Juliette continues, 'I've got to dash, the click and collect is broken.' I've been watching him the whole time Juliette's been talking, and he still hasn't looked up. 'But Tristan, you let me know if you want a break or help with anything. Zoe's ... nice.' I think this is her way of saying annoying. 'Hey, she's as friendly as her hair is purple.'

At this Tristan finally lifts his head. His eyes catch mine and widen, and I can't help but feel a confident smile parade across my face. Yes, Tristan. It's me. The girl with the purple hair. What are the chances?

Juliette dashes off and I motion to let Tristan take the seat by the till, while I hover beside him. As he slumps there, staring into nothing, I can already feel the negative energy oozing from him. He looks like he needs a friend. Maybe a friend like me. I don't mean to sound full of myself or anything, but I'd love to be friends with me.

Step one, I need to initiate conversation.

'You want to go on the till first?'

He looks at me, his brow lowered, jaw tense. Eventually he nods, gets off the chair and stands by the till. I was hoping he would at least respond vocally, but it seems like speaking isn't something he's planning on. Hmm. So far, conversation: zero.

Suddenly it gets busy on the tills, so I have no choice but to halt my conversation-making plans while Tristan serves customers. He's quick and efficient – he obviously knows what he's doing, and needs no help from me, which is annoying. If he needed help it would have given me an excuse to speak to him, or to try to close the iso-lated distance he is careful to keep from me. Instead, I just spend the next hour watching him, without him even looking back at me once. He keeps his eyes on the cus-tomers and the till, concentrating as he works – although I don't think he really is concentrating. His expression remains distant and his hands keep drumming on the counter.

I'll work him out eventually. It's what I do best.

When it finally dies down, I take advantage of the quiet and practically jump on him, shuffling close, getting all up in his personal space. It's conversation time, my friends.

'I'm Zoe,' I say, flashing my teeth at him. He turns his head towards me, but stays silent. 'And you're Tristan, right?' He looks at my name tag, and then moves his eyes down to his own name tag, pinned on his apron. He returns his gaze back to me before nodding slowly.

I think he's challenging me. Good thing I like a challenge.

'So, you know how to work the tills, hey?'

God, Zoe, what was that? It sounded like a bad pick-up line. Come on now. You are not one to waste time on small talk. 'You're quite the topic of conversation around here, you know.' This might not have been the best choice because his eyes narrow at me. Be careful, Zoe. You don't want to scare him away. Approach him like he's a baby deer. Slow, careful steps. I try again. 'So, what's the deal with your name?' I ask.

He stares at me intently, eyes scanning my face. 'What do you mean?' he finally replies. He speaks. The boy speaks, people! This is a start, at least.

'Well, I just wondered why you're called Tristan.' Slow, careful steps, remember.

He frowns. 'Why are you called Zoe?' Fair play, man. 'I don't mind my name,' he mumbles, still frowning.

'I'm going to be honest with you here, Tristan. I personally don't think it suits you.'

Without lifting his eyebrows, he asks, 'Why doesn't
it suit me?'

I shrug my shoulders. 'It just doesn't.'

'But you don't even know me.'

'I know just from looking at you that you aren't
a Tristan.'

'Well, maybe you don't suit Zoe.' His voice is strange,
quiet. He sounds kind of helpless.

'But I do, though,' I say confidently. 'Can I call you
something else?'

'No.'

'I'm going to call you Tree.'

'That's not my name, though.'

'Good thing nicknames exist,' I say, nudging him with
my elbow. He doesn't look impressed.

He scrunches up his face. 'Tree isn't even a name.'

'Says who? It is now. You like it?'

Tristan looks at me for a couple of seconds before he
says, 'Okay.'

Okay? I can tell he's trying to end the conversation, but
not on my watch. I can keep going all day. 'So where were
you born?' I ask, cupping my head in my hands.

The frown returns. He likes to frown. Note made.
'You're very nosy.'

I feel an amused smile play on my lips. 'I do love noses.'

'What?'

'Nothing.'

This conversation is slow. It's forced. But there is something about this guy. I've decided that I'm going to be friends with him whether he likes it or not – and luckily for him, once I've decided something, I stick with it.

Chapter 9

Tristan

I'm at work, and I'm sitting with that girl from the hospital waiting room with the purple hair, who apparently works here, too. She's trying to make conversation with me, like she wants to be my friend; she doesn't even know me.

Friends aren't the problem. I have friends. Or I *had* friends. Most of them left Surrey after finishing their last year at university, which is just about the time I went into hospital, but a group of them came to visit once. Like it was a good surprise or something. Nearly the whole group was there: Jake, Anthony, Liam, Harrison, Jonny, Chloe, Karl, Pete ... everyone. Talking to me as if it hadn't been months. Hugging me, telling me they'd take me to the pub when I was out. Talking about their interviews, their internships, their jobs, their new squeaky-clean, degree-filled lives, not realising they were making me feel even more pathetic about mine. I didn't want them to come. I didn't ask them to. They wouldn't have understood, but as soon I went into hospital, I realised I couldn't have friends around me again. Not ever.

'I've decided we're going to be friends, Tree,' the girl says, as she starts doodling happy faces on a notepad.

'It's Tristan, and I don't need friends,' I reply, my eyes compelled to follow her slippery-smooth pen work.

She turns towards me and grins. 'That's why I'm doing the deciding. So, why were you at hospital the other day? Other than to steal cigarettes?'

I narrow my eyes at her. What is she trying to do? 'I think you know why I was at hospital.' I'm not stupid. I know she knows all about me – she already said I was the current topic of conversation here.

'Yeah, I do,' she says with a grin. She has a distinctive voice – kind of husky, and slightly posh. 'I just thought I'd ask anyway. Wouldn't you rather tell me, than have other people do it?'

I feel the defensiveness already boiling up inside me. Who does she think she is? 'Well, you were at the hospital, too – what was your reason?' I say, to avoid answering.

She chuckles, like it's a question she was waiting for. 'I was visiting my gran. She's pretty ill.'

'Is she okay?' I ask, assuming that's what normal people would ask. Honestly, I'm not really interested in knowing.

'Nope. She's in hospital, so of course she's not okay.' She's rolling her eyes. 'I like visiting her in hospital, though. I like people-watching. I like the waiting room. I like the coffee machine. I like meeting new people. And the doctors are nice, too.'

She's scraping the barrel here. It's like she's trying to find things to enjoy about going to the hospital. 'Seriously?'

'Yeah,' she says smiling again. 'Seriously.'

I watch her carefully. She must be fairly new to the supermarket – she definitely wasn't working here before I went away. I'm sure I would have noticed her.

'Plus, it's a private hospital,' she carries on. 'It's obviously going to be an amazing hospital.'

I snigger under my breath. 'Just because a hospital is private doesn't make it amazing,' I say. Does she really think I seem like I've been to an 'amazing' hospital?

'Well, my dad had a friend from work who went there, and he got really good care,' she says.

I just nod, before turning my head away. I'm not going to lie, I don't really care about her dad's friend. I don't really care about anything she's saying.

'Are you going to tell me why you were there? Was it like a counselling session or something?' she asks, clearly not taking the hint.

I roll my eyes, exhaling a heavy sigh. 'I was getting discharged.'

'From, like, being there ... '

'Getting discharged after being sectioned.'

'They have a mental asylum at St Heaths?' she says, her eyes widening at her mistake the moment she said it.

I exhale another heavy breath, feeling my fists clench a

little. 'It's called a mental health institute. Not an asylum. I was there for six months.'

'Oh. So, how do you feel now, Tree?'

'Please don't call me that.' She has a strange face, almost elf-like. She has nice eyes though, very blue. Maybe too blue.

'Are you still depressed, Tree?' she says.

'Yes,' I reply, continuing to watch her. Because what else can I say?

'What made them let you out?'

'Because I know . . . ' Because I know how to play things now. 'Because I'm not as bad as I used to be.'

'Why were you in the waiting room when I saw you?'

I rub a hand along my face, letting out a sigh. How many more questions can she have? 'My brother was supposed to pick me up, but he forgot. It stressed me out.'

'Stress isn't good for the heart.'

Is she taking the piss? 'Well, sometimes you can't help it.'

'When I'm stressed I do yoga.'

'I don't do yoga.' I can't take this girl seriously.

'Maybe you should try when you're feeling stressed.'

'When I'm stressed I smoke.' I pause for a second, to inhale and then exhale. 'That's why I stole the cigarettes, I just needed a smoke. I don't usually steal. All right?'

If I've got to work with her, I don't want her thinking I'm some thug.

Not that it really matters what she thinks.

She watches me carefully, twisting her mouth to the

side. I stare back at her. She has her hair pulled into a high ponytail, and is wearing giant hoop earrings again. This time they are yellow. How is she getting away with wearing those with Juliette around? 'What about your parents . . . Did your da— mum. Couldn't your mum have picked you up?'

'Smooth.'

Her cheeks flush. 'Sorry.'

She really has had the *full* low-down on me, then. She knows I was shut away, so obviously she knows about Dad. But then who in this town doesn't have the full low-down on me?

'I don't have a mum,' I explain.

Usually when I tell people this they get sad, or quiet, or even embarrassed, but not Zoe. She jumps up from her stool and grabs on to my apron. I try to move away from her touch. 'Oh my God. Do you . . . did you have two dads, too?'

'What? No!' I step back.

'Oh,' she says, looking deflated.

'It's my fault my mum died.' She lets go of me. I think I scared her. Good. 'She died giving birth to me.'

'Ooohhh,' she says, exhaling. She even smiles slightly. 'That's not your fault.'

'Well, I still feel guilty. If I weren't alive then my mum would be.'

'Life works in mysterious ways, but you should never feel guilty for living it.'

My chest tightens. I rest both hands carefully on the surface. Why is she talking like that? 'Did you say you have two dads?' I say in a rush.

'Yeah,' she says with a confident smirk. 'I have two dads.'

'Your parents are divorced, then? You have a dad and a stepdad?'

'No! Like you, I don't have a mum but mine is probably alive whereas yours . . . isn't. Ah, shit, sorry, that was insensitive. I guess I do have a mum, biologically, somewhere out there, but I don't think she deserves that title.'

'You're not making this clearer.'

'Oh, sorry. I have two gay dads. They're husband and husband.'

'Oh,' I say, before kicking myself at the surprised tone of my response. I try to make it better by adding, 'That's cool.'

'No, it's just . . . normal.'

'Well . . . It's not that normal, is it?' I can't seem to stop digging holes.

She shrugs her shoulders. 'It's my normal. Who's to say what's normal and what isn't?'

'I guess it's the majority in most cases.'

'Okay,' she says again. 'But who wants to be normal?'

Me. I want to be normal. That's all I want.

I glance up at her and she's just staring. Her eyes sinking into mine. I don't like it. 'So how did it . . . how did it work, with two dads?' I ask, clearing my throat as my voice starts to get croaky.

'They used a donated egg and a surrogate, which means the person who carried me is not my mum. I was just renting her out for nine months. I'm only related to one of my dads, but they're still both my dad, equally. Being biologically related to someone doesn't automatically make you any more of a parent, you have to earn that title.'

'Okay.' She's rambling again, and I'm starting to wish I never asked. I don't really know why I did.

'I actually don't know which one I'm related to. Although Paul is from Mauritius, and I don't look mixed race to you, do I? And I also have the same eye colour as Jerry, so it's fairly obvious. Plus, there's the fact that my sister looks nothing like me and is a mini version of Paul. So they clearly did one for each of us. Paul and Jerry are my dads, by the way,' she adds with another smile.

This girl likes to talk.

Chapter 10

Tristan

I'm greeted by Misha when I get home. Jeez, I'm so happy to see him. Before yesterday, I hadn't seen him for six whole months, but he still remembered me. He was just as excited to see me today, so much so that he only went and peed on the floor.

'Good boy,' I whisper as Luke puts paper towels down. He's definitely the same mutt, neutered or not. He takes off, galloping toward the kitchen and missing the door, running straight into the wall instead. He's always been clumsy. It takes him a few seconds to get his head back in the zone before he dashes off again, eventually waddling back towards me, blanket in his mouth and his little paws slipping on the wooden floor as he places it on the sofa.

I look at Luke. I'm guessing he's just come back from the gym, because he's wearing one of his ugly tank tops, and his forehead is glistening with gross beads of sweat.

Luke's a personal trainer, which you might think of as a job that's good for you, but somehow Luke takes it too far. He's obsessive when it comes to exercise, which is surely unhealthy. 'Thanks for looking after him while I was away,' I say, letting my eyes reach his very briefly.

Luke looks taken aback, like he isn't sure how to respond. 'Of course,' he says bending down and stroking Misha. 'How was it being back at work today?'

'It was fine.'

'You know you can still give it time before you go back properly.'

For some reason, Luke doesn't think it's wise for me to go back to work at the supermarket. He thinks I need time. But what I need is to work. I need to be busy. We're not short of money because of the insurance payout after Dad died. But I don't want to rely on that – on money that's supposed to somehow replace a life. I want to work and earn my own money. My own independence.

'Have you thought any more about uni? They posted another letter.'

'No, I haven't, and you shouldn't be reading my letters.'

Luke also wants me to go back to university. But that's a lost cause. The damage has been done, and I couldn't face going back there. What would be the point? I'm not the person I was back then. I don't want a degree, or a career. I don't want to do anything with my life now.

Luke quickly jumps up. 'Hey, I have something for you,' he calls over his shoulder, walking into the kitchen.

'Okay,' I reply, my eyes focused on Misha, who keeps nudging my arm with his head until I stroke him again. That's Misha for you, he demands attention twenty-four seven. He does this thing where he needs one part of him touching you at all times for him to be content. My hand on his head, leg by his back, or even him putting a paw on my foot. It's like he needs to physically know I'm still there, to confirm I'm not going anywhere. I wish I could promise him that.

I can hear the tap running in the kitchen. Misha is now lying on his back on the sofa, belly on show, tail whipping me in the back.

'One a day, right?'

I turn around to see Luke standing over me, a cup of water in his hand.

I let go of Misha and stand up to face him. He's also holding something in his other hand. Something so small and delicate, you could hardly know how powerful it is. 'I picked up the prescription this morning,' Luke says.

I glare at him. 'Well, where's the bottle?'

Luke shuffles slightly before placing the water and tablet on the table, then sighs.

It clicks.

'You won't tell me where it is, will you?' I say with an incredulous chuckle, shaking my head.

Luke's eyes crease. 'Tristan, it's not that—'

'I'm out of that place. I'm out of that place in my mind, and I'm not in hospital any more. The hospital that *you* sent me to—'

'Don't start, Tristan.'

'I'm out, Luke. I'm better.' I'm trying to stay calm. In counselling, they always said to 'argue smart'. If you're going to argue, they'd say, keep it calm, keep it smart. Because if you raise your voice, and get angry, you'll look in the wrong, even if you were in the right. Because of the past, and the way you used to act. But it's hard to argue smart when you feel like this – so wound up, so furious. I know Luke doesn't believe what I'm saying. I don't even believe what I'm saying. He doesn't reply, just runs a hand though his hair.

'Do you think I'm going to overdose?'

'No, Tristan, you know it's not that ... It's just—'

'It's just what?'

Luke tries to reply but shuffles awkwardly again. 'I don't care where the bottle is,' I say with a sigh. 'I always took the pills after food, so I'll take it after dinner.' I move towards the table, but before I even get near Luke swoops in and snatches the tablet away. Seriously?

I chew my lip as I stare at Luke. 'You want to see me swallow it?'

Luke looks tired. 'Tristan, I'm doing what they told me. You have to understand that.'

'No, I don't,' I say. 'I don't have to do anything ... Do you think that I don't want to take them?'

'No.'

'Do you think I'm going to pretend to take them?' I'm shouting now. I can feel that beating in my head, a pulsing through my veins, and I'm almost glad because it drowns out the fact that I'm lying so unashamedly. 'What do you think I'm going to do?'

'I don't think you going to do anything, Tristan.'

'Don't you trust me?' I whisper.

'I want to.'

'Then just take my word for it. Take your own brother's word, instead of the doctor's. For once, Luke. Do you think I want to go there again?'

Luke's eyes shift uncomfortably from the pills to me to Misha, who has jumped down from the sofa. It's as if he can't look at me for too long. 'I need to do what I think is right.'

I start squeezing my fists together. I squeeze tighter and tighter until I feel a burn in the cut on my hand. I push in the sore point of my bandage. I keep pressing and pressing until my arm eventually spasms. I look back up at Luke. *Smart, Tristan. Argue smart.* 'I get it,' I say. I walk forward, taking the pill out of Luke's hand and swallowing it. It takes Luke a minute before he slowly places the glass of water on the table and steps back.

I turn away from him and lie on the floor next to Misha, stroking his fur in the same spot over and over. The room is silent. We don't speak. Luke sits down on the sofa and starts pouring himself a drink. His phone rings. I hear him quickly jump up, and walk out of the room.

I pull Misha closer to me. My throat feels dry. I can feel my stomach already starting to churn and bubble. I keep my eyes wide as they start to sting.

Don't.

It's inside me. How long until it starts to work again? It feels like a foreign object invading my body. I shouldn't need it. I feel dirty. I stand up, pausing as my chest heaves heavily, before I manage to push myself upstairs.

I lock myself in the bathroom, plug the bath, and turn the taps on. I pace the room uncomfortably, my sweaty feet sticking to the floor. No, I'm not feeling better. I sit down on the toilet seat, and start clicking my fingers. Raking my hands through my hair. Stretching my neck. I can feel the heat from the water already hitting my face, feeding through my nose as I struggle to breathe. I feel it in my throat, my jaw, behind my eyes. It's not working. I rub my hands along my face and, leaning over the toilet, I stick a finger down my throat and throw up.

I'm not bulimic. Trust me on this. I'm a lot of things. but I'm not bulimic. It's just that my mind has made the firm decision not to take the pills any more, so my body has to go with it. I have to agree. I'm not proud of it, but I feel better.

I look at myself in the mirror and that's when I start to cry. This happens a lot, crying for no particular reason. I get upset often and most of the time I don't even know why. It's not about Dad any more – it used to be, in the months after he died, but it's not now. It's not about Luke, either, or my failed degree. It's not even about the medication, or hospital. It's not about anything. My sadness just comes from a hole. A hole that can't be filled.

I know what you're thinking: Tristan, you are pathetic. And I am. There are people with worse problems. There are people with cancer. People who have lost everyone. People with no food. People who are lonely, not by choice. People who have no money at all. People who don't have a home. People my age fighting for their lives. I should be thankful for the life I've got, not sad about it. I think about this a lot. I try to be thankful. I try to think how lucky I am. But then I only seem to get even more upset. Why can't I enjoy life? Why can't I be thankful?

Why can't I just be normal?

I've stayed in this bath a long time. So long that my skin is wrinkling up and the tub is cold. I rest my head under the water until I feel myself lying on the bottom of the bath. I grip on to the edge of the tub to hold my weight down. I wonder how long someone can stay under water until they drown. I wonder if it varies from person to person.

In my mind, I'm on a beach. It's West Wittering, where we used to go every summer. I can see Dad, and he waves at me. I can't lift my arm to wave back but I smile at him. His eyes glaze over me, and I follow his gaze to see Luke behind me. Luke takes a glug from his bottle of water, and chucks it to me before running up to Dad. I watch them playing football on the beach. I wish I could join them, but I can't seem to move. I can't stand up. I can smell the sea salt on the air. I can hear the seagulls chirping as they soar along their pathway through the sky. They start calling out. Calling for me. 'Tristan,' they sing. 'Tristan! Tristan!' Actually, it's not all as rhythmic as that. It's like they are shouting. Since when do they shout?

'Tristan, answer me.'

I can't. If I can't move how can I speak? 'Tristan! Tristan, you bloody idiot, answer me.'

I try to reply but I feel something in the back of my throat. It's choking me. It's filling me up. 'Tristan!' They shout again. 'Answer me! Open the door!'

It's not the seagulls I can hear.

I open my eyes and feel a pressure on my throat, seizing, burning, pushing. I throw myself up out of the water and suck in a huge gulp of air. I start panting as my body throws itself into heavy coughing fits.

'Tristan, answer me! Are you okay?' It's Luke. He continues to shout as he bangs on the bathroom door. I try to reply but my coughing bends me double over the tub, heaving up waves of soapy water.

'I'm fine,' I gasp, inhaling heavy breaths of air. 'I just . . . swallowed some water.'

'Jesus Christ . . . Jesus fucking Christ.' Then there's a pause, and his voice goes quiet, muffled through the door. 'You scared me, Tristan. You've been in there for hours, and then you weren't replying to me. You can't do that.'

'I'm sorry.'

'You can't do that, Tristan,' Luke says again.

'Yeah. I know,' I say between coughs. 'Sorry.'

That evening, Luke makes me a bacon and chicken salad for dinner. He texted me to tell me it was downstairs. As I'm leaving my room to take my plate back down to the kitchen, I see Luke standing by his bedroom door. He watches me, a beer in one hand and the other arm leant against the door. He doesn't let his eyes leave my face.

'What?' I say defensively.

He continues to watch me, his eyes telling me something I don't understand. His mouth twitches, he wants to say something, but he stays quiet. He runs a hand through his hair before taking a step away from the door.

'What's wrong?' I ask.

Luke opens his mouth, but then he pauses. 'Nothing,' he says as takes a swig of his beer. 'Did you like the food?'

Before I get the chance to answer he goes back into his room. Fine. I don't care. I start to head into my own room when I hear the downstairs toilet flush. Who's downstairs? For a brief moment I wonder if it's Sally, the woman who cleans our house, and I slowly head towards the stairs, passing Luke's room. He seems oblivious as he sits on his bed, casually drinking his beer. The toilet door creaks open and the sound of footsteps follow.

I turn away from Luke, who shows no signs of reacting,

and head down the stairs, which is when I see a petite red-headed girl. She looks about my age, and I think I might have even seen her before, around uni. She is clutching a tiny bag while wearing very high heels that tap on our floorboards. She throws me a smile as she walks past me up the stairs. Stunned into confusion, I follow her. I follow her straight towards Luke's room. He stands up and smiles at her, using his hands to brush her hair away from her face. He carefully cups her face, before guiding her mouth towards his. They instantly start kissing; and as he heaves her up on to him, she hooks her legs around his waist. With the redhead still clinging on to him, Luke moves towards the door. His blank eyes catch mine, then he slams it shut.

Gemma didn't last long, then.

Chapter 11

Zoe

I'm sitting on the pavement with Anais, waiting for her boyfriend to pick her up after coaching. Jerry's sending his usual stream of texts again, asking when I'll be home, what I want for dinner. What's new?

Anais is my go-to girl at coaching. She tends to keep herself to herself, but she's always lovely to me. We're shivering in the cold February air, when I hear, 'All right, Pebble?'

I turn my head to see Jack, our bleach-haired friend who coaches with us, walking towards us through the leisure centre door.

Jack always calls me 'Pebble'. When I first started, the coach told him my name and somehow he misheard. How someone confuses 'Zoe' with 'Pebble', I don't know; but even after he realised his mistake he carried on calling me it. I like it, though; it's completely random – just like the best things in life. Anais nudges me, and I can feel her eyes boring into me. I refuse to look at her, even when she says, 'Shall I leave?', with what I imagine is a smug grin.

I shush her, right before Jack sits himself between us.

'I didn't really get the chance to speak to you guys in all the badminton madness,' he says in his usual cheery manner.

'I noticed,' I reply, biting my lip, trying to hide the grin that always springs to my face when Jack is around. 'Lucky us.'

Jack chuckles and elbows me, but then his face grows serious. 'How was the doctor's the other day?'

I grit my teeth, throwing my eyes towards Anais, who doesn't seem to be paying attention. 'Fine,' I say, tightly.

'What did they say?' Jack asks, clearly not getting the hint about the unwanted change of subject.

I exhale heavily. The hint is there, Jack, take it, keep it if you want, but don't ignore it. We had one deep conversation, months ago now, and I made the mistake of getting emotional and opening up. I made him promise not to talk about it afterwards – a promise he seems determined not to keep. I know it's because he cares, but he needs to leave it alone.

I stare at him, angrily. 'Not much.'

'I'm just going to call Adam, one sec,' Anais says as she trots away, using her boyfriend as an excuse to give us 'alone time'. She's obviously oblivious to the turn our conversation has taken.

I roll my eyes as Jack shuffles closer. 'Sure you're okay, Pebble?'

'Yeah, I'm fine,' I mumble, avoiding his eyes.

'Did something bad happen at the hospital? You can tell me, you know.' He puts a hand on my leg. I really don't want to lose it with Jack, so I decide to distract him.

'We should do something together again soon, outside of coaching,' I say, squeezing his hand slightly.

His eyes light up. 'Yeah? Okay.'

'My friend from work is having a party in a couple of weeks, you could come?'

His mouth twitches, and there's a glint in his eye. 'I'd love to, do you want me to pick you up?'

'Cool,' I say, releasing his hand and standing up. 'I've already asked Anais, she's coming too.'

'Oh ... okay.'

'Maybe we can all get a lift together, or I'll meet you guys there?'

'Yeah, sure,' Jack says, standing up as well.

'Anyway, I'll text you. I've got to head – you know what Jerry gets like if I'm late. I'll see you next week?'

I turn around, before even letting him give me a hug or a wave. I walk towards Anais, who conveniently seems to have finished her phone call now.

'Got any news for me?' she says smugly.

'Yeah, I do – want to come to a party in a couple of weeks?'

Chapter 12

Tristan

I've had three days off work. It's been hell. I phoned up and asked Juliette for overtime, but she said she didn't need me. Bullshit.

Luke's redhead didn't stay long, but a blonde-haired girl made her way into our house the very next day, then the day after that I caught a glimpse of another redhead. Different girl, same hair colour.

Luke continued to deliver my pills to me, but he kept more distance. He didn't want to cause an issue like last time, and I didn't either. When he appeared in my doorway with a pill and a glass of water, I performed a simple trick. Pop pill in mouth, stick pill under tongue, take a drink, exaggerate a swallow. Spit out the pill when you get the opportunity. Unfortunately, this only works with capsule pills, if you try it with the other type they'll melt under your tongue.

Other than these interactions, Luke and I have spent

most of the three days keeping out of each other's way, quite successfully. We only had one argument, on my second day with no shifts, over a box of smokes. Can you believe that he stole my cigarettes? If I want to smoke I can smoke, I'm not a child. It was the packet I took from the waiting room woman, which I remembered would be in my jeans pocket. When I realised they were missing, I started to feel panicked. I couldn't deal with the thought that I needed them right at that moment and I couldn't have them. The doctors would tell me this is my anxiety again, but it's not. I just need my cigarettes, for God's sake.

I'd been looking for my jeans and found them in the laundry room, which meant Sally had done my washing for me. Sally has been our cleaner ever since I can remember. I like Sally – you can tell she's a good person, and is always around for a chat. I find her easier to talk to than Luke. In fact, our whole family finds her easier to talk to than each other. Dad got on really well with her and would sometimes invite her and her daughter round for a drink at Christmas.

I remember when Dad first died, though it's so weird to think that's two years ago now, Sally was the one who told me. I thought it was strange to see her knocking on the door of my uni house. Before I had time to process what she was saying she pulled me into her arms and she just held me. She hugged me for what could have been hours. I imagine that must be what it's like to have a mum. I don't think I've ever hugged Luke.

It wouldn't have been Sally who stole my cigarettes. She's a smoker, too. But if she ever found anything in my pocket she'd give it to me. We even used to have a smoke together when Luke was at work. I've only seen her once briefly these past three days, when she gave me a box of chocolates and another big hug as a welcome home present. But no cigarettes. Which means someone took them from my jeans before they were washed. And it's not like there are many people living in this house.

Luke claimed he didn't take them, and began lecturing me on smoking. Soon we were shouting. Then I said, 'I'll buy my own, I'll just go to the shop.' He laughed and said, 'Good luck walking in the rain.'

'I'll drive your car there,' I snapped back. But once I got outside, I felt the keys wrenched from my hand and Luke dragging me back inside.

Apparently I'm not allowed to drive any more. Well, that's just awesome.

After all of this, Luke apologised for shouting and went upstairs. Later on, some of his friends came round to watch the football. I stole their tobacco.

Yesterday, my friend Joe came round. We've been friends since we were little, and have always lived down the road from each other. Even though he went straight into work, and I went to uni, he'd still tag along with my uni friends, even on nights out, and fit right in. Sometimes better than me. We stayed best mates, even when he got a work transfer up north, about two years ago – not long before Dad died. Through all of that he made sure he stayed in touch.

Joe's back in Surrey now – but it's different. He took a day off work to see me and even though he had to be up at five the next morning, he took me to the pub we used to go to when we were younger and bought a round of the beer we used to drink. But things weren't how they used to be. It was like I had a big stamp across my head that said 'mentally unwell'. Joe just shuffled on his seat, forcing out awkward questions, as if we were strangers on a first date.

'So how are things with Luke?'

'Yeah, fine.' I'd decided he didn't need to hear about our latest argument.

'You watch the football yesterday?'

'Um . . . no.' Since when did we talk about football?

'It's been ages since we saw each other, Tristan.'

'I know, I'm sorry.'

'Don't be sorry. It's just . . . crazy, you know?'

'Yeah, I know.'

I know what Joe wants to say, but won't. Depression is a sour word that offends people when it's spoken aloud. I can't even talk to my best friend any more, and I know it's my fault. I'm the one who changed. I changed everything.

I see Zoe as I start my Thursday shift. She isn't working, though. I'm on the tills when I spot her through the window. Standing by the sports field. I know it's her instantly by her ridiculous hair, and I can also tell it's her from the clothes she's wearing. She has on a baggy white jumper half-hidden under vertically striped, multi-coloured dungaree shorts, and under those are fishnet tights, and chunky black DMs. Why does she want to look like that?

I don't know why I'm still watching her. I think she's watching the athletics training on the field, but then I see her get something out of her rucksack and then there's a flash. It's a camera. But not a digital one. I can just make out from the way she winds it on that it's one of those plastic disposable ones that you would take on school trips. I didn't even know they still existed.

As the group she's watching start running a relay, I see her body twitching as if she's going to jump in there and join them. She bounces up and down slightly, her arms gently pumping, and though I can't see from here, I can just tell her eyes are wide with excitement. When the race ends she throws her arms up in the air, celebrating on her own. There's no other spectators, no one to high five, hug or cheer with, and I think she realises this because she slowly stops jumping around and sinks to the floor. She crosses her legs, hands picking at the ground, her eyes still not leaving the field.

After my shift, I bump into Zoe again. Or, more accurately, she bumps into me, intentionally. I'm in the cloakroom, getting my things out of my locker, when I hear her.

'Hi, Tree.'

I almost jump out of my skin when she appears right next to me. 'Jesus Christ,' I mutter.

'Nope, but I do get told I look like him.'

'What are you doing here?' I ask her, a little bit too aggressively.

She rests her arm on my locker door. 'I work here. You know that.'

'No, what are you doing in the men's cloakroom?'

She shrugs. 'I thought I'd say hi.'

'You're not allowed in here.'

She raises her eyebrows, turning the sides of her mouth up. 'You should try breaking the rules now and again, it makes life a lot more exciting.'

'But women aren't allowed in the men's cloakroom.'

She rolls her eyes. 'Come on, Tree.' So she's still calling me Tree, then. 'We're in 2018, those rules are so old-fashioned. Lighten up.'

Lighten up. If only I could.

Looking at her makes me uncomfortable. I'm not the biggest fan of eye contact at the best of times, and right now her eyes are barely giving me space to breathe. She's wearing another set of hoop earrings with her work outfit, which catch the light of the cloakroom glare, making them even more painfully colourful.

'You going home?' she asks. I'm slightly scared to answer in case she takes it as an invitation. She shuffles closer to me. 'Well, I'm guessing you are,' she says. 'So I'm glad I got you in time.' She hangs off a locker door, tips herself even closer to me and sighs exaggeratedly. 'I literally just came all the way from a lecture, I'm exhausted.'

Why is she lying? I know she's been out in the field for the past two hours. I've been watching her. 'Okay,' I say slowly, unsure how to react to the lie, but at the same time not really that bothered. As usual, the attempt to put an end to further conversation only results in more questions from Zoe.

'Where did you go to university?'

'Surrey.'

Her eyes widen with excitement. 'Oh my God, same. How weird is that?'

'Not that weird, considering we both live in Surrey.'

'But, see, it is quite weird, *because* we both live in Surrey. Most people go away for uni. So, you did Business Studies, right?'

I roll my eyes and nod. What didn't people tell her about me? And why does it even matter what I studied? It means nothing now anyway.

She tilts her head. 'Are you going back? To retake your last year? Because you failed it?'

It's straight to the point with this girl. I shake my head. 'Why?'

'I don't know. I don't think I could do it. Especially not now, I've missed nearly a year already.'

'Does that mean you're going to work here full time?'

'What are you studying?' I ask her, trying out a different tactic in an attempt to stop the endless questions from her side.

She twists her mouth. 'I'm in my final year of Sports Science,' she says. Her tone of voice has suddenly changed. It's flatter now.

'Do you enjoy it?'

She wrinkles her nose. 'I used to.'

'Too hard now?'

'No,' she says loudly. 'It's easy. I'm good at it. It's just different now. I don't think I want a career in this sort of stuff any more.'

'But at least you get a degree.'

'I suppose so.' She pauses before she looks up at me and perks up again. 'But it's fine, things change.'

Oh, I know about that. 'Yeah, sure do.'

'Change doesn't have to be a bad thing, though.' Out of nowhere I feel her hand touch mine. I quickly swipe it away.

'Calm down,' she whispers. 'Hold out your hand.'

'I'm okay, thanks.'

She frowns. 'I wasn't asking you a question. Open your hand.'

My eyebrows lower. 'Why?'

'Don't you trust me, Tree?'

'That's not my name, and no.'

'You don't trust *me*?'

'I don't even know you.'

'I work with you.'

'You've worked with me once.'

'But this is just the start, we're going to be working with each other all the time. Meaning we are going to continue to see each other.'

I sigh, wondering how rude it'd be to leave her without saying goodbye.

She carries on smirking. 'Look, I have something for you. And if you open your hand, you'll find out what.'

Because I'm annoyingly curious, I eventually give in, giving her my hand and opening my palm. This is when she places a slightly rugged cigarette packet in it. I squint as it sits in my hand, and realise it's the packet I stole.

The packet I accused Luke of stealing from me. Shit. He wasn't lying. Now I feel guilty.

I notice Zoe has drawn a big smiley face over one side of the packet. It's the same kind of smiley face she was drawing on the notepad.

'Smoking kills,' she says with a smile.

'When did you steal these from me?'

'Oh, I don't steal,' she says with wide, innocent eyes. 'It was you who stole them.'

'Come on, it's not like I robbed a bank.'

'But you still stole them,' she says, taking one step closer.

'And then dropped them when you got all angry with the bus shelter.'

I feel heat rise to my cheeks. So she definitely did see me punch the bus shelter.

'Remember, outside the hospital?' she grins. 'It was weird, and then you stormed away—'

'Yes. I remember,' I cut in. 'Wait a minute. You said smoking kills?'

'Yes,' she says with a firm nod of the head. 'I'm glad you're taking note of it. I'm sure it's hard to give up smoking, but starting with the right mindset is probably the first step.'

'No,' I scrunch up my face. 'What I mean is if you're so against smoking, why did you give them back to me?'

'I told you, I don't steal.' Her face has suddenly gone serious. 'And I know these weren't even yours in the first place, but I needed to give them back anyway. What were the chances we would see each other again? Let alone that you'd be working on the same till as me. How crazy, right?'

I rub a hand through my hair. 'Yup. Very crazy.'

'I think it's fate,' she whispers.

I sigh, rotating the small card box in my hand. I look back up to her. 'Thanks for giving it back.'

'No problem, Tristan.' She lifts up the disposable camera from earlier, and before I know what's happening I feel a flash in my face, and with that she leaves the cloakroom.

On my way home from work, I run my finger across the smiley face on the packet, but it doesn't even smudge. It must be permanent. I hate anything permanent. It's the worst kind of thing. With a heavy sigh, I open the box.

What the hell?

I'm staring at a row of small white cylinders. They could be mistaken for cigarettes, but they're not. I take one out and feel my nose start to twitch. No way. I roll it through my fingers before slowly lifting it to my mouth and cautiously taking a bite. They are candy sticks, the kind that kids used to pretend to smoke. She must think she is hilarious. I run my finger along that stupid smiley face before chucking the packet on the ground.

Chapter 13

Zoe

I glide up to the chocolate bars. We have a connection that cannot be broken, a Romeo and Juliet thing, a mac and cheese pairing, a salt and pepper duo. Chocolate and I go together like a love story and there's no denying it. I pick up a big bar of Cadbury's, slide my way up to the trolley Jerry's pushing and pop it in. Jerry picked me up from work earlier, because it was raining. Even though I was totally happy walking in the rain. He told me he needed to go food shopping, then drove us all the way to the giant Tesco down the road. It's like he forgets I work at a supermarket. I won't lie, spending my free time food shopping with my dad isn't my most favourite thing in the world. But hey, I know he likes any chance to spend what he calls 'quality time' with me. He peers into the trolley and frowns.

I feel myself copying his expression. 'What?' I say, now

with my eyebrows raised. 'It will make me happy, Jerry. And happiness is very important in the growth and development of a child.'

'Good job you're twenty then, and *not* a child,' he says, playing me at my own game.

'I'm going to be twenty-one soon,' I say with a proud smile.

'That just backs up my argument.'

I sigh angrily. 'Come on, Jerry.'

'Come on, Zoe.' He's good at this. We've been here many times before. Doesn't mean I won't continue to try. He can't disrupt true love. What if they did that to Romeo and Juliet?

Oh. Wait. They did, didn't they?

I look at him and smile sweetly. 'What about Fruit and Nut? Practically healthy.'

Jerry shakes his head.

'Jerrrrrrry,' I moan. I know I'm acting like a teenager, but there's a tendency for that to happen when you have to live at home with your parents and little sister. Jerry sighs, resting his hands on the trolley. 'You can have one *small* bar of dark chocolate,' he says. '*Small.*'

'Fine,' I mumble, as I start rolling away, purposely leaving the Cadbury's bar in the trolley. You know, just in case. And if he does take it out, it's fine. I'll stock up at work, I get discount for a reason. It's just more of a treat when Jerry buys it for me. As I start sliding away down the aisle I bump into my little sister. I say 'little' because she's three years younger than me, but she is actually about five inches taller. Leia is always up for a supermarket trip.

'Watch it, loser,' Leia says.

I stick my tongue out at her, grab a bar of dark chocolate and swiftly turn around. I glide up to the trolley, throw the chocolate in, and that's when my wheel slips from beneath me. I feel my balance giving way, so I save myself by pulling Jerry's trolley towards me. The unfortunate thing about this decision is that Jerry, who's leaning on the trolley, nearly falls over. Once he composes himself, he stands up and sighs. He does a lot of sighing these days. I'm sure it's not good for his chest.

'Do you have to wear those wheel things?' Jerry asks.

By 'those wheel things' he means the pair of shoes I'm currently wearing. You know, those trainers that have the wheels in? Fabulous invention. They are also banned from supermarkets – I know, call me a rebel.

'You mean my Heelys?' I say innocently.

'*My* Heelys,' Leia says. 'That I haven't worn for five years because they are too small for me.'

I shrug my shoulders as I start rotating circles around her. 'I can't help it if I have sweet petite innocent feet.'

'I also haven't worn them for five years because they are for kids. *Kids.*' Leia says this as if it's a good point to make.

I lean my head back and smile. 'But we are all kids at heart, little sis. There's nothing to be embarrassed about here.'

'Start acting your age.'

'I don't need to act anything. We're not all actors, Leia.'

'What are you saying?'

'We don't all put on a show like you.'

I can feel Leia starting to get worked up. She folds her arms and opens her mouth to reply, but Jerry cuts in. 'How was college?' he asks.

'Boring,' Leia says, as she chucks something in the cart, uninspected by Jerry.

'How was uni, Zoe?'

I shrug my shoulders. 'I don't know. I didn't go.'

I hear Jerry sigh again. I've already pissed him off. Well, what did he expect? Does he want me to lie? I stare at him, feeling my mouth tighten, before forming an exaggerated smile. 'I spent most of my day watching the athletics team.' Jerry turns his head towards me, and now his mouth is tight. 'They're okay, but they could definitely be better. I think the relay team is lacking a key member.' I feel Leia's eyes on me now. 'They're practising because they are going up against the Manchester team soon. I'll probably go watch. Be supportive. If they win that, they go into nationals, you know.' I can still feel both sets of eyes on me. But they don't speak. I don't let them. 'That will be cool for them. Nationals. Can you imagine that? I'm sure that'll be something that will stay with them their *whole* life. Like for ever. Once in a lifetime. I thi—'

'Remind me that we need to go to the pharmacy after this,' Jerry says, cutting me off. Distraction techniques are Jerry's tactic of choice. I don't reply; instead, I continue to stare at him for a few more seconds before I start talking again.

'The sprinters are fast. Which is good. But I think the long-distance runners need work.' I'm talking quickly, I don't want him to interrupt me.

'Zoe,' he mutters. A warning.

'I've seen better, basically. Their speed is good, but they need to focus on their endurance.'

'Zoe.'

'That's an important thing, that is. Endurance.'

I pause, waiting for Jerry to say my name again. But he doesn't. He just watches me carefully, before saying, 'You should have gone to university today.'

Seriously? What's the point in arguing? I turn around and start walking away.

'Zoe. Zoe!' I turn around to see Leia running after me. 'Are you all rig—'

'Hey,' I say with a smile.

'What?'

I bend down, slip her Heelys off my feet, and hand them to her. 'Thanks for letting me wear your shoes.'

Leia looks at the shoes in her hand, and at my odd socks resting on the supermarket floor. 'You can still wear them.'

'I don't want to,' I say with a smile. I turn around and start walking away again.

'What are you doing, Zoe?' Leia shouts.

'Tell Jerry I'm walking home!' I shout.

'But—'

'I'm a big girl, Leia.'

'But Zoe, Dad will—'

'Walking, Leia. I'm walking home.'

Chapter 14

Tristan

Luke can do one.

We had an argument, because he put a lock on his bathroom cabinet. That's where he keeps my meds. That's how much he trusts me. I got angry. I said nasty stuff. He said nasty stuff back. I started throwing things. And then there was pushing. Then he slapped me. He tried to say sorry but by that point I already had Misha on his lead and was out the door.

I have no idea how long I've been walking for, and I've mostly been going in circles. It doesn't matter, though; I highly doubt Luke is worried. I've done this a lot in the past – leave. Sometimes I'd be back at home within five minutes but other times it'd be days. Luke used to panic at first, but he eventually understood he had no control over it. No control over me. Just because Dad died it didn't mean he could replace him. It's not like I'm some stupid kid who can't look after himself. I'm just a stupid adult instead.

It's fine, walking. It's piss cold, proper winter weather, even though it's supposed to be March now. My feet are hurting, and the left side of my face is burning from where Luke slapped me, but it's okay – at least it was until the heavens decided to open up. I stop walking, and stand there in the rain like an idiot.

'Shit,' I mutter. It hasn't been raining for long and it's already getting into my shoes, soaking through my jumper, and making my hands cold and slippery. I pull my hood up, but it's pointless. The thin piece of jersey is going to do very little to protect me. I look down at Misha, who is running in circles. He always does this when he gets wet. Stupid dog. Then in full Misha style he stops, flops on the floor, and starts wriggling in a puddle like he's fully possessed. Well, this is bloody great. I look around, searching for options. I glance towards some nearby trees – maybe I could shelter there for a while? But then I remind myself that I'm in England. Meaning the rain could last for a few seconds, or it could last for a few days.

Walking into the park wasn't a good idea. There are no shops I can go to, no cafés, no restaurants. Just grass. Pavement. Trees. Not ideal. I sigh, turning around in defeat. 'Come on, Mish,' I say as I start walking. But he doesn't follow. Instead, he pulls me backwards, legs shaking, tail wagging, as he stares in the opposite direction. I look up, following his gaze across the park to see someone slowly walking through the rain. They're too far away for me to work out if it's a man or a woman, but it doesn't look like they are wearing very much. Not that smart, considering we're only just out of February. I give Misha one last firm tug and turn around again, and this time he listens and starts following me back to our house. I am already dreading what Luke is going to say. And Sally. I know she just wants what's best for me, but I can't be dealing with her playing 'Mum' right now.

'Hey!'

I turn around with a frown to see the person – a girl, it turns out – running at me through the thick wave of rain. I find myself squinting through the water droplets as she moves closer, and suddenly I know who it is. It's Zoe. The girl with the purple hair. She is completely soaked through, wearing a big, vibrant shell-suit jacket, over high-waisted shorts. It seems she's not very good at dressing for the weather.

Her mouth stretches into a chattering-toothed smile. 'What are the chances?' she shouts over the rain, before shuffling herself closer to me. 'It's like the world wants us to be friends.'

I lower my eyebrows. Now I understand why I didn't notice it was her at first. It's the hair. Now it's wet and hanging by her face, it looks almost grey, not purple. She's clutching on to her soaked arms as she continues to shake. I move my eyes to the ground. She's not wearing shoes, just some odd socks that are so drenched they are almost see-through.

'You all right, Tree?'

I lift my eyes to hers, feeling a frown of confusion still tight on my face. 'Are you following me?' I shout back.

Apparently, she finds that amusing, because she bursts into a fit of giggles. 'Don't flatter yourself,' she yells, then her face goes serious. 'Are *you* following *me*?'

'No,' I snap. I look around. There's no one else out here. Why is she chilling in the rain alone? How did she even get here with no shoes on? 'What are you doing here in the rain?'

'What are you doing out here?' she shouts with a smile.

Jesus Christ, why can't she just answer my question? I nod my head towards Misha. 'Taking my dog for a walk.'

'Same.'

I take a quick glance around, but she very clearly doesn't have a dog with her.

She catches on to my confusion. 'Oh yeah, without the dog,' she says. 'I'm just going for a walk.'

I lower my eyes to her feet again. 'Why aren't you wearing shoes?'

'I didn't want to,' she replies, almost as if that answer needs no further explanation.

'You're . . . strange,' I reply, as my eyes scan her.

She doesn't seem offended. She stretches her mouth wide so that I can see all her teeth grinning back at me. 'All the best people are,' she shouts with a failed wink as a droplet of water splashes into her eye.

The rain has slowed down. It's at a level that's not pain-ful any more, but it's still heavy, it's still cold and it's still wet. And have you realised we are casually having a con-versation in the rain? It's not that easy, when your ears are full of water. It's also pretty stupid, too. I decide to head back to the house, and tilt my body slightly, indicating that I'm going to leave, but Zoe doesn't take the hint. She just stands there, smiling at me.

'Well, I'm going to go back to my house now ...' I say.

'It's cold, isn't it?' she replies, still not moving.

She seems a lot colder than me, shaking heavily beneath her clothes. Her skin is starting to look pale. 'Where do you live?'

She twists her mouth. 'I live opposite the garden centre.'

Did I hear her right? That's nowhere near the park. 'How far is that from here?' I swear it's a long walk.

'Maybe half an hour, if I'm slow. What about you?' she replies, casually.

'I live near here, about ten minutes. Maybe even less.'

'Ah, that's good, Tree,' she says with a smile. She isn't giving up on this Tree thing. 'I'll see you next week at work, hopefully looking a lot drier.' She must finally have taken the hint, because she turns around, and starts walk-ing off in the opposite direction.

But for some reason, I don't leave. I watch her as she walks away slowly through the rain. Why am I not walk-ing? She's well and truly soaked. And it's still raining.

Half an hour is a long time, especially without any shoes.

I run a hand through my hair.

Bloody hell.

'Zoe!'

She turns around.

I let out a heavy sigh.

You're an idiot, Tristan.

'Do you want to come back to my place?'

Chapter 15

Zoe

'So, you live with your brother?' I ask him, walking quickly to keep up.

'Yeah,' Tristan replies, showing off the full range of that large vocabulary of his.

'You stayed at home for uni?'

Tristan looks back at me and lowers his eyebrows, as if I asked a stupid question. 'No, I lived in a student house. It was nearer uni and, you know, the student living is ninety per cent of the experience.'

'So you moved home after your second year?'

'No, I went home after ...'

'Oh shit, your dad. Sorry!' I clap my hand over my mouth. 'But hey! This is so cool, because we did the same thing. I was in halls but I'm spending my third year at home. Just like you did. Now that's freaky stuff! Seriously, what are the chances that we would both have done that?'

Tristan stops walking. 'Was living in halls too expensive?'

I feel my mouth start to twist. 'No.'

'So what made you move back home?' he says.

'I'm just spending my last year living with my family. Family is important to me, and I missed them,' I reply, nibbling on my lip, wishing I'd never brought the subject up.

'But if anyone was going to live at home for a year, it'd be their first, not their last.'

'Well, I don't like doing what everyone else would do.'

'I can see that. But what you're doing is weird.'

I shove my fidgeting hands in my wet pockets. 'Maybe I want to be weird.' I decide to change the subject. 'I think it's pretty cool we've lived so near to each other our whole life, even went to the same uni, and never met until now.'

He shrugs. 'Surrey is a big place.'

'But we live like a ten-minute drive from each other. It's *so* near. I could have passed you on the street, been on the same bus as you, sat next to you in a restaurant, and it wouldn't have meant anything as I wouldn't have known who you were. Don't you think that's crazy?'

There's a pause, before he says, 'Not really.'

Hmph. He's no fun.

When we get to his front door, he stands and holds his keys awkwardly. As he's about to open the door, he turns around and stares at me, doing that thing he does with eyebrows. Lowering them so much that you can barely see his eyes. 'This doesn't mean I want to sleep with you,' he says.

I cock my head slightly. 'Sorry?'

He exhales heavily through his nose. 'Just because I'm inviting you to my house, it doesn't mean I want to have sex with you. I don't want you to get the wrong idea.'

I can't help but smile. It's my natural instinct. A surprise, I smile. An awkward situation, I smile. A sad moment, I smile – purely because I don't know how else to react. It can get me into some sticky situations. 'Well, Tree,' I say confidently. 'I'm glad we're on the same wavelength, as having sex with you was certainly not on my agenda, at least not today.' I wink at him. But I don't think he's entertained.

Tristan watches me carefully. It's faded now, but earlier one side of his face was bright pink, as though he was blushing, but just on one side. He looked so odd, it was most entertaining. Now he gives me a firm nod before turning around and stepping up to the door again. And thank God, because I'm freezing. Really wet, too, and the longer we wait out here the wetter we're going to get. (See, I know science.)

I shuffle closer to him under the porch to get out of the drizzle as he fiddles with the key, but he swiftly backs up into me. He turns around, glaring. I take a careful step away from the shelter of the porch, back into the rain again. I suppose it doesn't matter. How much wetter can I actually get at this point? He pauses with the key in his hand again, turns around and watches me intently. He looks in pain. Or like he needs to go to the toilet.

'Sorry,' he eventually says. It's almost like he finds it hard to talk. 'I didn't mean to be rude.'

'About what?' I say, feeling my face scrunch in confusion.

'With the whole ... sex thing. I didn't mean it to come across ...'

'Oh, that. No. Stop being stupid. It wasn't rude.'

'No, it was,' he mumbles.

Can he open the door first, and then talk about this? He could be regretful inside the house, too, it doesn't just have to be an outside thing.

'I just ... I don't know. It didn't come out the way I meant.'

'Stop worrying,' I say, taking a step closer to him again. I can see he finds it uncomfortable, but I'm under the porch now, and finally sheltered from the rain. 'In fact, Tristan,' I say, trying to hold eye contact with him, something he clearly doesn't like to do, 'I think it was a wise thing to say, really wise, because I don't have the prettiest underwear on today. I'm wearing my granny knickers.' He watches me steadily, and I can't work out if he believes me or not. But then he mumbles something else, before quickly opening the door and stepping inside.

Finally.

Tristan has a nice place. It's a town house that's modern inside with big, tidy rooms. The kitchen is shiny, the oak coffee table is glistening, the pictures on the walls polished. But something about it doesn't feel right. I can tell even Tristan doesn't feel comfortable here. It's a lovely house, yes, but that's the thing – it's a house, not a home.

There was no sign of his brother when we walked in, but there was someone else in the house with us – a petite woman walking around doing numerous little jobs who smiled kindly, if a bit curiously, at me. It turns out she is the cleaner, which explains why the house is so spotless. She seemed friendly, and kept trying to talk to Tristan, asking him where he'd been. But he just shrugged her away, so I didn't get to speak to her much before she left, shouting her goodbyes down the hall to Tristan and Luke as she went.

Anyway, I'm sitting on the sofa now as Tristan stands there by the door. Doing nothing. Saying nothing. Just standing there. I know he keeps staring at me, but it's hard to catch him in the act because every time I look at him, he quickly looks away. Now, I rarely feel uncomfortable, but with Tristan hovering there, watching me in silence, I'm starting to wish I was back out in the rain again.

'We have a shower.'

I start and turn towards him. 'Well done?' I say slowly.

'You can use it ... the shower.'

'Oh, I see.'

He still stands there by the doorway, not moving. 'So ... do you want a shower?'

I grin. 'Why, are you saying I need one?'

Tristan glares at me. I'm learning he's not one for a joke.

'I would love a shower. Thank you, Tree.'

'Why do you call me that?'

'Because I like trees and I like you.'

'I like smoking but you don't see me calling you Cigarette.'

I feel my mouth curve into a slight smile. 'And I'm glad you don't.'

There's a pause before he says, 'You can wear some of my dry clothes, too.'

The shower is warm, enveloping me in a fuzzy bubble of heat as the steam clouds the room. There's something nice about going from cold rain to hot running water, it's like a pleasant shock to the body.

I can't believe I'm naked in Tristan's shower. I find myself giggling as the water runs down my face and drips into my mouth. I don't know why it's funny, but I'm laughing again. Maybe it's because he's been naked here, and now I'm naked here. It's a guy's shower, that's for sure. No hair conditioner, exfoliator or the like, only men's shower gel. I don't mind, though; I love that mannish smell.

When I get out, I change into the clothes Tristan has left out for me: a dark top of his and some tracksuit bottoms. The clothes drown me, but I don't care. I'm cosy, and it was kind of him.

I come back into the living room where he's now sitting, but he doesn't say anything. Has he been just sitting here the whole time? We may have descended into silence again, but I think that proves something. I think that proves we are secretly friends. We don't need to go to the effort of small talk.

As conversation isn't on the cards, I decide to look around the room. There's fitness stuff everywhere. Obviously, I head towards the treadmill and slowly stroke my fingers along the machine. This might make me a massive nerd but I know it's a NordicTrack Commercial and that it's expensive. I'd do anything to be able to try it out. I run my fingers along the frame again, I even close my eyes.

'It's Luke's.'

I turn around to see Tristan standing behind me (at a distance, might I add). I try to hold his gaze again but he drops his eyes to the ground. I can see that eye contact makes him feel weird, but he was watching me first. He has pulled his sleeves down so that they are covering his hands, and starts to pick at the material. 'The treadmill,' he explains, 'is Luke's, my brother. All of the exercise stuff is.'

'Luke has good taste in equipment. I like him.'

Tristan doesn't appear to like that answer because he scoffs and slumps down on the sofa. 'You can use it if you want.'

I quickly withdraw my hand from the machine. 'No, I'm fine.'

'I can tell you want to.'

I move towards the sofas and sit opposite him. He continues to pick at his sleeves. 'Maybe I do, but I'm not going to.'

'Why?'

I feel myself smile at him. 'There doesn't have to be a reason behind every decision we make.'

His eyebrows fall. 'So you're not going to go on the treadmill, just because.'

'We can go with that.'

'Are you just being difficult?'

'Maybe,' I say, matching his frown with yet another smile.

The kitchen door suddenly flings open, and out gallops the dog, bashing straight past the coffee table and stopping by my legs before deciding to shake his whole body, spraying lovely wet dogginess all over me. The world really wants me to be drenched today.

'Shit, sorry,' Tristan mutters, grabbing on to Misha.

'It's fine,' I laugh, leaning down and rubbing Misha's wet fur. What do I care? Water dries at the end of the day. The dog flops his head on me.

'Sorry,' Tristan says again before latching on to the pup's collar, tugging him away from me. The dog clearly loves me, because he refuses to leave. 'Misha, come on!'

My eyes light up. 'Misha Collins?' I say, mouth open with excitement.

I don't think Tristan understands. 'What?'

'Castiel?' I go on.

He just frowns at me.

'Tree, do you like *Supernatural*?'

He shakes his head.

'Oh.' Well, there goes my excitement. I push Tristan's hand away from Misha's collar and pull the dog close to me again, kneeling down next to him. As usual, Tristan snatches his hand away from my touch. He slowly sits back down, and I can feel him watching me. 'So why did you call him Misha?' I ask.

'I didn't,' he replies. 'Luke did. Maybe he reads *Supernatural*.'

'*Watches Supernatural*.' I correct him. 'Well, he suits his name perfectly,' I say, leaning in so that I'm rubbing noses with this adorable – albeit stinky and slightly dumb – dog. 'He's a little angel.'

I hear another scoff from Tristan. 'I doubt that's why Luke named him that,' he says.

I glance up at Tristan, and I can tell that instantly makes him feel uncomfortable again.

'Tree, do you think dogs are dying?' I ask.

This catches him off guard, and he squints at me. 'What sort of a question is that?'

'Not a rhetorical one,' I say.

'I don't want to think about my dog dying.'

'I'm not saying your dog, I'm saying dogs in general.' He doesn't reply, so I have no other choice but to elaborate. 'Usually dogs only live to be around … what, twelve? But if that was a human, people would say they died too early. For example, if someone you know is going to die at twelve, everyone would say they are *dying*, not living. Which leads me back to my original question, does this mean that dogs spend their life dying?'

'That is the strangest thing to ask. Or even think of,' Tristan says, slowly shaking his head.

'Thank you,' I reply, with a smug smile. I don't think he meant it as a compliment, but I can't help that I took it as one.

'Dogs have a lifespan of twelve years, whereas humans don't,' he says simply.

'Correct. But we don't know how long our lifespan is going to be.'

'Well, so far, you and I have both outlived twelve. I think that answers the whole human lifespan question.'

'But that's where you're wrong. Because even though dogs have a shorter life span, I think that they live a much bigger life than humans.'

'How can you say that?' he asks, almost laughing.

'Just because you have a long life, doesn't mean you have lived. A lot of people waste their life without realising. Someone might have lived till they were one hundred, old, grey and wrinkled, but that still doesn't mean they lived a big life. You know, they might have just . . . existed, for the most of it.'

I realise that Tristan has gone silent, his eyes drifting away. And that's when I ask myself why I'm talking to a boy with depression about life and death.

Tristan looks back up to me. 'Is this the sort of stuff that keeps you up at night, Zoe?' I can't help but feel a flutter of excitement inside me at him saying my name. I think that's the first time he's used it, not counting the time he yelled it across the park earlier. I like it. I like it a lot. One step closer to friendship . . .

'No, not all,' I reply confidently. 'I sleep pretty easily at night.'

'Lucky you.'

'Anyway, what I'm trying to say is that you don't know how long you're going to be around, so I like to make sure I'm actually living, while I'm still here.'

'It's not always that easy,' Tristan mumbles, picking at his sleeve again. I know this conversation is making him uncomfortable, but I seem stuck on the subject.

'Our future is unknown, you know? You could lead a dog's life, elephant's life, or even a tortoise's life. You just have to take each day like it's gold dust. The thing is, everyone wants to be the tortoise. Everyone wants to live to a ripe old age, live to be one hundred. Personally, I've never been jealous of a tortoise's slow-paced life – but that's just my opinion.'

Okay, so much for changing the subject. The thing about me is once I start talking it's hard for me to stop. I just want him to understand what I'm saying – I don't want him to think I'm trying to be mean or something.

'So . . . you want to live a shorter life?' Tristan asks. He's watching me intently, his eyes not afraid to maintain contact with mine any more.

'Do you?' I ask.

Tristan looks down. He doesn't reply, but I can hear him exhale heavily. He's not going to answer because he doesn't need to.

'Well,' I reply quickly, filling the silence, 'I want the longest life I can ever live. I love life. I just want to make sure I'm living it.'

Silence again. Shit. I've dug myself a hole. Why did I decide to talk about all of that? I can't even imagine the sort of battles he has going on in his head. I don't know his thoughts. His reasons. His feelings. I lower my hand and start stroking Misha again, in the hope he can deliver some puppy magic to this painful situation.

Now I don't know if this is Misha, or just brilliant timing, but at this very moment the door to the living room flings open, and in walks a tall, muscular man followed by a girl, wearing a short, skin-tight dress and very high heels. I guess the guy is Tristan's brother, and he kindly confirms it for me, by saying, 'Hey, little bro. You're back.'

He doesn't look that much like Tristan – he is tanned, with caramel-coloured hair, and muscles show through his T-shirt. Their eyes are the only similarity. In colour, yes, but also because they both have a dullness, this look of something missing, something dead, drawn-out, tired. And like Tristan, Luke doesn't look the healthiest, either, despite the tan. Hmm. Remind me to use my sanitiser when I get home.

I can tell he isn't like Tristan in personality, either – they don't seem to have much of a brotherly connection. He slumps on to the sofa next to Tristan, pulling the girl down close to him. Tristan quickly gets up, and sits next to me on the smaller sofa. His brother and the girl start whispering. She rubs her hand on his thigh. It's a high-intensity flirting situation. That I feel I shouldn't be watching right now. Tristan doesn't say anything, but sinks into his seat stiffly, looking like he wants to disappear. I get my phone out of my pocket to keep myself busy in the awkward silence and I notice I have three missed calls from Jerry, a WhatsApp from Leia and even a missed call from Paul. Let's pop that back in my pocket. Tristan's brother suddenly turns his attention away from the girl and looks at Tristan with a dazed smile. 'We cool?' he says with a slight slur.

'How did you get drunk so quickly, Luke?' Tristan says, his eyes not focusing on anyone.

'I'm not drunk,' Luke replies. 'Just tipsy, that's all. Hey. Hey, Tristan, look who I bumped into at the pub!' He points to the girl next to him, and smiles. 'It's … It's Gemma!'

Tristan shifts his eyes slightly, but doesn't say anything. The girl smiles. 'Wooooo. It's meeee!' she says. 'I told you I'd see you soon. And … your brother. I bought him shots.'

'Ssssshots!' Luke shouts, lifting his arms up.

'Shotssss!' Gemma says, joining in.

Well, this is strange, isn't it? Trust me, I'm not judging. Every family is different. I'm simply just stating a fact.

Tristan catches my eye for a couple of seconds before moving his hand to the middle of the sofa. He grips the sofa cushion, and I can feel the edge of his hand brushing against my thigh. I'm sure he's not aware he's doing it.

'Hey ... who's this?' Luke says. I realise he's pointing at me.

'Zoe,' Tristan says. There goes my tummy again. He says my name so beautifully. Zoeee. Zoeee. Especially for such a boring name. 'I work with her,' he adds. Okay, so he didn't introduce me as his friend, but he said my name, so that's a start.

'What a lovely name, Zoe,' Luke says. See, him saying my name doesn't have the same effect. I wonder why that is? Maybe because I don't want to be friends with him. 'I like your hair, it's purple.'

'It is.' I nod encouragingly, keeping my eyes on Tristan.

Luke turns towards Tristan and winks at him. 'You guys could make quite a cute couple, you know.'

'It's not like that,' Tristan snaps.

'Okay.' Luke throws his hands up defensively, slurring. 'Okay ... Just make sure you use protection, that's all.'

'Zoe's a *friend*, Luke,' Tristan says, eyes glaring at his brother.

Wait.

Tristan just called me – *me* – his friend. I did it! I actually did it. This is going to be a beautiful friendship.

'Okay, sorry. Would you like a beer, Zoe?' Luke's voice is really slurring now. He reaches behind the sofa and

113

brings out a six pack of beer on to the table. Sorry, but where did he just magic them up from?

'I'm good, thanks,' I reply.

'Okay. Tristan?'

Tristan stares at Luke and shakes his head.

'Gemma?'

Gemma looks at Luke and shakes her head. She then moves forwards, whispers in his ear, before latching on to his mouth. Luke looks at her with a devious smile, as he nods his head. They both stand up, hand in hand. 'I'm going to show Gemma something in my room, okay, Tristan?'

Tristan doesn't reply, or even acknowledge Luke has spoken. Luke waits a couple of seconds before giving up and making his way out the room still holding Gemma's hand. Once they clumsily traipse their way upstairs, I look at my new friend. This is even worse than the life and death talk. I look down to Misha, who is happily panting up at me.

'Sorry about him,' Tristan says.

'He was fine.'

'No, he wasn't. He has this thing about alcohol ...' He rubs a hand through his hair. 'He's a nice guy, it's just alcohol ... makes him behave like a dick.'

'I think it makes everyone behave like a dick.'

'No, he's different. He doesn't see what it does to him. He can't stop drinking. He has this idea that it helps him. It doesn't help him.'

'Oh.'

Is Tristan telling me his brother has an alcohol problem?

I think I've overstayed my welcome. I stand up. 'It's stopped raining, I should head home.'

Tristan gets up too. 'Yeah, okay.'

But then we both just stand there. I look around, about to get my shoes on, when I realise that I wasn't wearing shoes in the first place.

I should get my wet clothes. But I'm not doing that. I'm just standing here, staring at him, as he stares at me. What are we doing?

And why am I enjoying it?

'I'll give you a lift home.'

'You can drive?'

Tristan smiles, ever so slightly. 'Sure. I don't have a car, though. I use Luke's. Do you want a lift?'

I let a smile form on my face.

Chapter 16

Zoe

It's the day after I went to Tristan's house, and as soon as I get to work I spot him on the tills. At the sight of him I feel a warmth spread through me. I think back to yesterday, when he said he'd drive me home.

'I should probably get changed back into my own stuff,' I said, grabbing hold of the plastic bag with my wet clothes in.

'It's fine,' he said, as he took the keys out of his coat pocket. 'They're old. You can just keep them.'

So I did.

I swirl my way across the shop floor and stand next to him. He doesn't react, so I slam my hands down on the till happily. Still no reaction.

'Earth to Tree?' He turns his head towards me, staring at me with puffy, bloodshot eyes. He's been crying. 'What's wrong?'

Tristan doesn't reply. Obviously.

'Did something happen with you and Luke?'

Tristan chuckles, which feels so out of place against the backdrop of his drawn face. 'No,' he says in a quiet voice. 'Me and Luke are fine. He told me to say sorry to you, for, you know, making a fool of himself.'

'He didn't make a fool of himself,' I reply with what I hope is a reassuring smile.

Tree doesn't return my expression. In fact, he doesn't do anything except pull a shaking hand through his hair, staring around the empty supermarket. I'm glad it's empty, it means we've got time to talk.

'Tree, what's wrong?'

'We should be focusing on the customers.'

I look around at the deserted supermarket. I try again. 'Are you okay?'

He quickly turns his head, his eyes catching mine, and for the first time I don't like it. 'No.'

'Why?'

'It's nothing new,' he sneers.

What's happened? He wasn't like this yesterday. I suppose he wasn't entirely happy then either – I don't think I've seen him be happy yet – but he at least seemed himself. Seemed like the Tristan that makes me feel curious, interested, excited, not . . . like this. It's like he's just a shell of a person and the emptiness behind his eyes makes me uncomfortable. I don't like this feeling. 'What's wrong?' I ask, my voice soft.

'I don't know,' he says. 'I don't even know. I don't have a reason, I don't—' The words rush out and then suddenly stop.

I find myself speechless. Yes, me, speechless. I'm not used to this sort of stuff. I don't understand it, if I'm honest. How can you be upset and not even have a reason? I empty some receipt roll and stretch it out.

I don't know what to do or say so I start drawing on the receipt paper. It's a simple drawing. A smiley face. Again, and again, and again. It's already starting to make me feel better – until I feel Tristan watching me. Should I get him to draw a smiley face? Should I draw a smiley face on him? I just want him to have a smile on his face.

'I haven't been taking my antidepressants,' Tristan blurts out. I move my eyes up to him and inhale steadily.

'I thought you didn't take medication,' I reply, unsure if that was the right thing to say.

'I lied. I'm supposed to be taking them, but I haven't been.'

'Oh.'

I look around the supermarket. It's still empty, but I'm starting to wish it wasn't.

'I don't like the fact that I have to take something to make me normal. I don't want them to stop me being me, but then again, I don't like being me. It's confusing.'

I have to run what he said through my head a few times, and I'm still not sure if it makes sense. 'You shouldn't be ashamed of taking them,' I offer.

'I don't like them in my body. It sounds like I don't want to get better, but I do.' He turns towards me this time, almost abandoning his till. 'But I'm not . . . Better, that is. I never was better. I don't think I'm ever going to be better.'

There's a pause while I rack my brains. I can't understand why he is suddenly telling me this. All this time I've been trying to get him to talk to me, but I don't know about this sort of stuff.

'It's so tempting to give up.'

I'm properly panicking now. What do I say? I've never spoken to a person who feels like this, I don't understand *why* someone would feel like this. So how do I help?

'What are you planning on doing next, then?' I ask quickly, apparently deciding to change the subject altogether. 'What do you want to do as a career?' I feel my heart starting to pound, as I shuffle in my seat. 'I want to be an athlete,' I add.

His blank expression doesn't change, but it seems he doesn't mind the change of subject. 'You do training or something then?' he mumbles.

'I said I wanted to be an athlete, not that it's what I'm going to do.' I bring my hand towards my chest. It's really pounding. I'm starting to feel a little uncomfortable.

'So . . . you're not going to be an athlete?'

'No.'

'Are you not good at it?'

'No, I'm really good,' I say confidently. 'But my dads don't want me doing it.'

Tristan watches me carefully. 'Zoe, you're an adult, who cares what they think?'

I feel myself sigh. 'I think all parents have good intentions for their kids.'

I don't like this topic of conversation either. I lean over and draw a smiley face on the side of the till. He doesn't see me do it, his eyes are focused on some far-off place. 'What about you? You didn't tell me what you want to do.'

He scoffs, as if it's a stupid question.

Juliette chooses this moment to appear, her wild hair scraped back into a bun. 'Tristan, you can go on your lunch now,' she says, stretching her smile wide. Tristan wastes no time in logging out of his till. I think Ree and Anna were right about Juliette wanting to get into Tristan's pants, you know. It gives me another reason to find her annoying.

Juliette's face drops as she turns to me. 'Zoe, wait five minutes, would you? Trevor isn't here yet.'

'Okay, Julie, but I do have a lecture to attend in half an hour.' I flash a forced grin at her.

Juliette doesn't let the smile on her face slip, she just mutters 'five minutes' again, before wiggling away in her tight skirt.

I turn towards Tristan to give him a quick goodbye, but he's already left.

Alrighty.

When I finally get to leave, exiting through the prison doors of the supermarket, I spot Tristan like he's my prey. He's opposite the train station, leant up against the wall by the sports field, running one hand through his hair, fingers clutching on to his thin smelly smoke sticks.

'Enjoying your lunch?' I say, sneaking up from behind him.

He jumps, turning around and blowing smoke into my face in the process.

I hold my nose as I take a step back. 'Some of us want to be able to use our lungs, Tree!'

He just takes another deep inhale of his cigarette. 'You can't just shout at people.'

'I wanted to make sure you heard me.'

He shakes his head, before spitting on the floor. Lovely.

'What are you getting for your lunch, Tree?'

His eyes narrow. 'Why?'

'I just love talking about food.'

He crouches to the floor, stubbing out his cigarette. 'Unfortunately for you I'm not having lunch.'

'Why?' I feel concern hidden in my voice. 'You need to eat.'

'I do eat,' he says, mouth turned up. 'I just forgot my wallet today.'

'How did you manage that?'

'If I knew that, I wouldn't have forgotten it, would I?' He sighs, leaning back up against the wall. 'It's my fucking head. It makes me distracted. It blocks certain things out. I'm surprised I even made it here today.'

I rummage in my bag, fish out a tenner and hold it out to him. Tristan looks up at me, eyebrows pulled together.

'Here's your lunch.'

He stills looks at me, not saying anything.

'Like, the money isn't your actual lunch. I'm not saying eat the money, I'm saying use the money to buy food.'

'No, I got that,' he says slowly. 'But I'm not taking your money.'

'Yes, you are.'

'No, I'm not, I don't want it.'

'Okay, well, I'm going to give it to you for selfish reasons then.' I push the tenner into his hand, and then hold it to his chest firmly. 'It gives me good karma, plus I get a little selfish buzz out of doing nice things.'

Tristan watches me carefully. 'I'll pay you back,' he says.

'I would usually say no, but if you pay me back it gives me a reason to see you again, doesn't it?' I say, clicking my finger at him, followed by a good old cheesy wink.

'Zoe, we work together. I'm going to see you again.'

I take a step closer to him. 'Lucky you.' I feel a smile creep on to my face. But he just frowns. Again. I refuse to frown back, so I poke my tongue out at him, turn around and start walking across the car park. I'm about to reach the station when I hear him.

'Zoe, wait!' It does that thing. That thing where my stomach drops and I feel all strange. I turn around to see him walking towards me.

'Now you *are* following me,' I say with a grin.

'Where are you walking to now?'

I look around sarcastically. 'The airport,' I say with a twitch of a smile. I'm hilarious.

I walk further through the station gate, sitting on a bench on the train platform. He follows me. Standing awkwardly, keeping a careful distance.

'I mean *where* are you going?'

'Oh, uni,' I comfortably lie. I notice his head quickly drops. 'Shouldn't you be buying your lunch?'

'I will, but for now ... can I just wait with you?'

I'm taken aback but I try to hide my feelings by placing a confident smirk on my face and patting the bench next to me. 'I was wondering when you'd ask.'

He sits down next to me – slowly, carefully – and then does nothing. I want to turn my head to look at him, but I can't. I can't make any sudden movements in case I scare him away. I must stay careful and quiet. But you can only be quiet for so long before the silence starts becoming painful, so I make the move, and turn my head towards him. He stays put. He's still sitting next to me, hands fiddling in his lap, foot tapping on the floor, head bowed.

My heart aches. This is a sad boy.

'I wish I could make you happy.' I wasn't planning to say it out loud, but there we go.

I mean it, I do want him to be happy. Mainly because it's uncomfortable for me to act differently around him when he's sad. I don't like it, I don't know what to say, how to react, what to do. I just want to be normal with him.

'It's not that easy,' Tristan mumbles, eyes still on the floor.

'We could do something that makes me happy, and maybe it'll work for you too?' I suggest.

'What makes you happy?'

'Being active.' I feel my excited eyes beaming from my face, my heart already beating with excitement. 'Laser Quest. Paintballing. Trampolining.'

'Okay, let's do one of those, then,' he says uncertainly.

But I'm the one frowning now. 'Um . . . well, we can't.'

'Why not? You said yourself they make you happy.'

'They do.'

'So why can't we just—'

'You can't always just do stuff because you want to. Otherwise I'd be an athlete, wouldn't I?'

'Paintballing has nothing to with athletics.'

'I didn't say it did.'

Tristan screws up his forehead, narrowing his eyes at me.

'I have a train to catch,' I say, raising my eyes towards the sign on the platform. Two minutes to go. Am I happy or sad about that?

Tristan runs a hand through his hair, face still scrunched up. 'Why do I talk to you, Zoe?' he says angrily. 'You really annoy me, you know that?'

I keep my voice light. 'You talk to me because I'm your friend.'

'I don't do friends.'

'You introduced me to Luke as a friend.'

Tristan exhales heavily, the sound of it lost beneath the rumble of my train as it approaches the platform. I stand up. 'I'm going to take you to a place that will make you happy.'

He clenches his teeth. 'Where?' The train stops in front of the platform.

'If I tell you it's not a secret,' I say, getting a pen out of my pocket. I grab on to Tristan's hand. He goes tense, but doesn't pull away this time.

'What are you doing?'

'Hold still,' I say as I roll up his sleeve and start writing my number. Once I'm done, I look at him and stick my tongue out. Hearing the beep, I jump on to the train before the doors close. I look through the window at Tristan, who's still watching me in confusion. I slap my palm up against the glass, winking at him as the train moves away. His eyes don't leave my face the whole time.

Chapter 17

Tristan

The smiley face on her palm is the last thing I see as the train pulls away, drawn in black marker pen with the word 'smile' underneath. Who does she think she is? Does she seriously believe happiness is such a simple thing? That it's as easy as smiling?

I stand on the platform, hands in my pockets, earphones in. I'm staring at the floor, concentrating on the yellow line. The one you're supposed to stand behind to keep you safe. My stomach jolts every time a train speeds past the platform. I'm pretty sure it happens to everyone – feeling the wind sweeping up from the dusty track and through your hair, a lump in your throat, a shiver down your back. They go so fast, so bloody fast. What would happen if you were hit by that? At that speed? The way my body feels after a train passes me, the way my insides curl, the sick feeling in the pit of my stomach, the couple of seconds of numb thoughts – it's aching, it's sickening. The way it fuels questions in my mind, sparks something in my brain, terrifies me. It makes me want more.

I look over my shoulder at the other people on the platform and see an old lady sitting on the bench, picking at a loaf of bread and sprinkling crumbs along the platform, despite the fact there are no birds here. A woman with two children stands to the left of me, shouting loudly on her phone, holding one kid on her hip, the other in the buggy. She looks like a child herself. Neither seems to have taken any notice of me.

Before someone decides to point out that you're not allowed to smoke on train platforms, I inhale the last drag of my cigarette and drop it on the floor, stubbing it out with my foot.

My feet aren't just crossing the yellow line any more. They are completely over it, inches away from the edge of the platform.

Would you feel it?

My feet are edging over the platform now, I'm balancing on just my heels. I pull my hands into fists.

Would it be easy? I can hear the noise, a whirring through my brain, a tingle to my core, and I feel relaxed. I'm calm. I . . . I . . .

Step back.

Once the train passes, the feeling hits me. Slapping me across the face with a force that pushes me back towards the back of the platform. Lungs panting, heart beating, head pulsing, mouth gasping, body shaking.

What the hell, Tristan? What the actual hell?

The young woman stares at me. I wonder if she could tell what I was thinking; or if the old lady who is smiling at me as she shuffles on the bench saw me. Do they know?

As I sit on the train, my foot is tapping heavily on the floor.

I can't escape it. My nose is starting to tingle, eyes beginning to burn. I rub a hand through my hair. Not in public. Don't cry in public.

I haven't always been like this. I used to be happy. I really did. But I can't remember what that feels like now – it's like a foreign language that I used to know. I can't connect to it any more. It's impossible to translate.

Living isn't for me. I wake up in the morning and realise that I'm still me, that I still feel the same. So then I just spend the whole day looking forward to going back to bed in the evening, waiting for that quiet darkness, those precious hours where I'm nothing. Then I wake up with the hope that this day it will be different, but it never is. It never changes. I wake up and it's the same. I'm always the same. Waking up is the worst bit of the day.

Once I get home, I run upstairs and find myself

staring at the bathroom door, locked, somehow, from the outside. He locks the door now too? I can feel my arms shaking nervously either side of me. I decide to test my strength, and throw myself at the door. It's a bad move. All it does is hurt my shoulder. It turns out, however, that shoes are much more useful, and if you have enough determination you'll eventually break through the door. You'll eventually get into the bathroom, force open the cabinet and start rummaging through. You'll fling bottles out of the way, you'll throw things on the floor, until you find the bottle you need. My medicine. My antidepressants. I knew Luke had them in here. The fucker.

I pop the cap, and start pouring a generous amount into my hand. I need lots. Because I'm not the usual case, I don't fit the guidelines. I need more than the recommended allowance. I need more than the label says. I stare down at the hand holding the capsules. This will help. This will fix me. I look up at myself in the mirror – red eyes, sweaty stupid self – before looking back to my hand. This *will* help.

No, it won't.

All of this, all of it, is in my brain.

This is my brain's problem. I choose to be like this. I choose to be difficult. If I try, if I really try, I can fix myself. Why am I not trying? It's all in my head. It's all in my stupid idiot head. I don't need medicine.

The pills fall on to the floor.

Medicine is for people that are ill, and I'm not ill. I'm just not trying hard enough. I need to try. And in order to be able to try I need to feel something. Normal people feel something.

I reach out my hand to pick up the pills, then pause.

A dark line catches the corner of my eye. I look down at my arm, staring at the smiley face that has been drawn there. That Zoe drew. I run my hand along the Sharpie ink and focus on that simple doodle. She drew it so quickly, how did she get the mouth so perfectly curved? The two eyes so symmetrical? The tiny scribble is smiling up at me. I roll up the rest of my sleeve, and number after number slowly appears beneath the material. I'm eventually left with eleven digits in a misshapen font on my skin. A slow hiss of air escapes my mouth as I shake my head.

Just breathe, Tristan. Just breathe.

'Hello?'

'Erm ... Hey.'

'Who is this?'

'It's ... Tristan.'

'Oh, Tree! Hey! You sound different on the phone.'

' ... Do I?'

'Yeah, you sound dark and mysterious. But then again you *are* dark and mysterious.'

'Okay ... So, you said were you going to show me a place or something.'

'Oh yeah. I am. You'll totally love it. But I'm going to need you to drive us there.'

'As long as you promise to call me by my real name.'

'No can do.'

'Shall I come now?'

'Now? I'm at uni right now.'

'When do you finish?'

'Well, I have badminton coaching straight after. It's at the Riverbourne gym.'

'My brother works there.'

'Small world again, Tree.'

'Why do you do it?'

'To keep me busy. Plus, it fuels my inner exercise freak. I love it. I've been doing it since the summer. It's not like you to ask so many questions, Tristan. I like it.'

'You going to be home by four?'

'Come to my house for five o'clock. You remember where it is?'

'Yeah.'

'Okay, I'll see you then. I've got to go, make sure you save my number, yeah?'

She hangs up. I stare at my phone and slowly put it in my pocket. About ten minutes ago, Luke came home after working an early shift. I am staring at his car through the living-room window. I know his coat, with his keys in the pocket, is resting on the hook. Right now, he's upstairs

131

with a girl. This is my only opportunity to nab the car a without causing an argument.

I head into the hallway, retrieve his keys, open the door and leave.

Chapter 18

Zoe

He had scars on his arm.

He had real life scars along his arm.

There weren't many; they were small and faint, but definitely there.

I didn't want him to know I'd seen them, so I wrote out my phone number on his skin anyway. What else was I supposed to do? I wasn't going to say something to him about it. But the image is still playing on my mind as I walk through my front door.

'Beautiful fathers, no need to fear, your daughter is near. She's home. Safe, healthy and sound.'

Jerry comes to the doorway of the kitchen and frowns. 'It's just *father*, singular – Paul isn't home yet.'

I shrug my shoulders. 'That doesn't surprise me.' Paul is always home late.

Jerry looks behind me anxiously, as I kick my shoes

off by the door. He grabs on to me, pulling me into the house, and closes the door. 'Come on, don't hang around by the doorway.'

Confused, I follow him into the living room, where he peeks though the drawn curtains. He is anything but chilled right now. But then again, when is Jerry chilled?

'Jerry, what's wrong?' I ask, moving closer.

He quickly pulls the curtain closed, turns around and forces an exaggerated smile. 'Oh, nothing is wrong, Zee.' He only calls me Zee when *everything* is wrong. 'You know, I saw Rose when I went shopping today.'

I roll my eyes. Why does he do this? He knows I don't want to talk about her. About any of them. 'Did you?' I say with a sigh.

'She asked how you are.'

'I'm sure she did.'

'She misses you.'

'Jerry, can you not?'

'I'm just saying maybe you should contact her and—'

'Jerry, what were you looking at through the window and being all paranoid about?' I say, quickly changing the subject back.

Jerry sighs in defeat. He opens the curtain, indicating for me to peer out with him. I lean forward. I see what I always see staring out of this window: the houses opposite, the street lamps, the cars. 'Honestly, I have no idea what I'm supposed to be looking at.'

He tuts and points his finger at the window again. Nope.

Still can't work out what he's getting at. Is my dad start-ing to go senile? He's not old, but he's not young either. It could be around the corner ... 'The car, Zoe,' he mutters.

Oh, I see it; it's a red car parked on the other side of our road, right opposite our car. I feel like I've seen it before, but that's probably because I did just walk past it on my way to the house.

'Yes, I guess it's a nice car?'

'There's someone in the car.'

I turn towards him in mock surprise. 'Whoa. Someone in a car? No way. People drive cars? This is incredible.'

'Don't smart-arse me,' Jerry says with a sigh. 'The car has been parked out there for two hours now, the person has been in there the whole time.'

'I'm sure it's nothing.'

'But it's weird.'

'Maybe they are waiting for someone.'

'For two hours?'

'You worry too much, Jerry.'

'He keeps looking over at the house.'

I scrunch my nose in thought. 'How old is he?'

'No, Zoe,' Jerry says with a sigh. 'Not like that. It's just a young guy, probably about your age.'

Wait.

'You have to go outside to get a proper look at him, it's hard through the window, his windows are slightly tinted ...'

Jerry's voice fades off as I walk back into the hallway. I

knew I recognised the car. As I open our front door I feel a smile creep on to my lips.

'Zoe! Don't go out to see him.'

But I do go out to see him.

He is distracted by his phone, texting someone. I wonder who. Then I wonder why I'm wondering who. As I knock on the window he jumps, phone flying in the air and hitting him in the face. I can't help but laugh as he slowly brings his shocked eyes to my face. I open the car door and get in next to him. He doesn't say anything, just swallows. I smile. He doesn't.

'You know, you stressed my dad out.' Tristan's eyebrows contract. 'He saw the car just chilling outside our house for two hours and thought it was someone creepy.'

'Sorry,' he mumbles.

'Don't be sorry. My favourite activity is stressing my dad out.' He looks up at me, eyes reaching mine. 'Why were you so early, T?'

'So I'm T now?'

'Do you usually turn up places two hours early?'

Tristan rests his hand on the steering wheel and shrugs his shoulders. Okay, I can tell we're not going to get much conversation out of this subject. I feel my mouth twitch as I watch him. I find this guy so fascinating. I just want to find out more.

'Who were you texting when I knocked on your door?'

He frowns at me. He won't answer that one either. He's clearly not in the mood to talk. I'll let him take the wheel on this one, quite literally.

'You go straight on, then take the first exit at the round-about,' I say.

'Okay,' Tristan nods.

There has been a lot of 'okay's and a lot of nods on this journey. And, quite frankly, not much else. I'm starting to wish I was back at home. I do have an essay in for tomorrow. And my tutor told me I need to start 'pulling my socks up', which is always fun to hear. Oh well, I'm here now.

Tristan is a good driver – careful, safe, concentrated. A little too concentrated. I want him to loosen his grip, let it go, have some fun.

'So how come you don't drive?' he asks. He actually asked me a question. I'm shocked. He's the one instigating a conversation this time. I feel my stomach tighten in a knot. He's asking me a question and I'm struggling to answer.

'My dads can't afford a car.'

Tristan looks at me with a raised eyebrow, before pulling his eyes back to the road.

'What?' I ask.

'I didn't say anything,' he replies.

'Hey, Tree, I can't work you out that easily. You have to tell me what you're thinking.'

'Okay,' he says, turning on to the roundabout. 'It just doesn't look like your parents struggle with money. You have a big house in a nice area.'

'You live in a nice house, too, Tree.'

'I'm not the one saying my parents can't afford a car.' I feel that knot in my tummy again. 'Look, Zoe, I'm not saying I don't believe you but . . . '

'You don't believe me.'

'Okay. I don't. I think there is another reason you don't drive.'

'Yeah, you're right,' I say with a sigh. The butterflies start fluttering. 'My dads believe in working for yourself, so I have to save up for it. And I always spend the money I earn on things at work, and I'm a student, you know.'

'It doesn't seem like you live the student life, you don't have rent or food to pay for. Do you go out all the time or something?'

'No, I don't go out any more; I used to. Anyway, I don't earn any money from badminton coaching, and I only work part time, so I'm still short of cash most of the time.'

'Why didn't you just say that? I think it's good you're working for it yourself,' Tristan says, without taking his eyes from the road.

'Yeah, it's good doing it.'

'So, do you enjoy your coaching?' Tristan asks.

Another question from Tristan. This is going well. 'Yeah, I do, it's great fun.'

'What made you take it up?'

Hmmm. I'm starting to wish he wasn't asking so many questions. 'I don't know. I went through a phase in the summer. Wanted to do new things, wanted a change.'

He seems to accept this. After a pause, he says, 'So your parents don't even let you drive their car?'

'No. I haven't even learnt. I don't want to drive anyway. What's the point in learning if you don't have a car?'

Lies. Lies. Lies. I don't know why I don't just tell him the truth.

'I don't have a car. I know how to drive,' he says, glancing at me, and there's almost a smile in his eyes.

Chapter 19

Zoe

Once we emerge on to the flat, open rooftop of the building, I close my eyes and inhale, my heart already starting to pound with the thrill of it.

I can't believe I've taken Tristan here, to my special place. I hope he feels the same way I do about it. I'm already starting to feel breathless. But that could be the five flights of stairs. Fire escapes are a bitch to climb up. I turn my head to look at him, his hands in his pockets, standing awkwardly as he squints at me through the lowering sun. My heart pumps even harder. My eyes shoot to the ground.

'How did you find this place?' Tristan asks.

I turn around and stretch my arms up in the air. I always feel so good up here. 'I ran here once.'

'Ran?'

'Yeah. In the summer. I was angry. I was feeling all sorts of things, things that weren't healthy. I felt this pressure building up, so I did what I love doing. I ran. I just ran off the emotions. Then I stopped, completely out of breath, feeling sick and tired, and I looked up at the sun setting and it was beautiful. I wanted to see all of it, every last drop of the beautiful peachy-heated glow. I looked around and I saw this block of flats, and I decided I wanted to get to the rooftop. And I did. I got up here,' I say, pointing at the concrete beneath my feet. 'And I saw everything, every inch of the sunset. Of the town. And it was beautiful.'

'But you could watch the sunset from anywhere. What makes this place so special?'

'It was the last place I ran to. I haven't sprinted any-where since.'

'Why?'

I shrug my shoulders, still staring at the view. I'm not going to tell him that I also came here with Rose. We were having a bit of a life panic and stayed till the sun set drinking orange juice and prosecco. But it doesn't matter because I don't talk about Rose. She's not in my life any more. It doesn't count.

'I don't understand you.' Tristan is slowly making his way towards me. 'If you like running so much, why don't you just do it?'

A small sad smile finds its way to my lips. 'I don't have the time any more. Just because you like something doesn't mean you can always do it. Running isn't important.'

'Even if it's not important, you can still run. No one is going to stop—'

'Can't you see why it's amazing?' I say before he can continue his line of questioning, finding more flaws in my reasoning. I grab hold of his hand, dragging him towards the edge of the rooftop with me. Finding the small gap in the railing, I sit down. I look over the edge to see my feet hanging from up high and get a rush to the head, then look back up at the sunset. I feel in control, I feel powerful. I feel like I could do anything up here. I could rejoin the athletics team. I could run a marathon, I could fly. I have no boundaries. Being up here puts everything in perspective. It makes me realise how beautiful life is.

'I feel so good up here,' I say, swinging my legs in the wind, hugging my body as the cold air hits me. I glance back at Tristan, who slowly and carefully sits down next to me, and drops his feet over the edge one at a time. His eyes aren't focused on the beautiful peachy glow that is gobbling up the sky; instead, he's staring straight at the ground far below his feet. 'Do you feel it?' I say, as I shuffle myself next to him, trying to get his attention back. 'Isn't it great?'

Tristan stays quiet.

'Tree?' I say, as I shiver in my coat.

Nothing.

'Tree!'

At this he suddenly turns and lifts his head, his eyes squinting with some emotion I can't understand.

'Do you like it here?' I ask, grinning at him. But he just lowers his head again, looking back to the ground far below him. 'How do you feel?' I say, inching myself closer, my body touching his now.

'I feel ...' He pauses and starts inhaling some heavy breaths. 'I feel like I want to let go.'

'What?' I ask him, half giggling. But he stays serious.

'It's like I don't see things the right way,' he whispers. 'Death ... draws me in.'

That's all I need to hear. I quickly but firmly take hold of his hand and scooch us both away from the edge; then I stand and lead us into the centre of the roof. He doesn't question it, just follows me as I sit us both down in the middle of the concrete. The middle is safe.

He doesn't look at me, I don't think he wants to, and I can't blame him.

This is your fault, Zoe. You're an idiot. Why the hell did you think it would be a good idea to bring him here?

I do see the world differently to him. I saw that rooftop as another reason to live. He saw it as another reason to die.

Tristan is running his hand along the cement floor, stroking his fingers along a spot marked with lots and lots of smiley faces. He looks up at me. 'Was this you?'

I smile, my teeth chattering in the cool evening air. 'Yeah.'

'You like smiley faces.'

I nod my head. 'I also like Sharpies,' I say, bringing one out of my pocket. I lean down and add a new face to the collection. 'I draw a new one every time I come up here.'

Tristan looks at all the faces, as if counting, then back at me. 'Why do you draw them?'

'I'm not sure.'

'You don't know?'

'I've told you before, there doesn't always need to be a reason why we do the things we do.'

He doesn't seem to like that answer. He lowers his head and stays quiet. I look back at the sky; the sun is starting to set, and as the sky gets darker the warm glow is infused with deeper tones of red, pink and orange. It's comforting, despite the increasing cold. 'I wish you could see the world the way I do,' I say with a sigh. I feel his eyes on me, but I don't turn to look at him. I'm captivated by the light. There will never be more beauty than this.

'I do,' he mutters. 'We are literally looking at the same thing right now.'

'No, we're not.'

'Yeah, we are.'

I stare at him. 'Tristan, even with your eyes wide open you can still be blindest person in the room.'

He sets his jaw. 'Maybe it's you who's blind,' he says. 'You can't see what the world is really like.'

That can't be true. Can it? Perhaps it is normal to only see things negatively. 'Well, if that's the case I'd rather be blind than see it with clear eyes.'

'Can you stop speaking in riddles,' Tristan says as he gets a cigarette out of his pocket. He lights it, puts it in his mouth and exhales a puff of grey smoke. I can't help but hold a hand to my lips as I try to protect my precious organs.

'Smoking kills,' I mumble, shuffling away slightly.

Tristan sucks in another breath. 'I know,' he says with the added company of smoke. 'That's the point.'

For someone who says very little, Tristan is insanely good at shutting me up. But I'm also good at changing the subject.

'If you only had one day to live . . .' I stop and flinch at my poor choice of words, before deciding that I've said it now so I may as well carry on, 'what would be the one thing you'd want to do?'

I pause, assuming he won't answer that.

'There's nothing I'd want to do,' he replies.

'I know what I'd want to do,' I say quickly, trying to gloss over my bad choice of topic. 'I'd want to do a colour run.'

Frowning, he throws his cigarette on to the concrete. I wince as he stubs it out on one of my smiley faces. 'I don't know what that is.'

'It's a race, usually for charity, where volunteers throw powdered paint on you while you run along the track.'

He's still frowning. 'Why would anyone want to do that?'

'It's running and colour, two of my favourite things.' Tristan looks blank. 'It's supposed to be *fun* – running, raising money for charity *and* getting colour thrown on you. For me it almost sums up life.'

'You think life is colourful?'

I turn towards Tristan, and I'm the serious one now. 'Yes.'

'Well, it's not,' he says, too confidently. 'Life is dark and everyone knows it. People wear black to funerals for a reason.'

'What reason is that?'

'It's to remind everyone how dark life is.'

I exhale angrily. 'No, people wear black because they are sad.'

'Who isn't sad?' Tristan asks me.

'Me. I'm not. I'm not sad,' I say a little bit too loudly. 'I don't understand why funerals have to be so dark and depressing. It doesn't make sense.'

'It makes total sense.'

'No, it doesn't. If everyone wore black to my funeral I'd be annoyed.'

'What would your funeral look like then?'

I feel myself smile. Not a question that most people would smile at, but I'm not most people. I'm excited to tell him my answer, I've thought about this. 'Everyone would wear big, bold, bright colours, and they'd be smiling. There wouldn't be a sad moment, because I will have lived the best life I could. I want it to be like a party that I should be at. But technically it's a party all about me, so that's even better.'

'How do you know you will have lived the best life you could?'

I shoot my eyes to him. 'I'm already doing it.'

Tristan scoffs. 'So everyone would be in a graveyard dressed like they are going to a bloody party?'

'No!' I shout loudly. 'I'm not being buried in a grave-yard. I'm on the donor list so hopefully all my healthy organs will be used to save other people. And then I want my ashes buried in the soil of a newly planted tree. So I will nourish and help the tree to grow. I'll become that tree.'

'Please don't tell me this has anything to do with why you call me Tree.'

'Keep on dreaming. I call you Tree because that's the name I think you suit. Anyway, when I die, I want good to come out of it. I want my death to enable others to live. That's why I'm donating my organs. What else am I going to do with them when I'm dead?'

'I get that, but what the hell is the tree bit about?'

'I want to be a tree because they are important to the earth. They keep us alive. Keep us breathing. So even though I'll be dead, I'll be breathing through others. It's basically life after death.'

Tristan's frown returns. 'You have it all thought out, don't you?'

'Yep.'

'Why is that?' he asks.

I look at him carefully. His wise eyes squint in the pinky light of the setting sun, which stipples strands of his hair with highlights. 'I dunno. I just do. Haven't you ever thought about it?'

I bite my tongue. Another stupid question. Why do I

keep asking this poor guy questions about death? Tristan doesn't answer for reasons that I already know. I start panicking. If I keep doing this, he won't want to spend time with me any more. I want to be friends with him, not enemies. I need to think of something to say. Anything.

'Let's go to Laser Quest!' I shout.

Tristan looks up at me with a determined look in his eyes. 'Okay,' he says.

Oh. I didn't think he'd actually agree. My plan to take us to safer ground has, once again, backfired.

I feel my face fall. 'Really? Well . . . I don't want to.'

Tristan continues to stare at me. His eyes are blank. 'Yes, you do,' he says.

I can't lie again, so I exhale and say, 'We can't go. It's getting late. We won't make it in time.'

'So why did you suggest it in the first place?' he asks.

I look up and lock eyes with him. 'I was curious to see what you would say.' His eyes don't leave mine. He says nothing. Just stares.

'Why are you staring at me?' I ask. I'm starting to feel self-conscious.

He doesn't take the hint and continues to watch me. 'You're a strange one,' he says.

I feel my mouth curve. 'All the best people are.'

Chapter 20

Zoe

I take a picture of him with my camera. Standing on the rooftop in the last squeeze of the sunlight. March breeze watering his eyes. The cold air reddening his nose. He doesn't react. He's leaning against the barrier and something has caught his eye.

'What the hell?' Tristan says absently as he looks over the edge of the rooftop. He doesn't give me an opportunity to ask what's wrong, because by the time I open my mouth he's heading back down the fire escape. I peer over the edge to see someone leaning against Tristan's car. He has his arms folded as he scans the street. It's Luke. Now Tristan's down there too – that was quick. Luke gets off the car and walks steadily towards him, but Tristan backs away angrily. They are talking. Well, not talking, arguing. I can't hear what they are saying from up here, but I don't think it's particularly charming.

Okay, I know what you're thinking: Zoe, you've been nosy enough, just wait up here and let them deal with their family business alone. But Tristan's my lift home, and as selfish as it is, I need him to remember that. It's colder now the sun has set; I don't want to walk.

Once I reach them, they seem to have calmed down. Tristan is slumped on the floor by the wall, and his brother is standing opposite him, maintaining an awkward distance. Neither of them seems to notice me.

'. . . I took a taxi,' Luke says.

'Still doesn't answer my question,' Tristan mumbles.

Luke sighs. 'Stop driving my car, Tristan.' He sounds tired. He looks tired.

'How did you know I was here?' Tristan says, still sulking by the wall.

Luke runs a hand along his face, avoiding Tristan's gaze 'I . . . I enabled the GPS app connected to your phone.'

'*What?*' Tristan gets up and steps towards Luke. 'Luke! You're stalking me?'

'No,' Luke says, also taking a careful step forward. 'I just want to make sure I know where you are.'

Tristan starts shaking his head, and even from where I stand I can feel the anger rising and straining inside him. He starts pacing. 'You're a dick,' he mutters harshly.

'Don't overreact.'

'Overreact? Since when do I overreact?' He continues to walk back and forth but his movements are more abrupt now, jerky, uncomfortable to watch.

'It was what the doctors—'

'What the doctors suggested; yes, I guessed that.'

'I don't want you to take off and for me to have no idea where you are again. Hear nothing from you until I get a phone call saying that—'

Tristan pushes him in the chest. 'Why don't you believe I'm better? Why don't you believe me?'

Luke watches him for a couple of seconds before looking down to the floor. 'Because you're not better.'

Something inside Tristan snaps. He turns and walks towards the car, clenched fist raised, and we all know what's coming. But just before his fist makes contact with the car window, Luke grabs hold of his jacket and pulls him away. Tristan stumbles backwards before shrugging him off.

'Just leave me alone,' he says, giving Luke another push.

'Tristan,' Luke sighs.

But Tristan doesn't stop there, he pushes him again, palms shoving Luke in the chest.

'Calm down!' Luke suddenly grabs hold of Tristan and pins him against the wall.

I can't work out what noise I made, but it must have been a loud one; within a second both of their heads snap towards me, catching me standing there witnessing this situation.

Tristan's eyes lock on mine. He shakes Luke off him and starts walking towards me. I don't say or do anything, I feel rooted to the spot. Once Tristan reaches me, he stops and stands close. The closest he's ever been to me. The back of his hand touches mine slightly. I forget the cold. 'Sorry,' he whispers. I try to catch his eyes, but he doesn't look at me.

'Who's this?' I turn towards Luke. He's frowning at me, his eyes lingering on my hair.

'This is my friend, remember.'

There it is again. I'm his *friend*. My tummy bubbles with warmth.

'You met her the other day,' Tristan says.

'Oh, yeah – Zoe, the girl with purple hair.' He rubs a hand through his own golden hair, before clapping his hands together as if he's wrapping up the conversation. 'I hate to be that person, but we have to head home now.'

I turn towards Tristan. He stays silent, but glares at Luke. His hand is still ever so slightly touching mine.

'Give me the keys.' Luke's hand is outstretched.

Wordlessly, Tristan reaches into his pocket and throws the keys at Luke, who rather impressively catches them with one hand. Luke starts shuffling towards the door, trying to indicate to Tristan to get in. Tristan moves towards one of the back doors, and opens it, staring at me. 'We need to give Zoe a lift home.'

I think I manage to keep my smile hidden.

The ride home was painfully silent. Tristan sat in the back with me, but said nothing, did nothing – the whole journey was a big fat load of nothing. I hated it. As soon as we got to my house, I practically jumped out the car, saying a quick goodbye to Tristan and thanks to Luke, before gratefully stepping into the beautiful comfort of my lovely, non-silent home.

Not long after I make a green tea and slump on the sofa, Jerry starts to give me an earful about not telling him where I was, and who I was with, and for ignoring his texts and calls. It's a fight we've been having a lot recently, and as usual I explain to him that as I am twenty years old, I don't need to tell him my whereabouts all the time. That I could be living in my own house like I had been for the last two years before moving home, during which time he had no idea of my exact location.

I feel suffocated. I feel coddled. I feel like I can't breathe. I storm halfway upstairs, but then pause.

Remember the rooftop. Remember the sunset. Remember life.

I turn around, walk back into the kitchen and swamp Jerry in a hug. I can tell he's surprised.

'Where's this come from?' he says as he slowly folds his stiff arms around my back. 'We were having an argument ten seconds ago.'

'I know,' I say as I place my head on his chest. He smells like he always does: strong aftershave mixed with the slight bitterness of coffee.

'So, what's with the unexpected love?' he questions.

'I just want you to know that I love you, Jerry,' I say

with a happy sigh. 'I'm just so grateful I have you in my life. I'm sorry I take you for granted.'

'What has gotten into you?' Jerry says.

'What's going on in here?' Paul is standing in the doorway between the kitchen and living room.

'Paul!' I let go of Jerry and run up to Paul, squeezing my arms around him. Paul's hugs are better because he's taller and more meaty. 'The same to you, my father-dad,' I say as I squeeze my arms around him tighter.

'I still don't get this "father-dad" thing,' Paul says, accepting my hug.

'I love you guys. So much.'

'Okay? Well, we love you, too, darling.'

'Whoever you were spending time with today, you can see them more often, I think,' Jerry says with a chuckle.

'Zoe, stop being strange,' Leia says, gliding in past Paul towards the fridge and immediately rooting through it.

I turn to her with a wide smile on my face. I let go of Paul and start making my way towards her. 'My lovely, lovely sister,' I say as I open my arms.

Leia clocks it's her turn next, and starts backing away. 'No way.'

I catch her and cling my arms around her, while she fights uncomfortably in my grip. 'Zoe, stop. Ew. Jerry, tell her to stop! Paul! Dad! Dad!'

But I don't stop; much to her dismay and to Jerry and Paul's entertainment, I pull her closer in. I don't want to take my family for granted. I need to remember all of these moments. I need to cherish them.

Leia is saved by my phone ringing. I let go, and get it out of my pocket. With a sigh, I walk into the living room, plonk myself on the sofa, let it ring for a few seconds more – I like to make people think I'm a busy woman who can't answer phones straight away – and then eventually answer.

'Hello?' I say as I start fiddling with a cushion I've never seen before. Jerry must have bought it from one of the vintage shops he loves so much. The person on the other end says nothing. But I can hear their breathing. 'Hello?'

'Hi.'

I know that voice. 'Tree?'

'Hey, Zoe.'

How is it that he seems to say my name differently to other people? He makes it more than just a name. I try to bite away the smile on my lips. 'I forgot to save your number, sorry.'

'It's fine.'

'Are you okay?'

'Yeah.'

Still not one for words, then. 'So why did you call me?' I ask, laying my head down on the cushion. It's pretty soft.

'Thanks for taking me to that place today. It was cool.'

After our awkward rooftop conversation, I was expecting him to describe it as anything but cool. 'Oh, um. That's cool.' Stupid reply, Zoe. 'Thanks for letting me take you there.' Another stupid reply. 'It's special.' That will do. Now just don't say anything else. 'So was that all you wanted to call me about?' Or I can just ignore my own advice ...

'No,' he mumbles.

'Ooooh. How exciting, tell me more.'

'Well ... do you think ...'

'Jesus. Spit it out, dude.'

'Do you think we could do it again sometime?'

I feel a smile return to my lips. This time I don't bite it away. 'I am a busy and popular woman. But I'm sure I can fit you in somewhere.'

Chapter 21

Tristan

I know who I am, and I know what I do and don't deserve. I know what I can have and what I can't. So I know I can't have people close to me, and that's okay; I've accepted it. But am I at least allowed to feel good?

I think Zoe might make me feel good. I don't know why, and I'm not sure if I like it, but she just does. And maybe if I keep feeling good when I'm with her, I can open up again. I can eventually be the guy. The normal guy. The guy I used to be.

Since our trip to the rooftop, me and Zoe have seen a lot of each other. She's shown me her favourite vintage clothes shops and record stores, we've been out to dinner at a place she likes and sometimes we travel home together if we have similar shifts. I walk her home, even if it is in the opposite direction I need to go and makes my journey twenty minutes longer than it should be. We see each other a lot

157

at work, and it's got to the point that the shifts without her are boring. As selfish as it is, I find myself wishing she didn't have to go to uni so much; it would give her more time to distract me. The way she sees things, the topics she brings up, the things she does.

This doesn't mean I'm better. I told you this – I'm not going to get better. I still get the thoughts, the emptiness and the dark feelings. There are certain objects in my room that suggest to me possibilities I shouldn't even think about, and the crying is still something I have no control over. But for those small moments when I'm with Zoe, I forget about that. I stop thinking about myself, and start thinking more about her. It's impossible not to – she raises so many questions in my mind. Like how she can see things so differently to me; why she is the way she is; why she treats me the way she does, differently to every-body else. It's like she doesn't see me as a bomb about to explode, even when I know that's exactly what I am.

'I'm going now, love, see you on Monday,' Sally trills, perching in my doorway.

I turn my head towards her. I've been in such a daze, I didn't even notice her cleaning her way around my room. 'See you Monday,' I reply.

'Be nice to your brother; he works hard, you know,' she says in that calming tone of hers. What shit has Luke said about me now?

'I'm always nice,' I say, but even I can't keep a straight face at this. Sally chuckles as she heads down the hallway.

'Sally?' I shout, too lazy to get up from my bed. Sally's face pops back around the door.

'Yeah, sweet?'

'Is it just Luke down there?'

Sally shakes her head, 'Nope, his friends are still around.'

'Oh. Okay.'

'Don't shut yourself away up here, hon. Go downstairs. You know his friends. They don't bite.'

'Yeah, they do.'

She smiles at me, throwing in a reassuring wink. 'I also brought some lasagne for you boys – even more of an excuse to go downstairs now.'

'So, who's the friend you're waiting for?' Gaz, a friend of Luke's from the gym, asks me as he rests a heavy hand on my shoulder. I shrug him off and turn away from the window that I've been staring out of. I place my empty bowl on the coffee table. Sally does make a good lasagne. I go back to Misha on the sofa, and start rubbing his head, much to his delight.

'Her name's Zoe,' Luke answers, his eyes steady on me.

'Oh, a girl, hey?' says, nudging me.

'You got yourself a girlfriend, Tristan?' Alex, Luke's other friend, pipes up.

I sigh. I used to like Luke's friends, they've known me since I was young. Treated me almost like I was their younger brother, and they've been there for me and Luke over the years, especially when Dad died. But I'm not so sure how I feel about them any more. Every time Luke is with them he has another bottle in his hand, and he gets praised for it. He is seen as the legend in the group for always being the last one to stop, as if that's a good thing.

'They are just friends, apparently,' Luke says.

I've already had enough of this awkward conversation. If Zoe doesn't arrive soon, I might just go back and hide up in my room till she does. I lower my head and focus on giving Misha attention.

'Just a *friend*, you sure about that?' Gaz says.

I nod my head, not trusting myself to reply.

'We all know about *friends*. Luke's had lots of *friends*.'

'It's not like that.'

'Have you been friend-zoned, Tristan?' Alex says, leaning forward and resting his beer on the coffee table.

I try to keep my tone even. 'I'm not looking for a girlfriend.'

This, apparently, is hilarious, because everyone laughs, all leaning in to pat me on the back again. 'We've all heard what you were like at uni, we've all heard it, Tristan,' Gaz jeers.

'I think Luke takes his inspiration from you,' Alex chimes in, rewarded with a roar of laughter as they both nudge Luke.

I roll my eyes.

I've had a few girlfriends in the past. So what? Okay,

I've been with more than a few. But that was then, when all I cared about was girls, alcohol and sex. That was old Tristan. Old Tristan isn't present Tristan. As much as I wish he was. I don't want a girlfriend now. I don't even want friends. I don't want anything any more. There's not space in my brain for any of that. But what about Zoe? Zoe's just … just …

'Wait, do you like guys now?' Alex asks.

I shake my head. I don't think so. The thought has crossed my mind before, but I feel nothing when I look at guys. Then again, these days, I feel nothing looking at girls. Maybe I'm asexual now? Anyway, I used to want to kiss girls. I used to be totally head over heels for them. I used to feel that tingle in my stomach, heart beating, the other tingle elsewhere. I liked those feelings. And I liked sex. A lot of sex.

No, I'm not asexual. I wish I was, though, at least it'd make more sense.

'Oh, you'll find the right girl sometime soon.' Gaz opens another beer.

'He doesn't have to be with someone,' Luke says. I look over at him in surprise. Is he defending me?

'We're just going out for a pizza,' I say, trying to move the conversation on.

'Sounds like a date to me,' Gaz says. Luke shoots him a glare. Gaz ignores it and slides a beer towards me across the table. 'Want one, Tristan?'

I reach for it, but Luke snatches it out of Gaz hand. 'He's

fine,' Luke says, not even looking at me. Now it's my turn to glare at Luke. But my glaring is quickly interrupted by two brief knocks at the door.

Before she can knock the third time I jump up and open the door to see Zoe standing in front of me. She immediately throws her arms around me in a hug. I stand there for a few seconds before wrapping my arms tentatively around her back. I'm still getting used to her constant touching.

She pulls back, blinking her big bug eyes at me. 'Hi, Tree,' she says with a trademark smile. Her purple hair has been pulled into two high buns on either side of her head with stray pieces falling across her face. She is wearing bright pink lipstick that stands out even more against her green-check matching top and skirt. The top is cropped, showing her midriff. (Does Zoe have abs?) The skirt is short. Very short. But it suits her. She's finished off the outfit with white plastic knee-length boots. She looks her usual weird self. But there's something extra different about her tonight. I can't put my finger on it.

'Tree?'

I slowly close my mouth. 'Yup?'

'Am I allowed inside?'

'Sorry,' I say, moving away from the doorway. As soon as Zoe steps in I notice all eyes on her, and I start to feel awkward on her behalf. But I don't think she feels awkward. She smiles warmly at Luke and his friends, before placing a hand on her hip. I can tell she likes the attention.

All the guys are grinning back, except Luke. He is frowning, his eyes focused on her knee-length boots.

Oh crap.

I grab on to Zoe's hand and start pulling her towards the stairs but I'm not quick enough. 'Only going out for pizza?' Luke asks, eyes still on Zoe.

'We wanted to make an effort,' I say, looking towards Zoe for confirmation. She doesn't hide the confusion on her face. For God's sake, Zoe.

'How will you get there?'

One of my feet is tapping the floor. 'We're going to walk into town.'

'Walk? She's wearing heels.'

'I'm very good at walking in these shoes, Luke.' Zoe flashes another smile.

'If she gets tired we'll get a taxi,' I say.

'You'll call me if you need me, right?'

'Yes, Luke,' I say, cringing at the way he's treating me like a teenager and making everyone in the room feel awkward. I don't let him ask any more questions. I pull on Zoe's hand and drag her upstairs to my room, shutting the door behind us, and breathing out an exaggerated sigh. I look up to Zoe, who's staring down at her hand still clasped in mine. I quickly let it go and rub my sweaty palm on my jeans.

'Sorry,' I say with a nervous laugh.

Zoe looks up at me and presses her bright pink lips into a smile. 'Don't be sorry,' she says. She looks around the room like she's never been here before even though she has, a couple of times over the past few weeks, and she does the same things each time. She makes the same comment about how my walls are bare, my room is empty, it's lacking character, it's boring.

There's a pause. As Zoe continues to look around the room I do the same. My eyes focus on the window, or, more accurately, the curtain pole just above it. It used to have curtains on it, but I broke it when I was angry one time, tearing it down completely. I prefer it this way, though. There is something nice about not having curtains, about being able to look straight out of a giant window all the time.

'Luke doesn't know about the party, then?' Zoe says as she flops down on my bed. Zoe was invited to the party by Ree, one of the girls she hangs around with at work. I wouldn't have gone, but Zoe wanted me to, so I said I would. I know, I don't know what's wrong with me either.

I move over and sit on the bed next to her. She gets her camera out and takes a quick picture of me. I'm momentarily blinded. It's something she always does, at the weirdest times as well. 'No, Luke doesn't know.'

Zoe grabs me and pulls me down next to her. 'How come?' she says.

'He's just a little bit protective at the moment.'

'You're twenty-two, Tree.'

'I know, but like I said, he's protective.'

'It's just a party at Ree's house. You should tell him, I'm sure he'd rather you were honest.'

I roll my eyes. 'No, I'm not telling him.'

'Why not?'

'I had an appointment at the hospital yesterday. It didn't go all that well.'

Zoe suddenly sits up and leans her head over mine, beaming an excited smile down at me. 'No way! Yesterday?'

'Yeah,' I say, shuffling myself to sit up opposite her.

'I was at the hospital yesterday, too!'

'Oh ... really? Were you seeing your gran again?'

Zoe's smile falters. 'Yeah ... I was.'

I can tell this isn't a good topic. 'Is she okay?'

She looks distant. 'I hope so.'

'Same.' I nod, because I don't know what else to say. I wonder how unwell she is, considering how long she's been there, but don't want to push Zoe on it.

She raises her eyebrows at me, as if I'm supposed to say something else. 'Remember, Tree?'

'What?'

'The hospital is where we first met.' She's back to smiling again.

'I wouldn't say we met at the hospital.'

'We pretty much did,' she says with wide eyes. 'Could you imagine how different things could be? I might not have even been friends with you!'

'Come on, it wouldn't have been that different – we

still would have ended up working next to each other on the tills.'

'No,' Zoe continues seriously, 'because I wouldn't have been so keen to talk to you, and I wouldn't have given you back your cigarettes, and I wouldn't have asked you about why you were at the hospital—'

'Okay, but I don't think seeing each other at the hospital specifically led to us being friends.'

'Yes, it did. Everything happens for a reason. We both were at that hospital for a reason. It all started at that hospital.'

'I don't believe in that sort of stuff.'

Zoe rolls her eyes before flopping herself down on the bed again exasperatedly. 'Okay, spoil sport,' she says. 'So why was the appointment so bad?'

'Luke knows I'm not taking my antidepressants any more.'

Zoe's smile drops. 'How does he know?'

'The doctor told him that, based on my behaviour, he doesn't believe I'm taking them.'

'Has Luke said anything to you?'

I run a hand through my hair. 'No, and that makes it worse.'

'Why?'

''Cause I think he's disappointed in me. He gave me some freedom a couple weeks ago, trusted me to take my meds myself ... and I just ruined that trust.' I groan as I start rubbing my eyes. They ache with tiredness. They always do. 'I'm just so shit, and I can't stop it.'

166

'Hey!' Zoe says. I find her pulling my hands away from my face, forcing me to look into her eyes. They are super blue today. 'Stop being so self-pitying. You're not shit, Tree.' She shuffles along the mattress. 'You have a springy bed.' I nod my head. 'Can I bounce on it?' Before I get to answer, she is already up, taking huge leaps in the air, causing the whole mattress to shudder. She stretches her hands out to me. 'Come on, Tree!'

I'm still on my back, looking up at her.

But Zoe isn't one to take no for an answer. She grabs on to me by the wrists and pulls me up. She's surprisingly strong for her size and I have no choice but to bounce with her. At first it's awkward, and I don't enjoy it, though there may have been a split second where a smile snuck through. But as quickly as it started, it's over. Zoe drags me back down to the mattress again. She turns to me, her chest panting.

'That wore me out,' she says, flashing a smile at me. 'My heart is beating so fast. It's either you or the bouncing.' She quickly pulls my hand to her chest. I try not to tense.

Her heart is beating fast, like it's going to beat out of her chest.

There's also the fact that I'm quite literally touching her boobs here. I pull my hand away quickly.

Zoe crosses her legs and smiles at me. 'So, Tree,' she says, obviously not fazed by the boob touching. 'How are we getting to Ree's house? Taxi?'

'I'm driving.' Zoe cocks her head. 'I'll use Luke's car.'

'Will he let you?'

'He won't realise, he's going out with his friends tonight.'

'Hmmm,' Zoe says, a hint of excitement in her eyes. 'Okay.'

'We have loads of beers in the fridge, you can take some.'

'I'm fine,' Zoe says standing up. As she does, I'm reminded how dressed up she is. I feel my fingers start to twitch. I shove my hands in my pocket.

'You look nice, Zoe,' I say, in a short whisper.

Zoe turns around and beams. 'I know, right,' she says looking down at her outfit and then back at me.

I follow her eyes down to my dark shirt and jeans. 'I feel slightly underdressed.'

'Hmmm, you are a little,' she says, continuing to look me up and down. 'Can I do your hair?'

I frown at her. 'I don't need anything doing to my hair.'

'You do.' Zoe narrows her eyes at me. There's something else. 'Have you ever worn eyeliner?'

I feel heat run to my cheeks 'I ... well.'

Zoe looks too excited for my liking. 'You have, haven't you?'

I exhale a heavy sigh. 'I went through a phase.'

'I knew it,' Zoe whispers. 'You look like the sort of guy that would.'

I shake my head. 'No, I don't!'

'You do.'

'I was younger. I don't know. It was weird.'

'No, it wasn't.'

I stare at her. 'You don't know, you weren't there.'

'Boys wearing make-up isn't weird,' she says. Her face is serious. 'So why did you stop wearing it?'

'I'm not the guy I used to be.'

'Don't sound so dramatic, you're not in a movie. We all change, it's just what happens. Anyway, I bet you looked cool.'

I chuckle slightly. 'No. I tried to look like Billie Joe Armstrong, but failed.'

Zoe gasps. 'You used to like Green Day?'

'I . . . Well . . . I guess I still do.'

I don't know what I like any more. I don't know if I even like anything. I just can't remember the person I was, what it felt like not to have a constant darkness folding itself over and over in your head. I can't remember what it felt like to be . . . just me.

She beams me one of the weirdest smiles, eyes sparkling. 'I knew you liked Green Day,' she hisses. 'I bloody knew it. I'm always right, what's up with that?'

Chapter 22

Tristan

Parking the car on the side of the road, I flip down the sun visor and look at myself in the mirror. I can't help but sigh. Somehow I let Zoe put eyeliner on me, and backcomb my hair. I look stupid.

'You look like Jared Leto.'

I roll my eyes at Zoe. 'No, I don't.'

Zoe unplugs her seat belt, and bounces up and down in excitement. Leaning in, she lifts her camera and with a blinding flash takes a photo of both of us. 'Yeah! You know, when he went through that hot eyeliner stage. You have his eyes.' Is that a compliment? 'Not his hair though,' she continues, tucking the camera into her bag before pushing her fingers through my crispy hair. 'Your hair is so much nicer.'

I turn back towards the mirror. 'I look like some young punk rock fan.'

Zoe laughs. 'You are some young punk rock fan.' She opens the car door and gets out. I open my door but stay put. It takes Zoe a few seconds to reappear, peering impatiently through the gap. 'You coming, Tree?'

I moan as I pull my hand through my hair.

'Tree, don't. You'll ruin it.' Zoe snatches my hand away.

I look up at her. 'You know this isn't a fancy dress party, right?'

Zoe lowers her eyebrows. 'Which is good, because neither of us is in fancy dress.'

'Zoe, I look stupid.'

'Just because something is different, doesn't mean it's stupid, and anyway I know you like it so you can shut up.'

I sigh. Because she's right. I do like it. It reminds me of the old Tristan. I feel strange but ... myself.

That still doesn't mean I'm ever going to be the old Tristan again, though.

As soon as we step on to Ree's drive, I'm already regretting this. It's loud, and there are so many people outside standing in the light from the porch: groups smoking, couples making out, even a guy already throwing up. Fuck. I haven't experienced this sort of stuff for a while now.

This isn't going to be fun.

'This is going to be fun.' Zoe is practically glowing with excitement.

'Yeah, that was what I was thinking,' I mumble, lighting up a cigarette just to do something with my slightly sweating hands.

As we walk up to the door I'm hit with déjà vu. I recognise this place. Have I been here before? Though I know Ree from work, it's not like we hang out together, and I swear I've never been to her house before.

My déjà vu is interrupted as Zoe tuts, and quickly pulls the cigarette out of my mouth. Once inside we move past the people hovering in the hallway and make our way to the centre of the living room. The sofas have been pushed back and groups of people stand in circles. A few of them I recognise from work, and I think I catch some people whispering as they look in my direction, a few even nudging their friends. But maybe I'm being paranoid. I'm good at that.

Avoiding their gaze, I focus my attention on objects around the room. I'm getting that déjà vu feeling again ... Although it's not déjà vu, is it? No, it's a bloody memory. I scan the rest of the room to confirm it, taking in the photo of a crying baby on a side table, the stupid hamburger phone, the grand old fireplace. I've been in this house before. My eyes drag themselves to the leather couch, where a couple are making out.

Shit.

I drag my hand over my face.

'You okay?' Zoe says, concerned eyes scanning mine.

I raise my eyebrows in response and nod my head.

'Yeah. I'm cool.' But I'm not cool. In fact, I'm very far from cool. You see, I haven't just been in this house before. I've had sex in this house. Right there, on that sofa, to be exact. And not just on the sofa, but hey, you don't need details.

Shit. Fucking shit. Did I have sex with Ree?

Yes, okay. Judge me. I used to be bad. I used to have a lot of drunken sex.

'Have you seen Ree?'

I turn towards Zoe, trying to keep the panic out of my expression. Has she been reading my mind? I run a hand through my hair. 'Umm ... No ... I don't think so.' Zoe grabs on to my hand, and drags me further into the house. A few of the people from work say something to me as I draw near, but I carry on following Zoe. All I can think about is being in this house. When exactly was I last here? My brain is so foggy. Did I really sleep with Ree? Who else would I have had sex with in *her* house?

Zoe stops in front of me and hugs a girl with dark hair. She steps to the side and there's Ree, wearing a black, skin-tight dress and jet-black lipstick to match.

'Thanks for coming, Tristan,' she says, with a smile.

'Thanks for inviting me,' I reply, looking at her carefully. No. I definitely didn't sleep with her. Am I mistaking this for another house?

'Did you guys just get here?' she asks. Ugh, small talk. I think about how I never get that with Zoe. It's never just small talk with her.

173

'Yeah, Tree parked round the corner,' Zoe replies.

Ree rolls her eyes. 'Stop calling the poor boy that name.'

Zoe grins. 'It suits him.'

I try to look like I'm paying attention as I steal more glances around the house. When I turn back I realise Ree is talking to me.

'My sister's somewhere here,' she is saying. I nod slowly, not understanding why the comment is directed at me. 'Oh, there she is. Alice, yo!'

Alice?

I turn towards the girl Ree is pointing to; tall and slim, perched by the stairs, chatting with a guy. The girl hears Ree this time, and turns around.

I swear under my breath.

The good news is that I'm not going crazy. And I didn't sleep with Zoe's friend. The bad news is I slept with her friend's sister.

I totally forgot Ree and Alice were sisters. As soon as I see her it all comes flooding back – the complicated relationship I had with Alice that didn't end so well. I close my eyes. Please don't walk over.

I open my eyes to see Alice walking over. That's just perfect. She stands next to Ree, and I notice how similar they look. She smiles at Zoe. 'Hey, Zoe,' she says. 'Who is this guy you've brought—'

She stops talking, presumably having worked out who the 'guy' is. (Spoiler alert. It's me.) Her smile drops. I can already feel my chest thumping. I can sense Zoe's eyes on me. I force a tense smile and raise my hand up to Alice. 'Hey, Alice,' I stammer.

She doesn't reply, just exhales a long sigh as she continues to glare at me. I can still feel Zoe's eyes on me. Alice folds her arms, kisses her teeth, says nothing.

'Want a drink, Zoe?' I ask, not even looking at her or waiting for her reply. 'Okay, let's get something.' I take hold of her hand and swiftly drag her away from Ree and Alice into the safety of the centre of the party. Locating the drinks table, I pull out two red cups from a stack. Then I start pouring the first alcoholic thing I can find into them.

'What was all that?' Zoe asks. I turn towards her with wide eyes. I don't answer but swiftly take a huge gulp of my drink. Whatever it is, it's disgusting. 'Oh ... You and Alice used to go out, right?' I feel my eyes narrow. I take another gulp and realise I've finished the drink. I pick up the other cup and hand it to Zoe. She takes it in her hand and stares into it, before looking back up at me. She shakes her head and hands it back.

'You want something else?' I ask.

'No,' Zoe replies, eyes still focused on me. 'You're not on good terms with Alice?'

'Have the drink.' I try to hand it back.

'I don't want it.'

'Yes, you do,' I say, but she's looking at the drink with concentration.

Zoe moves her eyes away from the cup and up to me. She smiles. 'I don't drink, Tree,' she says.

I raise a quizzical eyebrow. 'Don't you want to get drunk?' I ask.

'I don't need to,' she replies, before winking at me. 'I'm already drunk on life.' She passes me the cup, raises her arms up and starts dancing to the music. I stare at her, still holding the cup in my hand. I lift it to my mouth and down it in one. By this point Zoe has moved on to jumping up and down. I step towards her.

Chapter 23

Zoe

'And I've been working at Wagamama for about five months now, it's all right.'

I nod my head, taking a sip of my cranberry juice. I can't remember this guy's name, and we've been talking for quite a while now. Is that bad? We're sitting outside in the fresh night air, which definitely has the feel of spring about it. The days are getting warmer recently, and I'm counting down the days till summer. The best memories are always made in the summer.

I watch the guy carefully; I'm sure he doesn't remember my name either.

'What about you, Zoe?'

Okay, it seems he does remember my name.

Ah, crap, what was he talking about? I have totally shut off for most of this conversation, and have barely listened to a word he's said.

'Um ... What do you mean?' I say, taking another slurp of my drink.

'Like, what do you do on your weekends?'

I try not to let my face fall. Does he really want to hear more about me? For the past half an hour all he's been doing is asking about my life. I won't lie, it is a subject that I enjoy, but he is taking it to a whole other level. He's hardly talked about himself at all, and when he does it's to tell me about taking his little sister to dance class, or getting a second job to support his mum. What I'm saying is, this is a nice dude right here and I can't even remember his name. And unlike everyone else at this party I can't blame it on alcohol either; I'm completely sober.

I have no idea where Tristan is. I don't think I've seen him for a good couple of hours now. That happens at parties, doesn't it? People just separate without meaning to; it's not a bad thing because you get to meet new people. New people like the guy I'm talking to now. I look up at him and smile; he shoves his hands in his pockets. My teeth chatter slightly as I exhale a breath of foggy air.

'You cold?' he asks.

I shake my head. 'Not properly. I was just a bit optimistic not to wear a jacket – I guess it's not *that* warm yet.'

'Do you want to go back inside?'

I look up at him and take a step closer, maintaining eye contact. 'No, I like it here.'

'So do I,' he says with a smile, before quickly looking down nervously. 'Do ... do you want my coat?'

I shake my head, but he takes off his coat and throws it over my shoulders anyway. I instantly feel warmer. Still holding my smile, I take a step even closer, before threading my arms around his waist. It takes him a second before he eventually hugs me back, encasing me in his body heat. 'Now I'm warm,' I whisper.

I love hugs. There is something so special about them. Tilting my head back, I look up at the nameless guy, our faces close. I can feel his breath gently hit my face, and he smells of peppermint.

He's not as tall as Tristan.

I'm not sure why that comes into my head, but just like that, I'm thinking about Tristan and wondering where he is again. Has he gone home? We were dancing earlier, and he was behaving differently. Maybe it was the alcohol. He had actually started smiling at me, and even tried out a wink. I'd thought he had a twitch in his eye. 'Why are you pulling that face?' I asked.

He looked happy, but it wasn't real happiness. It was like a thin veil he had drawn over himself. He gulped his drink. 'Seen anyone?' he said.

'What?' I said with a laugh.

'Seen any guys that have taken your fancy?'

I'd stopped dancing, and stared at Tristan. Why had he asked me that? I felt a sudden flash of anger that I couldn't explain, but squashed it down, plastered a smile on my face and said, 'No. What about you, seen any girls?'

Tristan had shaken his head at me, laughed as if it was a ridiculous question and turned away, dancing again.

Anyway, it doesn't matter, because soon after that I found this lovely, warm nameless man who is standing in front of me. He's beautiful, he's kind, he's friendly. In the past hour or two that we've been chatting I haven't picked up a single negative vibe from him. That's rare, you see, because we all have negative qualities, it's what makes us human. Is this guy real? I continue to stare up at him, our eyes locking. I angle my face slightly as our noses brush against each other. My eyes are closing as I feel his mouth closer to mine, breath exhaling heavily. And then he kisses me. And I kiss back. His lips are firm but gentle on mine.

Now I'm glad Tristan and I split up during the party. After he made that comment I felt myself deflate. He went outside for his twentieth cigarette, and I wasn't going to just follow him again, covering my nose and mouth again, coughing from the smoke again, shivering in the cold again, and so I stayed on the dance floor. And that is when I met Mr Mystery Name, and then I went outside with him instead. I wonder if Tristan has met someone. I wonder if he even noticed I didn't follow him outside, or if he's looking for me.

Zoe, what are you doing?

Why are you thinking about Tristan while kissing this guy? This isn't fair.

I move my head back, and the guy pulls away. I can see

180

the hurt in his eyes. 'I take it you didn't like it,' he says with a nervous laugh.

'No,' I say, lowering my eyebrows. 'I did. I did like it.'

And that's true. I had liked it. His lips were soft and he tasted minty and delicious. But my mind was otherwise occupied. I hadn't felt much else besides his lips on mine. 'You're nice,' I say to him, wishing I could remember his name. 'You're really nice.' The guy looks down at me through narrowed eyes. He knows what's coming. 'But the problem is, I don't think I am.'

'No, Zoe. You are.'

I shake my head with a small smile. 'Not nice enough for you.'

I can't help but wince at the reaction on his face, as he slowly nods his head. This isn't a rejection, I try to say with my eyes, I promise. 'It's cool,' he says.

Then we just stand here, staring. I give him a last small smile, before taking off his jacket, carefully stepping away and taking myself back inside. I should find Tristan. See if he's okay.

As I walk through to the living room, threading my way through the drunken crowds, I'm surprised to realise how pissed off I am with myself for ruining the moment with the nameless guy. I can feel the anger burning its way through my body, my heart is beating quicker because of it, and I'm drawing long heavy breaths of air.

I scan the faces around me, the anger intensifying, turning outwards. Why am I looking for Tristan? Why am I even friends with him? He's not that nice to me. He's pretty self-absorbed, too. And selfish. He doesn't know how to think of anyone else but himself. And he's so different to me. He has more sadness in him than I thought was even possible. His moods are draining. So why on earth do I care about him so much? I ruined the moment with that guy because of him. He distracts me. Too much.

Ree walks past me. I quickly grab her arm and pull her back. She sways as she watches me through squinted eyes. She's drunk. Or maybe high. Probably both. 'Have you seen Tree?' I shout over the music.

'Don't you mean Tristan? Tree isn't his name.'

'Yes, okay,' I say, waving off her drunken questioning, 'Where is he?'

She blinks at me. 'If I went to China, they'd start talking Chinese to me, because I look like them.' She hiccups. 'But . . . But.' She moves close to my face. 'Let me tell you a secret.' Her breath stinks of something that I do not want to come too close to. 'I have never been to Asia in my life!' She explodes into a cackle of hiccuping laughs. 'I don't even know Japanese, I've never been to Japan.'

Ree always does this when she's drunk. Alcohol makes her have this weird epiphany about her ethnicity. I have no idea why she is talking about China or Japan, because she's Korean. I exhale heavily as I let her lean on me for balance. I rest one hand on her shoulder, supporting her swaying body.

'Hey, Pebble.'

I instantly turn to see Jack standing behind me, dressed in a black-and-white-striped shirt, looking as gorgeous as ever. Anais is standing next to him, her curly hair pointing at all angles.

'You guys came!' I let Ree go for a second as I ambush them in a quick hug.

'The coaching group back together again!' Anais says, with a big grin.

'I'm so glad you guys made it,' I say, as I wrap my hand around Ree's shoulder, supporting her again.

Jack's eyes catch mine, crinkling as he grins. 'I told you'd we come.'

'And youuuuu did,' Ree slurs.

Anais looks at Ree, biting her lip to stifle a laugh. 'Is Ree okay?'

'Yeah, she's fine,' I say, rolling my eyes at them, trying not to let my gaze linger for too long on Jack's face.

'I rate the outfit,' he says.

'Why, thank you,' I reply, attempting a bow while still trying to support Ree. 'Oh!' I shout excitingly. 'My friend is here! The guy I was telling you about!'

'The leaf boy?' Anais asks, nudging Jack, who looks unimpressed.

'It's *Tree*. I've been trying to look for him.'

'Oh yeah?' Jack says. I can tell he's getting bored, and make a promise to myself to dance with him later. Jack loves a dance, and other than badminton I haven't really spent much time with him the last couple weeks.

183

'Yeah, I'm not sure where he—'

Then I spot him.

He's halfway up the stairs, back pushed against the wall. He's with Alice, Ree's sister. His ex. It's pretty obvious what they're doing, and I'm sure I don't need to explain it to you, but he's kissing her, and she's kissing him. It's almost as if they think no one else is in the room. There are hands through hair, fingers tracing backs, movement with hips. And here I am, watching like it's some sort of video.

Why am I watching? It's nothing to do with me. But before I can avert my gaze Alice pulls away from him, leaning forward and whispering something in his ear.

A smile spreads across Tristan's face as he nods his head.

I can't make him smile like that.

Alice trails her hand down his shirt and on to the buckle of his jeans, before weaving her other hand through his hair and pulling his face up to her. They kiss again. Tristan lightly pushes her away, picks up his drink, and with his free hand links fingers with Alice, and then they walk upstairs.

I move my eyes back toward Jack and Anais. Jack squints at me. 'You okay?' he says. I look down at Ree to avoid his gaze. She's crying now, for no obvious reason. 'I feel you,' I mumble. 'Do you want some water, Ree?' I ask more loudly. Ree sniffs before nodding her head.

I look back to Jack and Anais. 'I'm going to sober her up a bit; I'll meet you guys later.'

'You better, we want to see Zoe on the dance floor,'

Anais says with a grin. Jack looks confused, he goes to open his mouth to talk, but I quickly turn my head away. I tighten my grip and start half leading, half dragging Ree towards the kitchen.

'This has been a good party hasn't it, Zoe?' Ree says, as she starts chewing on a baguette. (Don't ask, I have no clue where it came from.) I rip an end of the baguette off and stuff it into my mouth. I think she's sobering up. 'I kissed this pretty girl earlier but then I lost her.'

'Well I'm sure you'll find her again, Ree.'

'No. No. She said I . . . I was the first and only girl she's kissed, you know.'

'Oh, so you converted a girl?'

'If we kept kissing maybe. She went to the toilet and never came back. Why?'

'I don't know Ree, I don't know why people do the things they do, and why—'

'Oh my God,' a girl sighs dramatically as she enters the kitchen behind me. 'I need a drink, Laura.'

I turn to see Alice with a friend. She takes a shot before resting her head on the kitchen counter. Where's Tree? Why isn't she with him?

'He's fucked,' she says picking up someone's drink. 'I don't get him, I don't fucking get him.' Is she talking about Tree? I continue to munch on my bread as I watch them.

'What happened?' her friend says, and I'm glad she said it, because I, too, want to know what happened.

Alice rolls her eyes and sighs. 'He just freaked out.'

'What do you mean?'

'All I'm saying is, I remember why I broke up with him.'

'Didn't Tristan break up with you?'

'Shut up, Laura,' Alice hisses before exiting the kitchen as her friend follows after her.

'Zoe!'

Now I turn around to see Rose standing behind me. Oh god. I don't need this as well. Why is everyone at this bloody party? Why the hell is she here? She's not friends with Ree, she has nothing to do with this lot.

I pretend not to see her and keep my eyes travelling around the room, as if I'm still trying to locate the source of the voice, but she grabs on to my arm, turning me towards her. I bring my head down to look at her, still trying to avoid her eyes.

'It's good to see you, Zoe.'

'Mmm, yeah, you too,' I say, chewing on the side of my nail. 'You know Ree, then?'

'No, my brother is best friends with her sister.'

'Well ... oh, right. We've got to go and—'

'I saw your dad the other day!'

I start twisting my fingers through my hair, as I scan the room avoiding her eyes.

'Oh really? He never said anything,' I lie.

'You know, the rest of the girls are here,' Rose says

186

holding on to my arm again. I feel my stomach sink.

'I have to go and see if my friend is all right.'

'You should hang out with us some time, it's been so long since you—'

'I have to go, Rose,' I say quickly. I feel my nose start to tingle, I slide my arm out from her grip and swiftly turn my back on her. I wipe my eyes with my hands, and blink heavily before looking back at Ree. She is still happily chewing on some bread, chatting to Anna. Anna? Where did she pop up from? I haven't seen her for the whole party. She looks pretty sober. Deciding that she can look out for Ree, I take one more look at them before swiftly leaving.

I find Tristan in Alice's room. He is leaning against the wall, eyes glazed, wearing just his pants. I sit down on the bed opposite him. It takes a while before he realises I'm there, and even when he does, he still doesn't say anything. He just stares at me, his red eyes blinking rapidly.

'Are you okay?' I ask, not letting my eyes leave him.

'It was fine,' he mumbles.

'What do you mean?'

'We had sex. It was fine.'

Something stings. I push the feeling down. I'm sure it's just Rose who's thrown me into a bad mood. My eyes move to the floor. 'And so ... what's the problem? You didn't want to have sex with her?'

'No, I did. I wanted to. But it wasn't the same as it used to be. I thought I would feel things like I used to, but I didn't.'

'Oh well, maybe you don't have feelings for her any more?' I'm not sure why I'm saying that.

'Then, after, she just went and ruined it.'

'What do you mean?'

'It was fine, then she got upset because I didn't want to cuddle her.'

'Come on, Tree, all girls like to cuddle after sex,' I reply with a short laugh. But Tristan doesn't seem entertained.

'We did.' His voice is monotone. 'But then she started trying to talk to me. About what we were, and what I used to be, and how I hurt her. She said I played her about, how I only came to her house once and she always used to come to mine. She just kept trying to talk about everything. Trying to drill her way into me. But I didn't want to talk about that. I couldn't talk about that. She didn't understand.'

'So why didn't you—'

'It started getting foggy up in my head. Dark.'

I try to understand what he is saying.

'I told her to stop, but she wouldn't stop. She wouldn't fucking stop talking as if I was the old Tristan, as if I was still that fucking Tristan from before. It made me angry. So angry. So I ... I ...'

I notice that his fists are clenched. My body tenses. 'Did ... Did you do something?'

He must hear the tone in my voice because he looks up at me with shock in his eyes and shakes his head. 'No. I wouldn't ... I would never ... But I wanted to ... I realised I wanted to do something, and that freaked me out.'

'Tree, that isn't good,' I whisper.

'I know. I'm sorry.'

'Don't apologise to me.'

'I pushed her off and started to leave but she wouldn't ... She just kept talking about how she felt like she could fix me, and she missed me, and she knew that this was just a phase. She thinks I love her and that she loves—'

'And then what happened?' I ask quickly.

'I lost it. I started shouting at her. I wouldn't stop shouting, then I started crying. I think I scared her. I scared myself ... I just totally lost it. I lose myself ...' Tristan pauses as his voice begins to crack. He lowers his head and sniffs. 'I'm sorry ... I'm sorry, Zoe.' He's slurring.

'It's okay.'

'I'm just so fucked up, aren't I? I feel like I'm being eaten alive inside, it's like I'm always walking around numb, in my own bubble, just trying to constantly fight back tears, tears I don't even understand why I'm crying. I can't work my head out.' I move my eyes to the floor, catching sight of his crumpled T-shirt. I lean forward and pick it up, and shove it into Tristan's hand. He looks up to me. 'You should go back to the party. I don't want to ruin your night.'

I form a small smile. 'No, it's fine, I've been finding it quite boring.'

'Did you not meet anyone?'

'No, I didn't. I've just been hanging with Ree.'

Tristan watches me with a pained expression for a few seconds. 'Do you want to get out of here?' he asks.

He doesn't know that I'd go anywhere with him.

Chapter 24

Zoe

'Get away from me,' Tristan shouts, as he walks further away down the street, holding his cigarette loosely in his hand. He's going to drop it on his T-shirt in a minute.

Luke pinches his nose and lets out a stressed sigh. 'Tristan, please just get in the car.'

'No.'

Here we go again.

I sit myself down on the pavement. I feel guilty for asking Luke to come, but I can't work out what else I could have done. It was only once we were outside by Luke's car and Tristan was struggling to get the key out of his pocket that I realised he couldn't drive us back, obviously – he's drunk. I don't know how I didn't realise it earlier. I knew he would be drinking, so why didn't I think about getting home? The answer is simple: it's because I'm Zoe. I don't worry about things. I never do. I just go with the flow.

Cross that bridge when I get there; it's how I've always been. And look where that gets you.

Tristan was trying to convince me he was fine while leaning on the car bonnet, and I was planning to call a taxi, when I noticed that his phone was ringing. He was too focused on trying to open the car door to answer it, despite the fact he wasn't even holding the keys. So I took his phone, saw that it was Luke, and I answered it.

'Just go away, Luke,' Tristan mutters, slumping himself down next to me on the pavement. He stumps out his cigarette on the floor; I kick it away from me. I watch Tristan silently, trying to work out how pissed off he is with me.

'You need to stop driving my car,' Luke says.

'No, you need to stop,' Tristan slurs.

'Stop what?'

'Yeah ... what?'

'Tristan, you're not making sense.'

'You're not fucking anything.'

Tristan finally got in the car. We're both sitting in the back seat. But now, instead of Tristan and Luke arguing, they've stopped talking altogether. We're in complete silence again. I would have preferred them to have another argument.

'Zoe? Where do you live? So I know where to drop you off,' Luke says, looking at me through the rear-view mirror.

192

'Oh I live just—'

'She's staying the night,' Tristan says, cutting me off. It's the first thing he has said this whole journey.

'What?' Luke says. I turn towards Tristan in confusion. Yeah, what?

'Zoe's staying the night,' Tristan says. He looks at me, and gives me a weak smile. 'If you want to?'

I nod my head cautiously.

'Don't feel like you have to.'

'No. I want to.'

Tristan stares straight ahead. 'Yeah, she's staying the night.'

I push my lips together to try to stop the smile that is spreading across my face, even though I'm not sure if I even do want to go back with him. I don't want to go back with him, do I? Maybe I should just go home.

'If that's okay?' I say. So much for going home.

I hear Luke sigh. 'Just be sensible, guys ... Jesus.'

'I *told* you, Luke,' Tristan shouts, probably a little too loudly, 'Zoe's a *friend*.' I feel Tristan grip my hand. 'A good friend.' He must've had more to drink than I thought. This isn't normal Tristan behaviour. I don't say anything, I don't even look at him. I just focus my gaze on his cold hand squeezing mine. The word 'friend' doesn't feel so good any more.

193

Once I get to Luke and Tristan's house, I head straight to the toilet. A girl's got to pee when she drinks a lot of cranberry juice. But this turns out to be another bad decision, as when I return they're arguing again. Of course they are. These two can't be left alone.

Not wanting to interrupt – or for them to see me – I watch them from the doorway.

'Why did you lie? Why didn't you just say you were going to a party?' Luke asks, sitting opposite him on the sofa.

'Because you'd give me a lecture about it.'

'You know it's only because I care.'

Tristan gets up and starts walking away.

'Tristan, come on. You can't just walk away from every conversation we have,' Luke says, following him.

Tristan stops and turns around. 'This is not a conversation. We never have conversations, only arguments.'

Luke runs a hand through his hair. 'You know I don't ... I don't think it's good for you to drink.'

'Hypocrite,' Tristan mutters.

'Tristan, don't do that,' Luke sneers as he moves closer. Tristan doesn't even look at him. 'You know why I don't want you to drink, it's just going to mess you up even—'

Luke pauses. He realises what he's saying, but it's too late, Tristan has already lifted his head. I have no idea what face he is pulling – I can't see from this angle – but I'm guessing it's not a smile. 'It's going to mess me up even more,' Tristan says, completing Luke's sentence. It's not a question, it's a statement. His words are serious, almost calm. It's highly uncomfortable.

Luke sighs. 'I didn't mean it like—'

'You did,' Tristan says, taking a step closer. 'But it's okay if you drink, isn't it, Luke?'

'Tristan, please.'

'It's fine if *you* drink.'

'Tristan,' Luke says through a tight mouth.

'Drinking messes you up too, Luke. You have problems too. You might even have more problems than—'

'DON'T YOU THINK I KNOW THAT?' Luke explodes. Then there is silence. Silence from me in the hallway (obviously). Silence from Tristan. And silence from Luke. I don't know what to do, so I pull myself back into the bathroom, carefully shutting the door and pretending that I hadn't witnessed that, wishing I had never witnessed that.

I press my back against the door as I breathe heavy gasps of air. Why am I the one freaking out? This has nothing to do with me. But maybe that's why. This is personal. This is family. Why am I here? Why am I getting involved?

Wondering what's happening out there now, I slowly open the door and peek out. Tristan isn't in the living room any more and Luke is slumped on the sofa, head resting on his hands. I quickly scoot past the doorway and creep upstairs.

Once I reach Tristan's bare, bleak room, I see him standing at his window with dead eyes.

'Tree?'

He doesn't respond.

'Tree,' I say, a little bit louder this time.

He slowly turns and looks at me. He stares at me blankly, just like he did when I found him in Alice's room.

'I think . . . I think I'm going to call my dad to pick me up,' I say.

Tristan's face crumples. And then I feel his arms around me. 'I'm sorry,' he whispers.

'Tree, it's okay. I just think I should give you and Luke some space—'

'Please don't leave me,' he says.

I try to pull away but he won't let go of me. 'I suppose I can stay, if you want?'

'Yes, I do want.'

I manage to pull away this time, looking at him and throwing him a short smile. 'Okay.'

Tristan throws back a smile of his own. It looks so foreign on his face. 'I can talk to you. You're the only person I can talk to. I don't know why.' I feel heat rise to my cheeks, and I stifle an uncomfortable laugh, but when I look back, he's not smiling any more. He slumps on the bed. I watch him curiously. I can't seem to connect with him.

'Tree?' I say, moving closer to him.

'When I kissed Alice. I felt nothing.'

I stay silent.

'The sex was shit.'

'Feelings change, Tree, it's okay,' I say, while standing awkwardly in the middle of his room.

'No, it's not that. I think she's beautiful.' I chew on the inside of my cheek. 'I used to feel something. I used to feel all sorts of feelings for her. I think I used to love her.' He lies back, his head resting on his duvet. 'I don't feel anything any more. I have no feelings.' I stay quiet as, yet again, Tristan has me at a loss for words. I start carefully placing some of his pillows on the floor. Tree lifts up his head. 'What are you doing?'

'Making a makeshift bed,' I say.

'I'm sleeping on the floor,' he says, sitting up.

'Tree, I'm not sleeping in your bed.'

'You're the guest, Zoe.'

'Exactly, so I get to choose where to sleep, and I'm not letting you sleep on the floor.'

I continue to prep my little bed on the floor; it's starting to look quite comfortable.

'Seriously, Zoe, you're not sleeping on the floor.' He sounds angry. Suddenly, I start to feel angry too. I can stand my ground. I drop the blanket, turn around and fold my arms. 'That puts us in a tricky situation because you're not sleeping on the floor either.'

Silence.

I smile to myself. He didn't see that coming. Tree looks to his bed, then back towards me.

'It is a double bed. We could both sleep here.' Oh. Is he

saying we could both sleep in his bed . . . together? 'Unless that makes you feel weird,' he says.

I quickly shake my head. 'Why would it?'

Tristan shrugs his shoulders. 'I dunno.'

'Cool.'

'Cool.'

'We can top and tail if you want.'

'Zoe, we're not five.'

He takes off his shirt and trousers, sitting in his boxers. I stare at him.

'Is it all right if I sleep like this?'

'It's your bed, you sleep how you usually sleep.'

He watches me, and I try to look back at him, trying to make sure my eyes don't linger on his body too long. 'You want some pyjamas?' he asks.

I lower my eyes. 'Erm yeah, a T-shirt and shorts?'

'Or you can sleep in your underwear too?' I lift my head up, feeling my heart start to pound. 'If that's how you usually sleep?'

I chew on my lip, nodding my head. 'Yeah. Okay.'

'Want me to turn away?'

I shake my head. 'No, don't be stupid.'

I carefully sit on his bed, unzipping my long boots. Then I go through a tired, nervous struggle taking off my tights. I unbutton my skirt, holding it for a few seconds as I swallow moisture back into my throat, then slide it down my legs and step out of it. I'm standing on his floor now, in front of him, wearing just my knickers and my crop top.

My heart is pounding its way up my throat. I swallow it down. Trying to steady my hands, I slowly unbutton the back of my top and lift it up. It gets tangled on the buns in my hair, and I feel panic fill my lungs. Then I feel his hands on mine, guiding my arms through my top as he carefully detangles me. Finally, my top is lifted over my head and there he is, staring at me. He steps back and sits down on his bed, watching me. I hold my hands in front of my body, not sure how to stand or what to say. If I can say anything. I can't find my voice. I hold my belly, trying to contain the butterflies that are actively taking flight inside me. My hand lowers, as I feel myself stroke the stretch marks that tiger-stripe their way down my tummy and on to my thighs. Can he see them? Does he think they are ugly? What about that varicose vein I have on my calf – is it obvious in this light? I wish I was wearing prettier pants. He still just watches me.

'Zoe?' he says quietly.

I move my eyes up to him.

'You're beautiful, you know that?'

I exhale a nervous breath of air. My eyes flicker; I don't know if he's being serious.

'I think I'm a little bit too skinny,' I whisper. 'I wish I had more boobs, bum and hips.'

'Any boy would be lucky to have you,' he says. I feel my mouth drop, as my eyes flick around the room. I don't know what to do.

He lies back on his bed, looking up at the ceiling so I

join him. As I lie down, I can hear Tristan chuckling next to me. 'Your bed is comfy, Tristan,' I say. He sniggers another laugh, triggering me to chuckle along too.

He laughs again, more loudly. I raise my eyebrows at him. 'What's so funny?'

'I don't know.'

'You're still drunk.'

'No, I'm not.'

'Yes, you are.'

'You weren't too drunk to have sex with Alice, were you?'

'No,' he mumbles. 'I was pretty sober then. I downed a few drinks once she stormed out the room.'

'Oh ... Okay.'

He smiles at me. 'Do you want to spoon?'

He hates touching. Is he just asking this because he's drunk? 'As long as I'm the big spoon,' I eventually say.

Tristan smiles. 'You can be the big spoon next time,' he says. And then before I can process what he's said, he rolls me over and wraps his arms around me. I lie there carefully, trying to not move too much. He pulls me tighter, my back touching his bare skin, his hands close, one on my chest, the other encasing me. I feel a warmth grow in the pit of my stomach as I feel his breath tickle the back of my neck. And then all is quiet. I close my eyes and try to relax. But I can't. My eyes flick open. I can feel my heart beating.

Beat. Beat. Beat. Beat.

It's getting heavier and harder. *Be-beat-be-beat. Be-beat-be-beat.* I'm sure Tristan must be able to feel it. I'm also starting to feel a little breathless, taking in long, deep breaths. My tummy is fluttering, my cheeks are blushing, head thumping—

Oh.

'Shit,' I mutter.

'You all right?' Tristan mutters close to my ear.

'Yep, fine,' I reply quickly, but I'm not. Because I've just worked something out. It makes a lot of sense, now that I think about it.

I like Tristan. I've known that for a while, but the problem is, I don't think I like him just as a friend. I think I like him more than that. I think I . . . Jesus Christ . . . I think I love him.

Love? This isn't a bloody movie, Zoe, this is real life. And why do you love him? It's Tristan, for God's sake, who barely acknowledged your existence tonight.

I don't know why, but I am.

I'm in love with this boy.

Chapter 25

Tristan

I wake up to one of the world's deadliest hangovers. As soon as I sit up, my head begs me to lie myself back down. But I push through and keep my eyes open, stretch my arms above my head and stare at Zoe sitting cross-legged opposite me on my bed. She's wearing one of my T-shirts—

Wait, what?

Then last night floods back through my brain. Alice, losing my shit, Luke picking us up, losing my shit again. My mind is foggy, I can't remember much after getting home. But Zoe must have stayed. She stayed with me the whole time. What have I done to deserve a friend like that?

I look across at her and chuckle slightly. As if I'm allowing myself to have friends. I guess she's an exception to the rule. I squint my tired eyes as I try to resist the urge to fall back down and nestle into my duvet. Zoe smiles at me.

Ah, man, my head really is pounding. I reach my hand up to my hair and—

'NO!'

Zoe is nodding at the hand that is now floating above my head. 'You don't want to smudge it,' she says. If it's even possible to frown more than I usually do, I'm doing that right now. I bring my hand down to examine it.

This is when I see black and bright pink nail varnish painted on my nails. I quickly pull my other hand in front of me to look at it and ... yup. Painted with exactly the same ugly colours. Oh, for God's sake. There even is a small, wobbly smiley face painted on the back of my hand. I glare at Zoe, who holds up two bottles of nail varnish triumphantly before stretching her mouth into an innocent smile. 'It suits you,' she says, before retrieving something from behind her back, lifting her hand and taking a quick picture of me with that blinding camera of hers.

I would usually complain, but right now I'm focused on my hands. I start rubbing my finger against my nails, but the colour doesn't budge.

'Oh, good, it's dried,' Zoe says. I glare at her. Her smile falls. 'Oh, I mean ... it looks like it's dried. What a shame.'

'Zoe, why did you paint my nails?'

'Well, what else was I going to do whilst I waited for you to wake up?' she says innocently.

'Where did you even get nail varnish from?'

'I brought it with me,' she says as if it's an obvious answer. 'Something you need to know about girls, Tree, we bring everything with us. I don't know why, we just do.'

She crawls forward, and raises her disposable camera in front of both of our faces as she takes another snap. I exhale a short laugh as I rub my tired eyes. I feel shattered. Maybe I deserve it for being such a mess at the party.

'I'm sorry about last night,' I say, looking down at my duvet.

'You don't need to apologise,' Zoe says. 'In fact, I'm sure that you ...' She's still talking but her voice trails off in my ears as I catch sight of the curtain pole above my bed, my focus that thin yet strong stretch of wood. My stomach drops as I try to swallow the lump that has risen in my throat. I quickly jolt my hand to my neck and stroke it, physically reminding myself to breathe. Just breathe, Tristan, just bloody breathe. I manage to gulp.

I turn my head back towards Zoe, realising that she is still talking to me. Well, was talking to me. She's not any more, now she's just watching me with wide, sad eyes.

'Are you all right?' I ask.

She doesn't reply, just continues to watch me, not even blinking.

I shuffle forward slightly. 'Talk to me,' I say.

Zoe stares at me with more seriousness than I've ever seen from her. It's worrying. She exhales. 'Tree, you scare me.'

What? I don't say it aloud; instead, I say nothing, all the while thinking that maybe I should say something.

'You scare me.' She says it like I didn't hear her the first time.

'What ... What do you mean?'

'I ... just worry that I'm making things more complicated. That I'm not helping you, you know?'

I shuffle closer to her on the bed, so that my knee is touching hers. 'You are helping me, Zoe,' I say, looking into her eyes. 'I'm just ... broken.'

She looks up at me. 'Well, then why can't I fix you?'

'Some people can't be fixed.'

She lowers her head and sighs, her eyes dazed and faraway as she stares out at nothing. After a few seconds, she snaps out of it and looks back up at me. 'You're not going to leave me are you, Tree?'

'What?'

'You're not going to leave me?'

'Of course I'm not,' I say, wrapping an arm around her. She doesn't react.

'Eventually you'll give in and then you're going to leave.'

I chuckle awkwardly, squeezing her shoulder. 'Where would I go?'

'Tree, I'm worried that I'm going to come into work one day and your till will be empty.'

I scan my eyes over her face, slowly, carefully, before forcing a smile. 'Well you don't need to be. I'm staying put.' I yank her arm and pull us both back down under the duvet. Zoe starts laughing, which is good; I like her laugh. I start laughing, too. But it's just a noise; not actual laughter. No, if you were to float up to the ceiling and look down at me, you'd see my smile disappearing and the fear creeping back into my eyes, even as I laugh.

Zoe wasn't talking about my till being empty because I wasn't at work that day, or because I'd changed sections, or even because I'd decided to move halfway across the world. No. We both know what she was implying.

I may have smiled, hugged her and shrugged it off. But honestly, I can't confidently tell her not to be worried. I don't know if that till will be empty one day. I don't know if I'm going to leave her. I don't know anything. It's not up to me. Not really.

Chapter 26

Zoe

It's been over a week since the night of the party, and I've seen a lot of Tristan – both on shift and outside of work, mainly at his house. He even met me outside of uni once, after a lecture. Just turned up and surprised me. I was supposed to go to badminton coaching that day, but I decided to skip it. I couldn't turn Tristan down after he'd made that effort to see me. Even if it did mean I received a moody text from Jack, upset that I hadn't shown up.

Tristan taps his fingers on the table like it's a drum, his eyes intently scanning the room. He's in a strange mood today. I look down at his hands, and the polish on his nails. By now it's pretty chipped, gone altogether on some fingers, but for the most part it's still there. That clashing pink and black. Seeing it makes me smile. I don't care what he says, I know he likes it. I grab my camera from where it rests on top of the menu and take a quick photo of him. By now he's so used to it he even pulls a face at the camera.

The Italian restaurant we're sitting in is hushed and practically deserted. Which I suppose is normal for a weekday afternoon. But it feels too quiet.

Tristan looks at me and grins. I throw him back a confused smile. What's up with him? He starts fidgeting with his hands again, rubbing them together before slapping them back on the table.

'You want to know something?' he asks suddenly, raising his eyebrows at me.

The more I look at him, the more I notice how bloodshot his eyes are today, like he didn't get any sleep at all last night. Though there is a smudged layer of eyeliner under his eyes that makes them look even more tired than they are. I knew he liked wearing it.

'I always want to know something,' I reply with a smile.

Tristan looks behind him, then back at me, leaning in closer as if he has some big secret to tell. 'Everyone at work thinks we're dating.'

I feel my jaw tighten. Ree and Anna certainly don't think that's the case. They think Tristan is messing me around.

'Isn't that funny?' he chuckles.

'Yeah,' I say. I'm not sure my own laugh is quite convincing.

'It's like people think a man and a woman can't be friends without them being in each other's pants.'

'I know,' I say, looking down at the table. 'Maybe they're just thinking about what you used to be like.'

When Tristan doesn't respond I look carefully up at him, and immediately regret what I said. It's like a curtain has come down over his eyes.

'I'm not that person any more,' he says, serious now. 'And it's a good thing too, because I was an arsehole to girls.'

'But I mean, do you think ... you'd like to date again?' I move my hand closer to his.

'No.' He shakes his head. I pull my hand away. 'I'm not looking for that. I don't think I could.'

'Not even one day?' I venture, trying to keep my voice casual.

'Zoe, you know this. I'm not normal.'

'Who wants to be normal?' I say with a not-quite-convincing smile. '*I'm* not normal, but I still want to date.'

My awkward chuckle is met with silence, and that's all the confirmation I need. You know it, Zoe. This isn't some date you're on. This is just Tristan agreeing to go for food so he can escape from yet another argument with Luke. He didn't turn up at my house today because he fancies me. And anyway, I'm supposed to be his friend – I'm lucky to be one of the only people he will allow himself to be friends with. I need to stop being selfish and be what he needs – a good friend.

'I met up with Alice last week.' His hands have started drumming again.

My stomach drops. 'Oh, you did?'

'Yep. I thought it might help somehow.'

'And ... did it?'

'Absolutely fucking not.' He's still tapping his hands and his feet have joined in, too, as he glances around the restaurant. 'If only she could *fix* me, like she's so sure she can. I think she even gets a kick out of the fact I'm so messed up.'

I keep my eyes trained on the table. He doesn't need fixing, he just needs support. He just needs understanding.

'But she can't, I'm not her charity project – and besides, I'm unfixable.' He says it flippantly, still drumming the table. He doesn't even seem sad about it. He's resigned to it.

The waitress chooses this moment to take our order. I glance up, instantly recognising her. *Oh, shit.* I look down at the menu, begging it to swallow me up. *Don't notice me. Don't notice me. Don't notice—*

'Zoe!' Rose exclaims.

I smile at her, and I can feel it's similar to the way Tristan smiles – small and tight. 'Hey, Rose, didn't know you worked here.' I really didn't. I grab the drinks menu and quickly look down at it, avoiding her eyes and Tristan's at the same time.

Suddenly all I want is to go home.

'First we see each other at the party, now here – that's fate, right?'

'Or karma,' I mumble under my breath.

'What?' Rose asks.

'Yeah, fate, Rose ... it must be fate.'

'How did you find the party? We didn't get to talk much.'

I force myself to look up. 'Yeah, I left early,' I say quickly, eyes flicking from Tristan to her.

'I miss you, all the girls do, you know. We haven't heard from you in ages.'

'Yep,' I say, exhaling heavily. 'I've just been so busy with work and uni, you know.'

'We should go out again, like old times.'

'We should, for sure,' I mumble, non-committal, eyes still focused on the menu. 'Could we order? We're in a bit of rush.'

'Yeah, sorry, what do you guys want?'

'Can I have a half pint of Stella?' Tristan says, with a polite smile at Rose.

'Can I just have tap water please?'

Tristan raises his eyebrows. He can be so annoying sometimes.

'You both ready to order food, too?' Rose says.

'I think so.' Tristan is still smiling at Rose. He seems to be smiling at her more than he has ever smiled at me. 'Can I have the pasta bake, please, and some chips?'

'All right, fries, curly fries or parmesan wedges?'

'Fries.'

'Okay,' Rose says, writing in her notepad. She turns towards me. 'What are you going for, Zoe?'

I sigh, feeling Tristan's eyes on me. I move my eyes away

from him and plant my gaze firmly on Rose. I forgot how pretty she was. 'The Bosco salad, please.'

Rose nods, smiles, takes our menus and leaves.

'She seems nice. Is she a friend?'

'She ... used to be.' I worry Tristan is going to press me on it, but he says nothing. At least I can always count on Tristan not to ask me endless questions about things I don't want to talk about.

I try to avoid looking him but my eyes eventually find their way back up to his. He is staring at me with a smug smile. 'When are you going to not order a salad and water for once?'

I roll my eyes. 'When *are* you going to order a salad and water for once?'

'I don't like salads,' Tristan says. Jesus, he is so bloody smug.

'Well there you go. I do like salads.'

'No, you don't.'

I frown at him, though he's right. They are bloody boring. 'Well, I care about my health,' I say.

Rose comes back with our drinks. She smiles at me. It's too friendly. I take my drink from her and immediately start sipping my water. I feel Tristan watching me again.

'So, what happened between you and that girl?' he asks once she's shimmied off.

I sigh into my water. So much for no-questions-asked Tristan.

'I really don't want to talk about it. People change.'

'Who changed, you or her?'

For God's sake. Why has he chosen now to be the nosy one for once?

'Last summer I just got so busy with work and uni that I didn't have time to see them as much, it's not a big deal,' I say, indicating the subject is closed.

But Tristan is still staring at me. I continue to chew on my straw. 'I think you need to live more, Zoe.'

I lower my drink. He's said it so seriously that I can't help but burst out laughing.

'Did *you* seriously just say that, to *me*?' The boy with depression. The boy who wants to stop living.

He doesn't say anything, but I can tell from his small smile that he's realised the ridiculousness of the situation. There's a silence as we sip our drinks. As I look around the restaurant, I have the sensation he's still watching me, and when I look back there he is, staring. I put down my cup and frown. 'Tree, what's up with you? You're in a strange mood today.'

Tristan just flashes his newfound geeky grin at me. 'Am I?'

'Yes.'

'Because I'm happy?'

'Well ... Yes. What's wrong?'

'Why is me being happy a wrong thing?'

He's right. It's not a wrong thing at all. It's good. This might mean something. This might mean he's starting feel things again. This might mean—

213

I pick at the tablecloth, before saying quietly, 'Do you think you are getting better?'

Tristan's smile falls. His eyes go cold again.

Don't be stupid, Zoe.

Tristan suggests walking our food off before we go home. I think he's stalling because he doesn't want to go back to Luke, but it means more time with him, so I don't complain. Sometimes I feel like I'm holding on to moments with him, dragging them out, praying for them to last a bit longer. Because who knows how many moments you're going to have with someone? Jerry has been trying to call me for the last half an hour, but I won't let him pull me out of this moment with Tristan. I just text him to say I'll be home late. I may hate his constant texts, but I don't want him to worry.

Tristan says he'll lead the way, so I follow. It's already dark, and with the harsh wind buffeting my face, you wouldn't think it's already April. But even though the roads are quiet, and the sky is gradually turning inky black, I have that feeling inside that I get walking down a sunny street. I don't usually like the dark, but walking with Tristan I feel safe. I'd walk all night if he asked me to right now.

Tristan strides at quite a fast past, which I find frustrating; I want to indulge in the stroll. We've mostly been

214

silent as we've walked, but now he says, 'I don't think I'll ever be better.' His voice echoes in the quietness of a Wednesday evening.

'What makes you think that?'

'I think I'm just built to be a sad person.'

I look down at my feet as they tap along the pavement. 'I'm sorry you feel that way.'

'It's okay,' he says, running his hand through his hair. 'It's hard to explain how it feels. It's like I'm split into two people, and the two sides are constantly fighting.' He takes a sharp right down a walkway; I don't have time to wonder where we're going, because he keeps talking. It's like walking is making him more talkative. 'I have my good days. But then when I have bad ones, they are really bad. When the bad side is winning, it seems like that's it, it's the end. Like there's no escape.'

'How can I help you?' It comes out as a whisper.

'You already help me. But it's wasted really.' I feel his hand brush against mine, but I don't dare look down.

Instead, I frown up at him. 'I don't understand.'

Tristan smiles. 'Okay, I'll explain – but don't judge me.'

'I never judge.'

He folds his arms. 'Well, honestly, I see this whole thing called "life" as a waste. I think I always will. It's not just about me being sad, it's so much more than that. It's a feeling that swallows me up, and the only escape I have is sleep, because when I sleep I don't hear the bad thoughts, I don't feel sick, or stressed; I don't feel any of it when

I sleep. But then I wake up and it starts again. I always hope that I'll wake up one day and it'll be different, but it's always there. I live my life dreading waking up, and looking forward to going back to bed in the evening. Tell me that's not a waste?'

His feet haven't hesitated or faltered while saying this; whereas I have to make a conscious effort to keep my feet moving. I feel my mouth start to twitch downwards. My heart strains. It aches for him. 'Things will get better.'

'Do things ever get better, or is that just in movies?'

'Are you taking your medication again?' I ask in a small whisper, aware that I have no idea how to navigate this situation or if I'm asking any of the right things.

'No.'

'Does Luke know?'

Tristan shrugs his shoulders. 'Probably. But there isn't a lot he can do about it.'

'Well maybe you should try taking them again? Maybe it'll help.'

'I've gone through it all before, I can't do it again.'

'Yes, you can. That's like someone saying if they don't win a race the first time, they won't ever win it.' I realise I'm getting angry. I want to help him, can't he see that?

'Taking medication for something like this feels wrong. It's like giving in. I can't fix my head myself, so pills have to do the job. Do you know how pathetic that makes me feel? It basically means I haven't tried hard enough.'

Can he seriously hear what he's saying right now? 'Tree, that isn't true. Depression is an illness.'

'No, it's a *mental* illness. Not a physical one. An illness in my head.'

'Still an illness. Tree, people take medication if they have an infection, people take medication if they need an operation. Do they feel guilty? *No.* It's because they need it and it's not their fault.'

'Those people don't choose to be ill. This thing ... It's in my head. In my brain. I've chosen to be like this. I just don't know why.'

'No, you haven't. No one chooses it. Mental and physical illnesses are still illnesses. One isn't worse than the other.'

'Stop trying to confuse me, Zoe.'

'All I'm saying is, you shouldn't see medication as a bad thing.'

Tristan looks up. 'I don't really,' he says. 'I just know I don't need it. Maybe for some people it works, but not me.' In the growing darkness, I feel him reach out and grab my hand. 'I've got you.'

I screw my face up in confusion. 'What?'

He stops walking and stares at me. 'When I'm with you, Zoe, you take the pain away. You remind me to be me. You're my medicine.'

I stand there silently as I try to process his words. My heart is beating and my thoughts are confused. I clutch his hand tighter. I mean to tell him that I can't be that for him; that he needs to start taking his antidepressants again; that he needs to tell Luke he's not been taking them. I mean to say all of this, but before I get the words out he smiles.

'We're here,' he says quietly, watching my face intently. His eyes piercing mine through the dark sky.

I look around – we're standing on the road that separates the sports field and the supermarket. I shake my head in confusion. 'You've taken us to work?'

'No,' he says confidently, taking a step on to the grass, letting my hand fall from his grip. 'I've taken you to the sports field.' He pauses, it's hard to make out his facial expression as he moves into the darkness, but I think he's looking very smug. 'It's time for you to stop watching from the sidelines. Show me your stuff, Zoe.'

'What?' I laugh, but take a step forward.

'Race me,' he says, with a slight smile.

I swallow the lump in my throat. 'I don't do that any more.' But even as I say it, I can feel the familiar tingle in the balls of my feet.

'I thought you were fast?'

'I am.'

'Are you scared I'll beat you?'

'No,' I say sharply. 'I just don't run any more, so why would I race you?'

He cocks an eyebrow at me, and starts stretching, before jogging on the spot. 'Do it because it's fun.'

My heart starts pounding in my chest. 'What are you doing, Tree?'

218

'Getting ready to race you, and win.'

'But you won't.'

'Okay. Prove it.'

I feel my breath get stuck in my throat. I close my eyes. I inhale. I exhale. And then I look at him. 'Okay. First one to the end of the track wins.'

I run, and it feels amazing. I feel free; I feel like energy is being back pumped into me – along with exhilaration, competitiveness – rather than being drained from me. My legs are pacing, arms pumping. All I can think is: I'm back.

I reach the end of the track first. Then we turn around and run again. I beat him a second time, and then when we do it once more for good measure, I beat him again.

Finally, we both flop down on the field; exhausted, hearts racing, looking up at the sky.

'You proved it,' Tristan says in a breathy voice.

'I told you.'

'So why don't you do it, then?'

I stay silent, staring up above. I want to run again. I will run again. I know it's for me; like a smoker's secret cigarette or an artist's painting, I can't just let it go. I need to do the things I enjoy. I felt more alive in those thirty-second sprints than I have for months. I need to do more of that; I need to start living again.

I stare at the stars sprinkled across the sky. I can hear Tristan's heavy breaths falling in time with mine. The smell of damp grass is weeding its way up my nose as cold creeps through my clothes.

'Aren't stars special?' Tristan says softly. I look away from the stars and back at him as he talks. 'Those tiny sparks of light in a mass of darkness.' He turns towards me, his eyes just visible in the darkness. 'I think you're my star, Zoe.'

I feel my breath catch in my throat, as I watch him carefully, trying to focus on his face in the darkness.

Then he looks back up at the sky. 'But there will never be enough stars. You look at the sky and even though the stars shine so bright, the sky is still dark.'

I look down at our hands, which are clasped together. My skin tingles where his palm touches mine.

And I know then that I'm loving a broken boy. A boy who will never be able to love me back.

Chapter 27

Tristan

I end up sleeping in Luke's car for the night. I just didn't want to go home, didn't want to talk to Luke and ruin how I was feeling.

I wake up in the car on the driveway. A groan escapes my throat as I sit up.

Luke is standing outside our front door, arms folded, staring at me. Before I took off yesterday we had another argument, and – like I always do – I ended up taking the car and heading to Zoe's.

I get out and shut the door behind me, leaning on the car and folding my arms to match his. A blur streaks past Luke out of the doorway and Misha runs up to me, head-butting me in the crotch. I bend down, trying to ignore the shooting pain I now have in my nether region. Thanks, Misha, you big weirdo.

I nestle my head in his fur and he scurries his body

about, too excited to know what to do with himself. 'Misha,' I mumble into his hair. 'Please take me away from here, I don't want to deal with this.'

But then it clicks. Maybe I don't have to. I look back at Luke. I don't think he's looking at me angrily, it's more like sadness. I stand up and take a couple of steps forward.

Luke opens his mouth to speak. 'Can I talk first?' I say quickly. Luke doesn't say anything. 'Look, I know I make things difficult for you.'

Luke goes to interrupt, but I don't let him.

'Just let me talk,' I say, putting a hand up, before realising that it's rude, so I shove my hands in my pockets. 'I just want to say I'm sorry. I want to say sorry for the argument we had yesterday; I'm sorry for not letting you know I was safe last night; I'm sorry for being a crap brother.'

'Tristan, you're not a crap—'

'Luke, please.' I sigh. Can't he see I'm trying? 'I just want you to know I'm sorry, and I'm going to try harder.'

Luke watches me for a couple of seconds. 'I'm going to try, too,' he says with a small smile.

I think I smile back, but I'm distracted by a screech of brakes from the road.

And then Luke isn't smiling any more. In fact, he isn't even looking at me, but over my shoulder. He's pointing, running. I hear a car horn. I hear a howl.

I turn around.

No.

I run into the road. And I see Misha. Lying there.

I collapse on to my knees and pull Misha on to my lap. *No, no, no.* There's blood on my hands. Blood on the road. Blood on Misha's fur. He's not wagging his tail. He's not licking me. He's not wriggling his body. He's not opening his eyes.

'Misha? Wake up. Misha, please . . .'

Chapter 28

Zoe

'So, what's the deal with your hair?'

I shift in my seat to turn towards Ree. I stayed over at hers last night, filling her in on my dinner with Tristan and our trip to the sports field the night before, and she's kindly dropped me into work this morning. It's been a while since we had a good old girl's night, especially just the two of us, as Anna couldn't make it. 'What do you mean?'

'You haven't dyed it,' she says.

'I know.'

'So it's staying purple?'

'Maybe. I haven't thought about it.'

We're parked up outside the supermarket and Ree switches off the ignition while we chat before my shift starts. 'You going to redo the roots?'

I scrunch my nose and peer at my reflection in the wing mirror. 'Nah, I'm just going to let it do its thing.'

'What's happened to you?' she says, eyes focusing on my hair. 'Trying something different?'

'Yeah, I guess.'

Ree cocks her head to the side appraisingly. 'Yeah, it will be like a purple ombré sort of thing. Anyway, I better go, I've got that baby shower to go to.'

'Yeah, don't worry about it. Thanks for the lift.'

'No problem.'

Once I say goodbye to Ree with a meaningful hug, I stride through the sliding doors and head towards the canteen. I have twenty minutes till my shift starts. I know Tristan is here somewhere because I texted him ten minutes ago asking if he was in today. He is, of course – he's always in. He replied to tell me he was on his lunch break, so I glide into the canteen to find him there, looking as Tristan-like as always. I sit down next to him heavily, slamming my hands on the table.

Tristan doesn't look up. He keeps on staring at the sandwich in his hands that he's not eating. It must be a Zoe-starts-the-conversation day.

'So, I visited my gran at the hospital the other day.' Tristan makes the effort to lift his eyes up and look at me. 'I was half expecting to run into you, because we seem to do that quite well,' I continue with a chuckle. His eyes drift across my face again, before returning to staring straight ahead of him at nothing. Not even his sandwich this time.

Um. Okay . . .

I grab a bottle of water from the vending machine and sit back down to drink it. It's quiet in the canteen.

Naomi heads straight for Tristan, asks him if he minds writing a note to say he'll cover her shift next week. He nods and I watch him as his pen slides across the paper, quickly scribbling the words.

'I like your handwriting, Tristan.'

His hand pauses. He heard me. Then he continues to write, hands the paper to Naomi, who thanks him and disappears. Still he shows no sign of speaking, so I continue to fill the silence. 'I love handwriting in general. I think of it like the equivalent of someone's voice.'

'How?'

Tristan finally speaks, and I can tell it's taken him a lot of effort. 'Well, everyone's handwriting is slightly different, and only you will have your handwriting. Someone else might have a similar style to you, but your handwriting will always be yours, unique to you. Just like someone's voice. It's another part of what makes you you.' Tristan's mouth almost slides up into a slight smile, but then his face suddenly drains of emotion. His head drops back down. 'Tree?'

No response.

'Tree, have I done something wrong?'

Tristan's eyes move up to mine as his brows furrow. 'No.'

'Well, what's— I mean, are you okay?'

His head lowers again. He rests his palms carefully on the table. 'Misha got hit by a car yesterday,' he quickly says.

Oh, shit.

'Is he . . . ?'

'They don't know yet.'

I know how much Tristan cares about his dog. My mind scrambles for a way to make this better. That's what I'm supposed to be able to do, as his friend.

But I'm not used to dealing with death. I've had it lucky. I'm not used to counselling. So instead of saying something, I just turn back towards the table, and sit in silence beside him, counting down the minutes till my shift starts.

Chapter 29

Tristan

I run my finger along the rim of the beer glass, then slowly lift it to my lips and take a sip of the wheat-filled bubbles, forcing them down my throat. It's only when I put my glass back down on the table that the noise in the pub surges back around me.

'Yeah, well, I told her that if she was interested she could buy *me* a drink this time, that's how you do it, you listening, Gaz?' Alex is talking loudly, followed by a roar of laughter from the whole group. I look up at Luke, who isn't as engrossed by the conversation as the rest of his friends. Instead, he's watching me. Clocking his gaze, I feel a pressure on my chest, so pick up my beer and drink again.

It was Luke's idea that I come out with his friends to the pub tonight. I came along, not because I wanted to, but because when I tried to decline he said he would stay at home with me.

I wish I could have just stayed at home. I wouldn't have been completely alone. Sally is at the house right now, finding jobs to do like she usually does. But Luke said it'd be a good distraction from worrying about Misha, and I thought he might be right. Misha will be having his second operation right now, and I don't even want to think about how much it's costing. We never took out pet insurance, so his treatment is costing the big bucks. But each time the vet mentioned the cost Luke didn't hesitate, didn't bat an eyelid. He just said, 'Whatever you need to do, do it. He's family.'

I'm sure Luke is draining the insurance money from Dad like nobody's business. At least I've got a job again now. I'll pay Luke back, eventually. But what if he's spending all this money and it's just going to go to waste? The vet said that if Misha doesn't respond well to this operation, it'd be cruel to let him live in pain, and they'd need to put him down. They don't put humans down if we're suffering, if we're in pain. Even when it's what we want more than anything, even if it feels like we are trapped in our body, just desperately trying to survive every day. Even if it means we have to forgo a comfortable way of saying goodbye to this world. Even if it means we could finally be in peace. They don't do that. Humans have to suffer.

There is another loud roar of laughter, as the whole group slams their empty drinks on the table. 'Another round?' Gaz says, standing up. The group respond by shouting as if they are apes.

It's ridiculous.

I used to be like that. I miss being ridiculous.

'You want another one, Tristan?' Gaz asks.

'He's fine,' Luke cuts in, his eyes still on me.

'Luke, let your brother answer for himself. Tristan, do you want a drink? It's on me.'

'I'm fine, Gaz,' I say. He turns to the bar.

'So, Tristan, how's uni?' Alex slides in to the left of me.

I suck in a deep breath of air. 'I didn't actually go back to uni, I'm just working now.'

'Come on, man, you've only had a year out, you were in your final year – you can't let all that work go to waste.'

'Alex,' Luke mutters.

My shoulders tighten. 'There's no point going back for me really.'

He must sense my discomfort, because he changes tack. 'Any girls you got your eyes on?'

Not this again. My eyes jump around the table. 'Not really.'

'Not really?' Alex questions.

'Alex, let him be, man.' Luke says it a little louder this time.

'Hey, what about that girl you see? The one who was round the other week. The one that calls you the funny name?'

'Zoe?'

'Zoe. Yeah, that's right!' Alex replies, nudging me in the

shoulder. He goes to wrap an arm around me. I'm feeling squashed. I need air. I need space.

'Don't get so close to him,' Luke mumbles, his eyes on us.

'Hey, we're only being friendly.' I can smell the alcohol on Alex's breath.

'Just ... leave him, all right?'

'All right. All right,' Alex answers, lifting his arm away. 'Just involving Tristan in the conversation. That girl was a good-looking bird, you know.'

I can feel my hands starting to tense.

'Oh yeah,' Gaz grins, returning from the bar. 'Cute, wasn't she? The quirky type.'

'Good legs on her as well.'

My teeth clench. 'Don't talk about her like that.'

'Guys, quit it,' Luke says warningly. He looks just as uncomfortable as me. 'You're not helping.'

'Oh, come on, Luke, we're only having a laugh.'

'Yeah, but I don't think this is going to make him feel better.'

'Better?' Gaz seems to click. 'Oh yeah, because of the dog?'

The dog.

Alex turns to me. 'Yeah, I'm sorry about the dog.'

'Misha.'

'Yeah, I'm sorry about Misha.'

'It'll be okay,' Gaz chimes in.

It.

It'll be okay?

231

'At the end of the day, it's only a dog,' Gaz says.

My chest is heaving now as I try to keep myself calm, and I know Luke's eyes are still on me.

'You can always just buy another one – you could get a puppy.'

I stand up. All eyes in the circle follow. I look down at my clenched fists, fingers pinched, knuckles white. *Keep it calm, Tristan.*

I take a deep breath in, before slowly uncurling each finger and opening my hand. Taking one last look at them I push past the booth and storm off.

'Tristan!' I hear Luke call behind me. 'Tristan, come on. Wait.'

But I can't wait. I can't be here.

I need to go somewhere else, somewhere I can breathe. I think of where Luke goes when he needs a release, and of running with Zoe.

I have an idea.

Chapter 30

Zoe

Coaching badminton can be boring at times. In fact, most of the time. There's not really enough for me to do, and all I want is to get in there and play.

I watch in a daze as the sweaty-faced kids play, their trainers squeaking along the rubber floor, their eyes lighting up as they make a winning shot. I can almost taste the victory, as one of them lifts their arms up in celebration. I miss that feeling. I whoop and raise up my own arms, but it's not the same.

But hey, coaching goes some way to help my inner competition freak, and I know it will look good on my CV when I graduate and apply for jobs in the future. Not that I know what kind of job that will be. I should start thinking really, as I finish university in only a couple of months – if I ever get around to finishing my dissertation, that is. I can't wait to say I've graduated – at least then I'll feel like I've accomplished something in my life.

Jack nudges me out of my reverie. 'You bored, Pebble?'

The stupid nickname brings a smile to my lips.

I take my camera from my pocket of my tracksuit bottoms, step back and hold it up. He strikes a pose, waits expertly for the flash before moving again. He knows the drill.

'Bored? Me? No. Loving it.'

Jack smiles. 'Yeah, I can tell.'

Jack volunteers here just because he wants to. Not as a distraction, not because he felt crap about himself, or because he lost his old friends. He's been doing it for three years now.

He grabs a racquet and starts bouncing a shuttlecock on the spot. Jack is good-looking – like majorly good-looking. He has the face and build of a model, and even got scouted by a modelling agency once, but said he wasn't interested. He wanted to focus on his course – he's studying graphics. I keep telling him he should contact them after he graduates but he just shrugs and says, 'Maybe.' But just you wait and see, give it three years and I'll be the one saying, 'Hey, I used to volunteer with him!' when his face is plastered across billboards on Oxford Street.

I catch the shuttlecock as he hits it too hard and it flies in my direction. 'Go away now, please,' I say. 'You're distracting me from my hard coaching work, as you can see.'

'All right, Queen Coach,' he says, smirking. 'I have to go and look after the ten-year-olds.'

'Tough break,' I say with a sympathetic sigh. They're a notoriously annoying group of kids.

'I know, right.'

And with a final shrug, Jack walks off to the other side of the hall. Even though I'm the one who told him to go, I already want him to come back. But I don't have long to mourn his absence as Anais appears, having set her group to do some exercise that requires minimal interaction from her.

'Jack hasn't declared his love for you yet, then?' Anais asks as I sit down on the floor. I just stare up at her blankly. 'You know he tells people he likes you?'

'Yes, you've told me that before.' Four times to be exact. I'm not sure I believe it, though I've always got on with Jack since I started here last summer. I look over at him. Did I mention he's beautiful? Jack has blond hair – almost ice blond – and it couldn't suit him any more if he tried. It goes with his strong jaw and pouty lips. It's what makes him have that 'Jackness' about him. The fact we both bleached our hair – I was silver-blonde back when we met – was something we immediately bonded over, sharing our top tips, the best products. And our friendship grew from there.

I definitely used to have a crush on Jack when I first started coaching last summer – how could I not? And at one point I did think he might have liked me, too.

Especially when a group of us went out clubbing one time, and we kissed. I even ended up going back to his house, but we didn't sleep together. And thank God we didn't, as I found out the next day he was completely wasted, and I still don't know if he remembers the kiss. Until recently, it was something that I found myself thinking about a lot. But those kinds of feelings have started to fade. I suppose it's since I met Tristan. Tristan makes me feel so different. And he makes me so curious. Plus, he doesn't know the stuff about me that Jack knows, which means he doesn't ask. Since meeting Tristan, I've decided to just be friends with Jack. I've realised that's all I want. That's all I'm supposed to want.

'When are you going to join us on a night out again?' Anais asks, with an innocent smile. 'Maybe next time you won't ditch us like you did at the party.'

I look up at her apologetically. 'Sorry.'

'It's fine, I'm sure the Tristan guy was much better company,' she says with a wink. I can't tell if she's joking or not.

'Tree needed me, I was being there for him.'

'I know, I'm only joking with you.' She slumps down on the floor next to me. As you can tell, we are *very* good at coaching. 'But it's obvious you're falling for a boy that doesn't like you back. What's up with that? That doesn't sound like a Zoe story to me.'

'I don't like Tree like that,' I say quickly, but I know it sounds unconvincing.

'Yes, you do, Zoe. You talk about him enough. Even Jack knows.'

I feel myself deflate, my stomach sinking. 'He does?'

'Yes,' Anais says, as she scoops up a stray shuttlecock and throws it to me. 'He told me that's why he stopped asking you to hang out.'

I catch the shuttlecock. Now I think about it, Jack has been quiet on that front, recently. He's been more distant. I have a lump in my throat, why can't I swallow it down? 'Jack and I only ever hung out as friends, Anais.'

'Come on! We both know it was more than that.'

My finger starts tracing the floor, drawing out imaginary smiley faces.

'Listen, you can say you don't like this Tristan guy all you want, but it's clear you care about him. Of course you care – you're Zoe, you care about everyone! But all I'm saying is that at least Jack would care for you back. From what you've told me, it seems like Tristan doesn't care about anything but his own feelings.'

'He has a lot going on.'

'Exactly,' Anais says, standing up. 'I'm not saying he's a bad person for it. But I just worry he's not able to care about you, Zoe. That's just how it is.' Without giving me a chance to defend myself, she walks back to the group she's supposed to be in charge of.

I'm left on my own. I feel weird. What she's saying isn't true, is it?

Tristan does care about me, right?

I join the group closest to me, shouting encouragement, but I can't focus on it.

Why does it matter what Anais thinks anyway? I look determinedly back to the game. I spot Jack's face on the other side of the court. He gives me a wave, and I stick my tongue out at him. He sticks his tongue out right back at me, without even questioning it.

Jack asks me for a coffee after coaching, buying me my usual green tea and not letting me pay. I like spending time with Jack, and no matter what Anais says, we are just friends.

We're by reception, signing out, when I see Tristan. Standing by the entrance, talking to security.

What's he doing here? Is he here to see me? I have mentioned to him a few times that this is where I coach – I never thought he paid any attention to it, but he must have. Before I can stop myself, a stupid grin is forming on my face.

He's wearing a hoodie, head lowered as he continues to talk to the security guy – he looks moody. I open my mouth to shout to him and wave, but something makes me pause. I close my mouth and shuffle back, deciding not to let him know I've spotted him. I turn around to finish signing out, when I hear shouting.

'Don't be an arsehole.'

That's Tristan.

I turn my head to see him, his nostrils flared and jaw tensed.

'Just let me in!' he's shouting, squaring up to the security guard.

Calm down, Tree, I think. *Stay calm.*

But it's too late, he's cracked. Everyone's attention has turned towards Tristan and the security guard.

'My brother works here. I've been here before with him. Why do you think I'm lying?'

The security guard, obviously used to this sort of stuff, isn't even batting an eyelid. 'Calm down, mate. We have a new security system in place. You need to be a member—'

'Calm down? I'm calm!' Tree shouts.

He's most definitely not calm.

Should I intervene? I look around nervously.

'I better help out.' I look up at the sound of Jack's authoritative voice. I wonder if he's recognised Tristan from the party, but I don't want to ask.

'No, Jack, I—' But before I can say anything, Jack is already standing opposite Tree, who is almost vibrating with anger now.

'Hey, mate, it's cool,' Jack says, in soothing tones, making me feel instantly calmer about the situation.

Tristan, not so much.

'No, it's not cool. It's really not.'

'Okay, talk to me,' Jack says.

'Just give me space. Can you leave me alone and give

me space.' Tristan has his fists clenched now, and is taking deep ragged breaths.

'Okay,' Jack says, stepping back, 'but maybe you need—'

'No!' Tristan shouts, shoving Jack in his chest. Jack doesn't push back, just takes another calm step away and mumbles something at the security guard, who nods at reception and gets out his phone.

Oh, crap. No. Don't call the police.

'What's going on?' Anais appears next to me, having obviously heard the noise from inside. Shit. Everyone is here.

'I, er . . . I don't know . . .' I mumble quietly. I find myself walking forward and pulling on Jack's arm. 'Wait, Jack, I know him,' I say.

Jack scrunches up his face in confusion.

'Zoe?' It's Tristan's voice. I turn my head towards him – he's squinting at me with red eyes. 'What are you doing here?' he says.

'What do you mean what am *I* doing here? What are you . . .' But I trail off at the sight of his blank face, and my stomach sinks. He wasn't here to see me, then. Okay . . .

'I volunteer here, remember?' I mumble.

'Wait, this is Tristan?' Jack asks.

Tristan ignores him, and just stares at me, the confusion on his face clear. 'You volunteer here?'

'Yeah . . .' I'm starting to feel self-conscious with everyone listening in on this conversation. 'You know this. I told you, Tree.'

240

Then it becomes clear that I'm not going to help the situation for anyone, because Jack puts a calming hand on Tree's arm to steer him away.

And in response, Tree punches him in the face.

Chapter 31

Tristan

The car door opens and I stare at the officer. He tells me his name is PC Smith, but I can call him Frank.

I look down at my throbbing hand. It hurts even more if I open and close my fingers and that's what I keep doing. Opening and closing. Open. Close. Open. Close. Open. Cl—

'Come on, Tristan.' I look up at Frank, who has authoritative but friendly eyes. 'Your brother's here.'

I sigh. I know, I shouldn't sigh – Luke being here is a good thing. But I still do. I unfold myself out of the back of the police car and walk along the pavement to where Luke is waiting. I glance back at the entrance to the gym. Zoe's not there.

If I'd known she coached there, I would have steered clear. I went to the gym thinking that it would make me feel better in the way that exercise makes Zoe feel better.

But she was the last person I wanted to see, not when I was like that.

Luke catches my eyes. He's sitting on a bench, dead eyes staring at me, running a hand through his hair. He stands up and shakes Frank's hand. 'Thanks,' he says.

'No problem. Now, like I said, I'm not taking you in this time, but we don't want to make this into a habit,' Frank replies, eyes directed meaningfully at me.

I nod my head, Frank turns to leave, and then we do the same.

'We have to walk,' Luke mumbles. 'I was drinking earlier.'

'Okay.'

So we set off, keeping a distance between us.

'I didn't think you'd be getting the police's attention again so soon, Tristan.'

'Me neither,' I reply. I look down at my aching hand.

'Why did you have to lose it at my work, Tristan?'

'I'm sorry,' I say, because I really am. 'It won't affect anything for you, will it?'

'No, it'll be fine, they know about you.'

My stomach sinks. They know about me. What does that even mean?

'Tristan,' Luke says. I can sense his eyes shifting from the pavement ahead of us to me. Not a good sign.

'Yes?'

'I have news about Misha.'

Chapter 32

Zoe

'I'm sorry about yesterday.'

I lift my head up from my till to see Tristan. I'm only on a three-hour shift today, and I've nearly finished it. So far, we haven't spoken a word to each other. I just want to get out of here, go to the library, and do more of my dissertation, which is going very, very slowly. I also need to revise for an exam tomorrow. I'm very behind at the moment, if you can't tell – and I don't need to get into this with Tristan right now.

'I'm sorry, Zoe.'

I continue staring at my till. Why does it have to be quiet today?

'Zoe ...'

I sigh. For God's sake. I turn to Tristan sharply. 'It was Jack you punched, not me.' I give him a short glare before turning back to my till. For the first time, I wish I was back working the tills on my own.

'Yeah. I'm just sorry … for making you look bad.'

I frown at him disbelievingly. 'You didn't make me look bad, Tree,' I snap. How can he be so obnoxious? 'It was yourself you made look bad.'

That was it, that was the end of the conversation. I'm just going to get on with my work now.

A customer comes over to me. I gratefully start serving them, but once they leave, Tristan starts talking again.

'You're right. But I'm still sorry. I'm so sorry.'

I keep my eyes planted forward. Stay resilient, Zoe.

But after a beat of silence I can't help it.

I turn to him, feeling my heart hammering in my tight chest. 'Why did you punch Jack? He did nothing wrong.'

He creases his forehead. 'I don't know. He was just in the wrong place at the wrong time.'

This only angers me more. 'No, Tree, he was in the right place at the right time. You weren't supposed to be there. You were the one that caused all the trouble.'

'I know that, Zoe. I just lost it. Sometimes that happens … I could have lost it at anyone and he touched my arm, so I just lost it at him. I don't know why. Honestly, it fucks me off as much as it fucks you off.'

I exhale heavily. I wonder about telling him how hurt I was yesterday. Thinking he was there to see me coaching. Right up until that oblivious look on his face when he saw me. I breathe out slowly again. Keep it to yourself, Zoe.

Tristan has moved off now, and I steal a glance behind

245

me to where he is, head lowered, arms carefully planted on the surface, concentrating. I'm not sure on what, though.

'Listen, Tree,' I start chewing on the inside of my cheek. 'You were an idiot yesterday.'

He nods. 'I know.'

'Like, a real big idiot.'

'Yeah, I was.'

'But I know you're going through a hard time, especially with Misha—'

'Shouldn't be an excuse.'

'You're right, it shouldn't, but sometimes we're allowed free passes,' I say. Tristan lowers his eyes again, but before he does I see the worry in them at the thought of Misha. 'Also, I think Misha is going to be okay, I really do.' Tristan doesn't say anything. 'Hey, do you know what the name Misha means?'

Tristan lowers his eyebrows in confusion. 'No.'

'One of the meanings is "little bear" . . . like teddy bear.'

'How do you know that?' he asks, still frowning.

'I googled it. I have this thing about names – but that's not the point. His name means teddy bear, right? I'm not embarrassed to admit that I sleep with a teddy bear, that it makes me feel safe. Misha makes you feel safe, right?'

Tristan doesn't reply.

'Well, what I'm saying is that my bear has never left me my whole life, just like Misha won't leave you. They don't – teddy bears don't do that.' I take a deep breath. I know I sound a little crazy.

Tristan is still staring at me like I'm making no sense. Maybe I'm not, but that doesn't stop me.

'Misha has a name that is too perfect not to mean anything. And it does mean something. It means he's going to stay with us for a little bit longer, he won't leave you until you're ready.'

Tristan's eyes lower, and I can feel the sudden sadness that washes over him. What did I do wrong? I suddenly panic. Misha is still alive, right?

Tristan must notice my panic. 'You're right, Misha's fine,' he says quietly. 'They had to amputate his back leg but he's alive. I visited him this morning. He's okay,' he says, his voice still small and his eyes sunken.

'Is he home?'

'He's coming home next week,' he replies.

'That's great!' I say. 'Why aren't you more happy about it?'

'I don't know,' Tristan says, his eyes rising up to mine challengingly. He starts shaking his head. 'I don't know, Zoe. I got told my dog wasn't going to die and I didn't feel anything. I didn't feel relieved, I didn't feel happy; I felt nothing. There's something wrong with that.'

'No, Tristan, it's perfectly norm—'

'Don't say it's *normal*, because it's not. Normal isn't being sad all the time. I can't keep on like this, having a future where nothing matters. I can't do it.'

I feel a sick flutter in my stomach. Because we both know what he's saying here. And that's not okay. 'We both said we didn't want to be normal, though, right?' I say weakly. He doesn't reply. I feel even more sick. 'You're coming to my house,' I add quickly, surprising myself.

Tristan frowns. Of course he does.

'I want you to come to my house,' I repeat.

'I've been to your house,' he replies.

'Dropping me off and picking me up doesn't count. You're going to come round for dinner with my family.'

'I am?'

'Yes, Tree, you are.'

'Why?'

'I love introducing my family to my friends, and you're a good friend.'

'I'm not. I was awful yesterday. *You're* a good friend, Zoe.'

Friend.

'Well it's great you think that, because I'm always going to be here. Okay?'

He looks at me, his expression pained.

'Tree, I said okay?'

His brow relaxes. 'Yeah. Okay.'

Chapter 33

Tristan

Wet tears dribble down my face as I try to choke the emotion back down my throat.

Stop it, Tristan. Stop it.

I hear the front door open, and my stomach drops.

Luke. What would he do? You'd ruin him. He'd have no one left. No one.

My body is arguing with my mind, and I'm so tired.

I manage to pick myself up from where I've been lying on the floor and walk over to my bed before the crying starts in full. Not the quiet tears like before, this is the proper kind. The kind where you forget who you are. I can't breathe as my throat tightens, cramps, chokes. I can't think, I can't talk, I can't anything.

It's the kind of tears where it seems like I'll never feel more pain in my life, I'll never get over this feeling.

One day I'm going to give in.

Chapter 34

Zoe

'So, what's your boyfriend's name? Is it hot Jack from coaching?'

'Shut up, Leia,' I say, as I lay a placemat on the table. 'And no, it's not Jack.'

'But I thought Jack was your boyfriend?'

'Tree is who is coming round, and neither of them is my boyfriend.'

'Oh, this Tree boy you're always with. And why is he coming round?'

'Because he's a friend.'

'So why do I have to be here?'

'Trust me, Leia, I don't want you here.' It comes out as less of a joke than I'd meant it to.

Leia slams the knives and forks on the table and runs upstairs, shouting for Jerry. Paul comes into the dining room and takes Leia's place with the cutlery.

'This is the guy you've been spending lots of time with recently, yeah?'

I pause with the placemats and look up at Paul. He isn't going to go all fatherly and weird on me, is he? 'Paul, you know he's just a friend right?'

'Yeah, I know that.' I'm not totally sure he believes me. 'He's a nice guy, right?'

I feel a flutter in my stomach. 'Yeah,' I say, placing down the last placemat. 'He just needs good people in his life.'

'Well, lucky he's got you, then.'

At this point Jerry appears. 'Mmmm, that shepherd's pie smells divine.'

Paul turns to me. 'Will he like shepherd's pie?'

I smile. 'He's not a fussy eater.'

'Oh, okay, good.'

'Zoe.' I turn towards Jerry. 'Catch!' he says, before throwing what looks like a paper bag at me. Once I have it in my hands, I realise what it is. A pharmacy prescription. I look back at Jerry.

'*Seriously?*'

'What's wrong?' Jerry says. 'I thought I'd collect it for you while you were at work.'

I look back into the bag, before giving him a quick scowl. I decide to let it go, even though in giving it to me now, he's clearly making a point. 'Nothing,' I mumble, as I fold my hand over the bag and walk past them.

But Jerry decides to push my limit again by following me. 'Also, while we're talking about it, I was thinking

251

today that maybe you should have a break from working –
just while your dissertation deadline is coming up—'

'*Not now*, Jerry.' I try not to shout it as I run up the
stairs. Tristan is going to be here any minute. I push past
Leia in the hallway, and dive into my room. I take a second
to lean in the doorway and catch my breath, before placing
the prescription on my vanity. I begin to walk out of my
room, but then I pause. I turn back to look at the white
paper bag.

Knock.

Knock.

The front door.

Knock.

It's Tristan.

'Zoe, your friend is here.'

'One minute, Jerry!' I shout, still staring at the bag.

'Shall I get the door?'

'No. One minute.'

'You can't leave him waiting!'

Jesus, I can't let Jerry open the door. Jerry is the least
Tristan-oriented type of person you can get.

'Leia!' I shout over my shoulder as I grab hold of the
paper bag and start searching my room. 'Leia, can you get
the door for Tree?' I hear the front door open. Thank God.
I open my knicker drawer, shove the bag in and close it.

'What's up?'

I turn around to see Leia, blowing a bubble-gum bubble
as she leans in my doorway. Shit. I run past her, galloping

down the stairs, only to see the front door already closed. I walk through the hallway into the living room where I see Tristan being bombarded by questions from Jerry and Paul. Jesus. The idea is to make him feel good about himself, not scare him off. I push past them and place myself between them. 'Hey, Tree.'

He gives me a weak smile. 'Sorry I'm late.'

'It's fine. Did you drive?'

'No, Luke gave me a lift. I don't drive his car any more.'

'Oh, good.' Was that the right response? I look down at Tristan; it seems he's made an effort, he's wearing a buttoned shirt with a jumper over the top. I bring my eyes to his face and smile. He's wearing a tiny bit of smudged eyeliner. Just a tiny bit. You would only notice if you stared at him.

I like to stare at him.

'I didn't know what to bring,' he says as he hands me a bottle of wine. I take it and look up at his face.

'Thanks, Tree,' I say with a forced smile, trying to ignore the pointed silence from Paul and Jerry. Tree shuffles awkwardly and I turn around to shove the wine into Paul's hands, before grabbing hold of Tree's hand and leading him out the room.

Chapter 35

Tristan

Zoe's room is the kind that people would take pictures of and put in a magazine. It's almost like one of those rooms people would pay to stay in as an 'experience', because it's so strange. There's a colourful sheet with an elephant on it pinned above her bed, wind chimes hang from every possible surface, and a hundred other patterns and colours feature throughout the room. No one wonder she thinks my room is boring.

'Nice room,' I say in response to her eager expression.

'Thanks! I basically just moved it all from my uni house when I came back home last summer.'

I still don't understand why she would choose to move home. It's one of the many things that doesn't make sense about her. Zoe keeps quiet as she stands by the door watching me. She's dressed reasonably casually tonight, wearing no make-up, a baggy patterned jumpsuit, and her hair tied up. I look down at my own clothes.

I feel myself going red so I turn my head towards a shelf taking up one side of her room. It is filled with trophies, badges and plaques. I move closer and trail my fingers along the engraved writing. *Zoe Miller National Athletics Championships. Zoe Miller First in Relay. Zoe Miller First in 100 Metres.* And so many more.

I turn towards her, her face now crumpled into a frown. 'You really did use to take athletics pretty seriously, huh?'

Zoe gives me a weak smile. 'You could say that.'

'You won a lot of competitions.'

Her smiles grows. 'Obviously.'

'There's something I still don't understand. If you are so good, why did you stop competing?'

I can see Zoe's mouth twitching from side to side. 'You don't have to understand everything in life, that's the beauty of it.'

'Don't go all quotey on me, Zoe. I know you enjoy it more than anything.'

Something flickers across Zoe's face, then she presses her lips into another smile. 'Competing was the best thing in my life, but ...' She moves across the room and sits down on her bed, which is so low it's almost just a mattress on the floor. 'I didn't have time any more – I had uni, and work ...'

'You can always make time for something you love, Zoe.' It's something I've heard Zoe herself say before.

'All right, smart arse.'

'Hey, I just want to work it out – that night at the running track … it was special.'

Zoe lowers her head and starts awkwardly rubbing her hands on the bed. Trying to keep busy. 'If you must know, I'm thinking about taking it up again.' I can see she's trying not to make a big deal of it, but she can't stop the smile spreading across her face. 'But I haven't mentioned it to Jerry and Paul yet, so don't say anything,' she adds in a rush.

'That's great!' I know I'm grinning too. 'Though I still don't really understand why you stopped in the first place,' I can't help but add. I can't shake the feeling there's something she's not telling me.

Zoe looks up at me, mouth tight. 'There's lots of stuff I don't understand about you, and I don't question you about it,' she says pointedly.

Fair point. I move away from the shelf, and sit next to her on the bed. Jesus, it's low. I turn towards the wall that her bed is pushed up against; it's covered with hundreds of pictures, some glossy, some dark and grainy, others vintage-looking. They're mainly of Zoe and her family, plus a few friends I don't recognise, and places she's been. She's captured every detail of her life. 'I take a lot of pictures.'

'I've noticed. Those cameras you use, they're disposable, right?'

Zoe smiles. 'Yep, so much better than a polaroid or a digital camera.'

'Why do you think that?'

She grins at me. 'You don't know what the pictures will look like until you develop them. And you develop them so far down the line, that when you get the pictures you're reminded of all the memories you've forgotten. And there, in your hands, for ever, you can cherish these important moments again and again. The real memories, not the posed, photoshopped or edited ones; these are pure, in the moment, one-take wonders. The real snapshots of life.'

I look back at the wall. There are a lot of photos here. How is she going to keep up with this for the rest of her life? That will be a lot of photos and a lot of cameras. As I look at the photos I notice something about Zoe – she has different hair in all of them. Obviously, purple isn't her natural shade, but her hair is a different colour in every single picture. She has gone through the rainbow: pink, blue, yellow, green, red, white blonde, jet black, half blue half green. I turn back to her, and somehow her purple doesn't seem so crazy any more.

'You used to change your hair a lot, didn't you?' I say.

Zoe smile, her eyes following mine towards the pictures. 'Yep. First of the month, every month.'

'Why?'

'Dyeing my hair is like my means of control. Sometimes I feel like my life is out of my hands.'

I start chuckling. 'Zoe, that is the biggest load of shit I have ever heard. You, out of anyone else, has the most control of your life.'

Her expression changes, and she grins at me. 'You think?'

'Of course!'

She flicks her hair. 'I also get bored very easily, which is another reason why I dye it a lot.'

I feel my eyes focusing on her. 'Are you going to get bored of me?'

Zoe turns her head towards me and smiles. 'I don't know about that, Tristan,' she says. 'I think you're far too interesting to get bored of.'

I look down for a moment; I think I almost feel a smile on my lips, but it's gone as quickly as it appeared. 'What's the next plan for your hair?' I say quickly.

'Eventually, when it gets so damaged from dying it, I'm going to shave it off.'

'Really?'

'I want to see what I'll look like. It is only hair at the end of the day. It grows back.'

I move my eyes back towards the pictures. 'You know, it's April.'

'I know that,' she groans. 'I'm really behind on my dissertation.'

'Yeah, but I met you in February. That means you've had purple hair for three months now. You've broken your cycle. What changed?'

Zoe watches me intently. 'I like my hair purple, I think I might keep it like this for a bit longer.'

I feel my mouth twitch. 'I like it purple, too.'

Then suddenly Zoe has one of her cameras in front of

my face again. I shouldn't be surprised. 'Smile,' she says. I try to, but I'm almost certain my face doesn't respond. Then, right before Zoe presses the button, I feel her turn her head and kiss me on the cheek. As soon as the camera clicks, she turns her head away again.

Chapter 36

Tristan

'That was delicious, thanks.' I take my plate into the kitchen and hand it to Jerry, who's standing at the sink.

'Hope you have room for apple pie,' Jerry replies cheerily, taking my plate from me.

I offer a smile in response before returning to the table, and squeeze my way back in next to Zoe.

As good as pie sounds, the truth is I'm starting to itch to go home. The meal was good, don't get me wrong. And it hasn't been awkward – Zoe's parents are both lovely, her sister is a little moody, but nice too. But I'm not used to this. Any of it. Sitting together as a family, making conversation, making each other laugh. At home, I eat my meals in my room; Luke eats out or in front of the TV. There's no family dinner stuff. Never was, even when Dad was alive.

'So, Tree, what do you want to do with your life?' I look

up at Leia. Where did that come from? It's clear Leia and Zoe are sisters.

I clear my throat. 'I ... erm ...'

'Not everyone knows what they want to do in life, Leia,' Zoe cuts in. 'Unlike you.'

I throw a small thankful smile to Zoe before looking back towards her sister. 'Why – what do you want to be?' I ask in a way I hope is polite.

Leia smiles at me proudly. 'A doctor.'

I can't help but snigger. I feel Zoe's foot kick me under the table.

'Is something funny?' Leia asks.

I look up at her and quickly bite my smile away. 'No ... No. It's just I don't understand why someone would want a job like that. In a hospital. A place so surrounded by death. Makes no sense to me.'

Leia narrows her eyes at me. 'Yeah, but it's also a place of healing, hard work and lives being saved. I don't know why someone wouldn't want to do that.'

'Well, doctors don't always save people. People do die. And you know who gets the blame? The doctors. Everyone blames the doctors, even if they didn't do anything wrong. They blame the doctors because they couldn't save their loved one – because it's their job to save them, but they couldn't.'

Leia holds eye contact with me. 'When I become a doctor, I'd rather those people blame me than themselves.'

At this point in the conversation, Paul and Jerry come

back in, Paul setting an apple pie down on the table and Jerry handing out bowls. I suddenly don't feel very hungry any more. I allow a huge slab of apple pie to be dumped on my plate, staring at it as the scent of sweet caramelised fruit wafts past my nose. I scrunch my face in the hope that I can block out the smell. But looking at the pastry leaking bubbling sauce causes my stomach to heave.

'We forgot to open your wine, Tree,' Jerry says, the bottle in his hand. 'But it's perfect to have with pudding, hey?'

I force a small smile as I sink lower in my chair. Jerry starts pouring some glasses, pausing at mine. 'Do you want a glass, Tree?' The answer is no. I decided that way before I got here. I'm not drinking tonight. In fact, I'm starting to think I might stop drinking full stop. I don't want to get like Luke. But because I'm too awkward to explain that, and I can't find the words to say no, I nod my head and let the dark liquid fill my glass. I'll just pretend I forgot to drink it.

'Jerry, pour me one,' Leia says, without looking up from her phone.

I look round at everyone on the table. Why didn't Paul pour Zoe a glass? I brought the wine mainly for her. And then suddenly I remember – she doesn't drink, does she? How did I forget that?

I feel myself sink even lower into my chair as I prod at my dessert. The conversation has gone quiet. I look up to see Paul, Jerry and Leia tucking into their apple pie, the sound of spoons scraping across the ceramic bowls. Everyone is digging into their food apart from me and Zoe. I look at her and she gives me a faint smile. I glance around the table again only to catch Leia staring at me, not with a smile, but with narrowed eyes, like she's trying to work me out. She smiles before taking a bite of her pie. 'So, what did you do today then, Tree?' she says in between mouthfuls.

I hate it when the conversation is directed at me. I roll my shoulders back, and place my hands on the table. 'Erm, not much. I had work, went to the doctor's, it was pretty boring.'

Wait. Why did I have to mention the doctor's? Idiot.

'The doctor's? Hope everything is all right, Tree?' Paul says as he reaches for the tub of ice cream.

'Oh, yeah, everything is fine.' I lower my eyes to the table, staring intently at my placemat.

'Glad to hear it. More ice cream?'

'No, I'm good, thanks,' I answer, looking at my obviously untouched pie.

'Zoe, that reminds me, don't forget to go to hospital on Thursday.'

I feel tension slice through the air. I turn to see Zoe, mouth clenched, staring at Jerry. 'Yeah, Jerry,' she mumbles. 'I know.'

I can feel another uncomfortable pause coming. To keep the conversation flowing, I say something, anything, quickly. 'How is your gran, Zoe? Is she all right?'

Zoe turns towards me with wide eyes, and everyone else follows. I can't hear the scraping of the bowls or the shovelling of pie into their mouths; everyone has paused. Zoe's eyes start shifting around the room, 'Erm ... she's ... well,' Zoe starts to stutter. 'She's—'

'She's, you know ... getting there,' Leia cuts in.

Zoe moves her eyes towards her sister. 'Yeah ...' she says. 'She's okay.'

Jerry and Paul don't say anything, and Zoe says no more. They all turn back to their pies and start eating, slower this time, more robot-like.

Something tells me Zoe's gran is not okay. I'd like to think she'd tell me if she wasn't, though. I could be there for her, right?

Chapter 37

Tristan

'*Coming out of my cage and I've been doing just fine . . . !*'

Zoe changed into her pyjamas once we got upstairs; she didn't give me a reason, she basically started stripping while I was in the room. I'd just turned to close the door and I felt her hand grab on to me, then I turned around to see her standing there in her bra. She pulled her pyjama top over her head and smiled at me.

She also didn't explain why she suddenly wanted to start dancing to music.

While I sit on a chair by her dressing table and watch her in fascination, she jumps up and down to the beat of the music. I say she's in pyjamas, but I'm not sure if what she's wearing really counts – knee-high socks and what looks like a guy's shirt. Whose shirt would it be?

Zoe keeps singing as she collapses on to the floor,

before picking herself up dramatically and making her way towards me.

And then she has pulled me up, clinging on to my hands as she bounces on her bed to the music. And I don't know why, but I find myself singing, even shouting, the words with her. They just come out of my mouth from nowhere. I'm joining in.

And you know what. It felt fucking awesome. I've changed my mind, I don't want to go home any more.

I flop to the floor as Zoe puts on another record. It's the Manic Street Preachers, 'Motorcycle Emptiness'. She sits next to me, singing along to the words. Then she moves forward, face still lit up in a wide smile while pretending her hairbrush is a microphone. *'Under neon loneliness motorcycle emptiness ... Life lies a slow suicide.'*

My eyes quickly dart up to Zoe.

Zoe stops singing. Her smile drops. The music carries on. Neither of us say a word, as Zoe suddenly stands up and turns off the record, leaving us in silence. But now there are no other lyrics flowing through my head. So instead I go back to that one word. *Suicide. Suicide. Suicide.*

'I got the record player for my birthday last year.' I turn towards Zoe, who looks just as uncomfortable as me. I can tell she's trying to lighten the mood. I make an effort to join in.

'I didn't realise you'd be *so* good at singing,' I say, with a slight chuckle.

Zoe rolls her eyes. 'Shut up, Mr Tree.'

I wrinkle my nose. 'I don't think that's quite how "Mr" works. What's your favourite song, Mr Zoe?'

Zoe suddenly frowns. We were having fun, weren't we? Even I was getting into it ... But it turns out she's just concentrating. 'That's hard,' she says eventually, her eyes narrowed in consideration. 'I like a lot of songs. A lot of artists. A lot of bands.'

'Well, name some.'

'Erm, David Bowie, Prince, Pulp, Queen, the Beatles. Abba.' She puts her hands to her face. 'Ahh, there are so many, I don't want anyone to feel left out.'

I bite my smile back. 'I'm sure they won't mind.'

She drops her hands and stares at me. 'But I will.'

'Okay, are we safe in assuming you like all upbeat pop songs?

'Well, no, that's not true. I do like happy songs, but I love a good sad song.'

What? Zoe, liking a sad song? 'Seriously?'

'Yeah,' she says with a smile. 'Sia, The XX, Lana Del Rey, M83, Coldplay, U2. They're classics to have a good old cry to.'

'Good' and 'cry' are not two words I've ever really put together. And since when does Zoe cry?

'Sorry, but I couldn't imagine you crying.'

'What? Tree, of course I cry. Crying is good for you.

You can't bottle everything up, or you'll explode. Crying is a good release.'

I don't say anything. If she knew how much I cried, I doubt she'd be saying it was a good thing.

'I also like Pixies!' Zoe suddenly shouts.

I look up at her, she's waiting for a reaction. ' ... Pixies?'

'Yeah, the band. That song is my favourite ... *Where is my mind? Where is my mind?*'

I can't help but laugh. It's a question I ask myself on a daily basis. 'I should probably go soon.'

'Oh okay, is Luke picking you up?'

'No, I'm getting the bus.' There's a pause. I move closer to Zoe. Our legs are nearly touching. 'Thanks for inviting me over. It was nice. Can't remember the last time I had a family meal.'

Zoe's eyebrows lower as she makes an earnest face. 'Anytime, Tree. Seriously. I hope it wasn't awkward. I know my family is quite intense ...'

'No. It was good.'

'Well, that's great, because it won't be the last time you come round,' Zoe says, the smile returning to her face.

I chuckle. 'Okay, Zoe,' I say, moving my eyes to the floor. But I can feel her watching me, her eyes lingering on my face. When I look back up she's frowning. 'You all right?'

'I'm always going to be here for you, Tree.' Her eyes are serious again.

'I know.'

'I honestly will. Don't think you can get away with doing anything stupid.'

I look up at her. I can't promise I'm not going to do anything stupid.

'I know a lot of people have left you in your life – I can't imagine what it felt with like your dad dying – but I'm not leaving. I'm not.' There's a pause. Our eyes don't leave each other. 'So please don't leave mine.'

I move my hand closer to hers. They aren't touching. But they are close.

'I don't want to.'

Which is true. I don't want to.

But you don't always get everything you want.

Chapter 38

Tristan

Around 9 p.m., after saying goodbye and thanks to Zoe's dads, I left and walked to the bus stop. Zoe walked with me and we stood there in silence for a while, with Zoe huddling in the cold next to me.

'You didn't have to come to the bus stop with me, you know.'

Zoe hugs her shivering body. 'I don't mind.'

She stands with me for a good ten minutes until the bus appears. And though I'm freezing cold too, when the bus stops in front of me, I feel my stomach sink. It's arrived too quickly.

I give Zoe a quick hug to say goodbye. Well, that was the plan. Instead, I hug her and I don't let go. She doesn't either. Even though Zoe is wearing a big padded coat, I'm sure I can feel her heart beating, heavy and fast, against my own chest.

We wait for the next bus.

When I eventually get home I'm greeted by Misha. The lovely stupid adorable mutt who I didn't know was coming home today. Luke must have picked him up while I was at Zoe's. I'm not even pissed off with Luke for not telling me, I'm just happy for once. He might be limping around on three legs now, but he's exactly the same – the same ridiculous dog. I don't even think he knows he's lost a leg – he just keeps hopping around happily as if nothing has happened, making my heart ache with love for him.

Looking at him like this, it feels like someone is finally on my side. Like someone is watching down on me and keeping him safe.

Maybe things are looking up. Maybe.

Chapter 39

Zoe

'So, he was a nice guy,' Jerry says placing a plate on the drying rack. I take it and start wrapping a towel around it.

'Yeah, he is.' I shine the plate until I can see my blurry reflection in it.

'Quite quiet, though.'

'That's just how is he, Jerry. He's not the most confident of people.'

'Ha! Couldn't be more different from you, then!' This comes from Paul, who's wiping the surfaces. I pass him the plate and he puts it in the cupboard he's stood by.

I ignore the dig. 'I think that's why we get on, because we're so different.'

'It was nice he asked about Gran,' Jerry says, trying to mention it innocently as he turns the tap off.

Oh God. Here we go. I look down and continue to dry a glass, putting all my energy and focus into it.

'Yeah. That's the sort of guy he is.'

'Bit weird though, isn't it?' Jerry's not going to drop this. I can tell he has his eyes on me, though I'm not going to look up at him. Because I'm busy. I'm drying this glass.

'I told you, that's how Tree is.'

'It's random, though. Considering there isn't anything wrong with your gran, with either of them for that matter. Touch wood.' Jerry places his hand on his head. 'Unless he knows something we don't?'

'No,' I mumble.

'Tree hasn't taken a trip to Devon and met Gran, has he?'

'No.'

'So that does make it strange?'

'Yeah.'

'Zoe, honey, I think the glass is definitely dry.'

I move my eyes to my hands. So it is. I'm almost burning towel marks in the glass at this point. I put it down on the surface and finally look at Jerry. 'Do you want to know why he asked, Jerry?'

Jerry gives me a short smile. 'I think I already know.' I turn towards Paul who is watching me with the exact same expression on his face. Jesus. Dad problems, am I right?

'Well, aren't you going to tell me that I shouldn't be . . . '

Paul shakes his head. 'It's *your* business, hon.'

Jerry can't help himself. 'Well, I think that maybe you shou—'

'It's your business, hon,' Paul says, repeating himself, eyes on Jerry.

Jerry holds eye contact with Paul, before sighing heavily. 'We're not going to tell you how to live your life, Zoe,' Jerry says. 'But you know that if you want to stay friends with that kid, you've got to be honest. Little secrets eventually turn into big lies.'

'Yeah, I know, Jerry.'

And then, with perfect timing, my phone chimes. I glance at the screen to see a text from Tristan. Tristan *never* texts me first. Ever. I don't mind, he's just not much of a texter. I excuse myself and run into the living room. Once I'm comfortable on the sofa I open the message, feeling a fluttering sensation in my stomach as heat rushes to my cheeks. I am so pathetic.

Thanks for having me. Sorry I was so awkward.

I look at the message again, a smile plastered across my face. Should I reply straight away? No. I don't want to seem too eager. But wait, why does it matter? We're friends. This is hardly the first time we've texted. I'll reply in a minute anyway. I throw my phone across the sofa and stand up, thinking I'll go have some leftover apple pie. But as I'm walking out the doorway, curiosity gets the better of me and I catapult myself back to my phone and type a message.

You weren't awkward. Anytime, Tree. Seriously xx

Was that an okay reply? He probably won't reply now. He's usually slow at replies.

I'll take you up on that offer haha

Oh. Okay. I smile and tap out a response.

All right. Well, what about the rooftop tomorrow? xx

I do love it there. The perfect smoking spot. ☺

Shut up! You don't even smoke that much anyway. My goodness has passed on to you xx

Hey. Don't get too full of yourself. I still smoke.

So is that a yes to tomorrow? x

Of course.

'Who are you smiling at?'

I lift my head to see Leia lying on the opposite sofa, laptop resting on her belly. I lower my eyebrows at her. 'What?'

'You're messaging someone on your phone, who are you smiling at?'

'I'm not smiling.'

'Is it Tree?'

'No.'

'You like Tree, don't you?'

'Leia, we're friends.'

'Oh my God. You so do. You're acting like a love-struck teenager now you live back at home.'

'No, I'm not!'

'I don't blame you, he is kind of dishy, but he's a little odd, too.'

'Shut up, Princess, or I'll get Jabba on you.'

Leia frowns at me. 'You're not funny, Zoe,' she says switching her attention back to her laptop. It's the *Star Wars* joke. It gets to her. I turn back to my phone to send another text.

So I'll see you tomorrow then? x

Unless I bail on you and go to Laser Quest, then paintballing, then afterwards have one of the world's greatest pizzas.

Ha. Not without me you're not x

Okay. Come with.

Very funny x

No, seriously. Let's do it tomorrow.

I pause. I feel my stomach churning now.

Next time. Tomorrow is the roof. It's calling us x

Okay. Misha is home by the way. The dumb mutt doesn't even know he's lost his leg.

Oh seriously? Ah, that's so great

It is. I feel great x

You do? So do I.

When we were at the bus stop, did you know your heart was beating fast? I could feel it against me.

I stare at his words, feeling my fingers leave my screen for second. What an odd thing to say. I start typing my reply but I pause. My fingers hover above the screen again as I look back at my words. I can't press reply. I have to change it. I can't reply with that. It'll be weird. But then, wasn't his reply weird?

You made it beat fast x

Sent it.

He reads it. He doesn't reply. That's fine, he doesn't have to reply straight away. He doesn't even have to reply. I don't care. It's cool.

It's completely fine.

Chapter 40

Tristan

She pushes her lips against mine, as she heaves herself on top of me, then starts kissing my neck. Delicate little kisses, travelling up my neck until she reaches my ear.

'Ready for round two?' she whispers in my ear. I pull my head back to look at Alice and sigh.

I'm not exactly sure how we got into this situation.

Just after I got back from Zoe's she texted me but I ignored it – I hadn't seen her for ages, I didn't want to see her either; I mainly just wanted to spend time with Misha, but then she showed up. And now here we are.

Alice starts kissing me again, and I kiss her back. But I'm not in the moment. I'm somewhere else. My phone buzzes. I lift my head up.

Alice continues kissing my neck. 'Ignore it.'

'Someone texted me,' I say sitting up.

Alice continues attacking my neck. 'Well, they can wait.'

'Maybe they can't,' I say more firmly, moving her off me and grabbing my phone. It's from Zoe. A little emoji. I stare at it for a couple of seconds, before putting my phone down and going back to Alice.

Her lips are on mine again, but still I'm not really there. I feel sick. I shouldn't be here with Alice, it feels wrong. I know it's because Zoe texted me – but me and Zoe are just friends. Just really close friends . . .

I focus back on Alice, who's now kissing my chest. This doesn't feel right any more. It didn't even in the beginning and now it feels plain wrong.

I push my mouth against Alice's anyway.

Chapter 41

Zoe

Just before I went to bed, I sent Tristan a little sticky-out-tongue emoji. Just in case he took my last text too seriously, or he thought it was weird. I was being funny. I was having a laugh.

The next morning I wake up to lots of notifications. I flick through messages from Anna, Ree, Jack, Anais, Naomi, and the guy I sometimes sit next to in lectures, asking something about my dissertation. But nothing from Tristan . . . I click on to messages. It says he's read my texts. But there's still no reply.

Chapter 42

Tristan

I walk through the front door, Zoe following me. Since the dinner at her parents' house, the last week with Zoe has been great. I've tried to help her with her uni work and I've gone round a few times, because apparently she needs company while she writes her dissertation. She says if she's on her own too long, her brain over-explores. And she was round mine yesterday; she brought her laptop with her and sat on my bed typing away while I watched TV. Even if we're not talking, just being in the same room with her is nice, watching her face as her brain ticks over thoughts. It might be my favourite type of company. We're going to do it again today.

That doesn't mean life has been great. When I shut the front door, I hear the sound of glass lightly clinking against the coffee table. Luke putting down his beer. I squeeze Zoe's hand as I try to quietly lead us towards the stairs. But by that point Luke has already entered the hall-way, and is standing in front of us with his arm around a girl. Her name's LuLu.

'Hey, Tristan,' she says. I've met her twice now, which is apparently enough for her to act like we're friends.

I glance up at her, carefully avoiding Luke's gaze.

'Tristan,' Luke says. I don't register him, as I grab on to Zoe's hand and give her a tug, hoping she'll get the hint.

She doesn't get the hint.

'Hey, Luke!' she says with her usual smile. 'How are you?'

I look up. Luke awkwardly shifts his eyes from me to Zoe. 'Yeah,' he says rubbing a hand through his hair. 'I'm good, Zoe. What about you?'

'I'm good, thanks,' Zoe says, stealing a quick glance at me. 'You don't mind me coming round, I'm not interrupt-ing anything am I?'

Luke looks towards LuLu before taking his arm off her and shoving his hands into his pockets. 'No ... not at all. LuLu is a friend of mine.' Luke's eyes shifting towards me again.

'I meant with Tree, like if you and Tree had plans,' Zoe says with another smile.

'Oh,' Luke says awkwardly, before looking at me again. He struggles to look at me for too long. 'No, not at all. Stay for as long as you like. I might get a takeaway later.'

'That would be—'

'We're going out later,' I say.

Luke raises an eyebrow, but doesn't say anything. I feel Zoe watching me. 'Yeah, I guess we are.'

I don't let Luke, LuLu or Zoe say anything more. I walk up the stairs pulling Zoe with me. I know she's going to ask me what's wrong. Ask what happened between me and Luke, and if we had another argument.

I hope she knows better than that now. Of course we had an argument, but what's new there? I couldn't even tell her what it was about. We now have arguments about the fact we have arguments, and they last for days now. I don't know what's happening to us. Luke is my only family. He's all I've got. So why can't we get on?

The force of the pillow hitting my face nearly makes me fall over. Zoe is perched on my bed, a grin on her face. She grabs another pillow and raises it above her head. I frown at her, and then I feel another hard lump throwing me backwards.

This is war now. I pick up a pillow and run towards the bed, ready to get my equal play at this game, when Zoe sticks her hand out to me. I pause.

'When I feel like I need to disappear, sometimes I pretend to,' she says with wide eyes.

My hands drop the pillow. 'What?'

'You are allowed to escape, you know. Sometimes everyone needs to escape.'

Where has this come from? 'No, Zoe. You can't. You have to just get on with it.'

I don't understand. She's the one who told me to not do anything stupid. She's the one who was telling me to stay strong. To see life in a different light. Now she's going back on her word.

'Yes, Tree. You can. If you want to disappear, you can.'

'Of course I want to, but I—'

'Just say and I'll take you there.'

'Take me where?'

'Just say it, Tree! Say that you want me to help you disappear.'

'But Zoe . . .'

'I'm not helping you unless you say it.'

'Fine . . . Will you help me disappear?'

Zoe grins and opens up her hand to me. 'Of course, it'll be my pleasure.'

I take her hand.

Chapter 43

Tristan

I look up as the sheet brushes my face. I turn towards Zoe, who opens her eyes, looking at me with a smile. 'This way you can disappear without hurting anyone,' she says.

I stare at her. Her idea of 'disappearing' was to pull the bed sheets over us. Beneath our white tent she turns on to her side, watching me, her wide eyes not leaving my face. 'Zoe, are you on drugs?'

She scrunches her nose. 'Tree, I don't drink, I don't smoke; do you think I'd take drugs?'

'I've taken drugs before.'

'And you also drink and smoke.'

Fair point. I look back at her as she shuffles closer to me. 'Tree. We all need to time to escape, even me,' she says. She's so close I can feel her breath on my face.

'We haven't *escaped*.'

'Yes, we have. Right now, it's just us here, away from the world.'

'We're still in my bedroom.'

Zoe's eyes focus on mine. 'You are way too literal sometimes.'

'I can't help it.'

She doesn't reply; instead, she just lies there, staring. So I stare right back. What are we doing? Why isn't she talking? My eyes move across her dark eyebrows, to the little freckles on her nose, then up to the deep roots that are showing through her bleach-damaged hair – so much longer than when I first met her – and back down her flushed cheeks, the little dimple she has on her chin, her pink lips. Her lips that are slightly parted. Her face that's moving closer. She moves her head towards mine and—

I sit up.

I push the covers away from my head and breathe in a gulp of cool air. Zoe emerges from the sheet but I turn away from her and sit on the edge of my bed, my head thumping.

What was that? Did she just try to kiss me?

I groan as I rest my head in my hands. I need to leave.

'Tree?'

Zoe is sitting up now, watching me carefully. She is chewing on the inside of her cheek, as she twists her hands on the bed sheet. 'Sorry,' she says.

Sorry? Does that mean she *was* going to kiss me? This is hurting my head. My brain feels like it's cramping.

'My parents liked you the other day,' Zoe says quickly. I look up at her. I can tell she's changing the subject like she always does, but I'm happy for her to. 'They thought you were nice.'

'They ... did?' I say, trying to hide the fact I'm still out of breath.

'Yeah.' She nods, moving her hand close to mine, but not touching. 'I think they liked you more than they like me, you know.'

I feel my eyebrows lower. 'I doubt that. Why wouldn't they like you?'

'You know they annoy me sometimes.' She pauses to chuckle. 'It feels like they care *too* much. I understand they want what's best for me. But this is my life, not theirs. I wish they'd give me some space. Let me do the things I want to do. The things that make me happy.'

I quickly move my hands away from the bed and shove them on to my lap. She's right. Zoe should be able to do the things that make her happy. That's why I can't let her get close to me. 'At least ... ' I mumble, already regretting what I'm about to say. 'At least you have parents.'

'Shit.' I immediately feel Zoe move past me and jump down from the bed. Her feet pace in front of me on the floor. 'Shit, Tree, I'm so sorry. I don't know what I was talking about. I'm not ungrateful. I like my parents. I love them.' She breaks off, guilt written all over her face.

'It's fine,' I say briskly as I get to my feet. 'It's just ... '

She pauses in her pacing. 'What?'

I shrug my shoulders. 'I can't.'

'Can't what?'

'I can't live the way other people want me to. I will never be able to.'

'Tristan . . . '

'You know I've started sleeping with Alice again?' It comes out in a rush. I'd promised myself I wouldn't tell her that.

Zoe watches me, and goes quiet for a few seconds. I think I see a pained look in her eyes but then it's gone. Now she's judging me, but still I feel relieved. 'Do you like Alice?' she says, her mouth tight.

I shake my head. 'No.'

'So why are you sleeping with her?'

'I don't know,' I say, because how can I explain? All I know is that I can't get close to Zoe like that. And that a part of me was hoping that Alice could make me feel the way she used to.

'Does she know you don't like her?'

'I don't know, we haven't spoken about it.'

'You can't mess people around like that. You're being unfair on her. You're just thinking about your feelings, not hers. You're leading her on.'

'You don't even know Alice! Why are you defending her?'

'Because you're not being fair. What you're doing isn't healthy.'

'Nothing I do is healthy. All I'm trying to do is get

through each day, like everyone says. But how can I move on when I don't value anything? You know this, Zoe. I don't value life, I don't value people. I'm not even going back to university. I wasted three years of my life and I don't even care. I don't care about anyone or anything.'

Zoe's eyes lower. She doesn't look sad. She looks almost annoyed. 'That's not fair, Tree'

'I know.'

She narrows her eyes at me. 'No, seriously. That's not fair. Not fair to you, and not fair to the people around you.'

I take a deep breath. Here it goes, someone else trying to play counsellor.

'I'm going to try and say this as nicely as I can, but life does go on, Tree.'

I take a step away. 'What do you know? You don't live my life.'

'I don't. But Tree—'

'If you're going to act like everyone else you can leave. The only reason I'm friends with you is because I thought you weren't like that, that you were different. You didn't treat me like I was sick in the head.'

'I am different.'

'No, you're being the same as everyone else. You're trying to be a fucking counsellor. Trying to pretend I'm normal. I don't need this from you. I don't want it. Okay?'

I can see I've hurt her, but Zoe takes a step closer to

me anyway. I can feel my body start to tense. 'Why are you being like this? You have so much potential – it's so annoying you can't see it.'

'Well, you annoy me too, you know that? You annoy me all the time and you don't see me telling you about it.'

'Okay, you don't need to be mean,' Zoe says, taking a step back now.

'I don't want your help.'

'Maybe you need it.'

'No.' I narrow my eyes. 'It has nothing to do with you.' I spit the words out.

'Yes, it does, I'm your friend.'

'Well, then act like one.'

'Why don't you act like one for once? You're a crap friend. Not just to me, but to everyone. I know you think the world is out to get you but it isn't, and that doesn't give you an excuse to act like a dick all the time anyway. Stop being a dick to your brother, stop being a dick to your friends. Stop pushing everyone close to you away.'

'I don't want anyone close to me.' I can feel my chest pounding now.

'Maybe that's the problem,' Zoe says. 'You're stubborn. You refuse to take your medication, even though by not taking it you're causing more damage to yourself than good.'

'Why are you bringing my medication into this?'

'Medication doesn't mean you've failed. It means the opposite. It means you're trying.'

'Stop it, Zoe!' I'm shocked by the aggression in my voice.

'You hold yourself down. Don't you understand how frustrating it is?' she says, taking another step back. I can see her chest is heaving as well now. Her eyes are narrowed. I've never seen Zoe so angry before. But I don't care. I'm the one that's got the right to be angry here. I can feel the pressure pulsing through my whole body. She needs to shut up.

'Well, you're one to talk,' I spit. 'You're all about living your life, and doing want you want to do. So why don't you just do more running if you love it so much? I saw you on that running track, you loved it, you missed it. So why don't you just fucking go paintballing? Eat a burger? Be an athlete? You're not living life either and you know it. You're scared.'

Zoe's face falls. She takes another step back so that her back is almost touching the far wall now. She glares at me. 'Shut up.'

'You're a hypocrite, Zoe. You can't say one thing to someone and do the opposite.'

'We're talking about you here, Tree, not me.' Her voice is starting to shake.

'What's the point? You don't understand me.'

'Well, then let me understand,' she says, grabbing on to my hand.

I push her off me. 'You can't. I don't even understand it. I want to die. That's not the way it should be. But that's how it is.'

'No, you don't.'

'What?' I click my neck, trying to ease the tension I feel growing. I should leave this room now. I look at the door.

'You don't want to die,' Zoe says calmly. I notice that her eyes are starting to gloss over. 'What you really want is to start living.'

And that's it, I snap.

I take a step forward and push her against the wall. Things happen quickly after that. I raise my fist, Zoe flinches and moves her head to the side, and I punch the wall.

Zoe gasps as she stares at me. I quickly lower my fist and take a few sudden steps away from her. Did I mean to hit her, or did I know she was going to move her head?

It doesn't matter. I could have hit her. I quickly open both of my fists. Her blank eyes stare at me.

'Zoe, I'm ... I didn't mean to ... I'm sorry.' I'm finding it hard to talk. It feels like I'm choking, I'm suffocating. Like I've cut off my lifeline.

Without moving, Zoe watches me, as a tear falls down her cheek. Her bottom lip quivers. And then without a word she walks across the room and opens my bedroom door. As she is walking out the door, she pauses. She turns around. Her eyes are red. 'Yes, Tristan,' she says, her voice too calm and controlled. 'Your dad is dead and it's clear it fucked you up. But once someone's dead they stay dead, they don't come back. And you're alive, and you still have a life to live. That's that.' She sniffs as she wipes her eyes. 'Your dad might be dead, Tristan, but it doesn't mean you have to be.'

And with that she walks out.

Chapter 44

Zoe

I'm running. Bare feet slapping on the ground. I didn't even stop to put my shoes on, I just left. I keep running, not caring that I'm bang in the middle of the road. I just keep moving my feet. My lungs are aching, feet cold and stinging. But I keep going until I'm physically forced to stop, bending down in the middle of the road. Gasping heavy breaths of air.

Suddenly running doesn't feel so good any more.

Once I get home I run straight up the stairs and climb into my bed.

I can't stop thinking about the moment Tristan's eyes changed, as he pushed me against the wall. He wasn't Tree then. It was like he was a different person. Would he have hit me if I hadn't moved?

I knew about Alice. Ree told me when I was round her house a couple days ago. What hurt the most was that he must have had sex with her straight after coming back from mine. I didn't tell Tree that I knew. I hoped he would he tell me himself if it was true. I'm not sure why I thought he would feel he had to, but I just hoped he would.

And then he did tell me, and now I wish he never did. It has broken my heart.

'Zoe, you okay?' I lift my head up from my pillow to see Leia standing in the doorway.

I nod my head, wiping my eyes. Leia sighs as she sits down on the edge of my bed. 'I'm fine, Leia,' I say in a weak voice.

'Is it Tree?'

'That's not even his real name,' I mumble.

'You don't say.' She gives me a crooked smile. 'It suits him, though.'

I nod my head again, as I try to prevent myself from crying. God, I'm pathetic.

'Did you like him, Zee?'

More nodding. 'I wasn't planning on it.'

'He doesn't like you back?'

'I don't think he likes anyone, Leia.'

'That's probably the best reason for a guy not liking you back, right?' Leia says, shuffling close to me.

I sniffle a snotty laugh. 'I guess. I don't understand it. I've never ... never felt like this.'

'Well, he's the one missing out, sister.'

'I'm not sure.'

'I am. And anyway your first love isn't going to be the one you have for the rest of your life, that's the way it works.' I'm not sure when Leia got so wise. 'He was like the starter. Your main course will come soon, and he'll be even better, just wait for it. And then dessert, phoaaaaaar, you're in for a treat with dessert, girl. I'm almost jealous.'

'I never said I loved him, Leia.'

Leia smiles at me. 'Okay. But you did.'

And she's right. I did. I still do.

Chapter 45

Zoe

Last night, before I went to bed, I texted him to say I was sorry. I don't know why, because I'm not. I'm not sorry about the things I said. He's the one who nearly hit me. He's the one who should be apologising, and I'm not sure I can even forgive him. But I wanted to message him, and that was all I could think of saying.

Maybe I am sorry, then. About it all. I'm sorry I fell for him.

He didn't reply to the text. So this morning I sent a random little cake emoji. I didn't know what else to send. Turns out it didn't matter because he read it and still didn't reply. I was hoping we could smooth things over before our next shift together but I have work today, and he usually works on Tuesdays, too. So we'll talk then. Hopefully.

I didn't see him on my morning shift. I guessed he must have swapped with someone. I had lunch with Ree, who told me her sister was pissed off. Apparently, Tristan has ended things with Alice, told her he was leading her on, and he was sorry if he hurt her feelings. You'd think I'd have been happy about this, but I wasn't. It just made me feel strange. I wish the whole thing with Alice never came up in the first place.

Now lunch is over, and he's still not here, though he should be in by now. I'm nervous about seeing him, but I've got to face him soon.

His till stays empty. I stare at that empty till and wait. I wait my whole shift. He never shows ups. At the end of my shift I ask Juliette if Tristan has booked today off, or swapped shifts with someone, but she seems just as confused as me. She says she has no idea where he is, that she tried to call him, but couldn't get through. He skipped work.

Because of me? Surely not.

At the end of the day, just before going to bed, I text Tristan asking where he was.

He reads it. He doesn't reply.

It's fine, I decide. He'll be in work tomorrow. He'll be in, and then he'll finally have to talk to me.

But Tristan wasn't in the next day. Or the day after that. And now, after three days of shifts and trying to keep myself distracted – trying to actually listen to my 9 a.m. lectures, failing to write more of my dissertation in the evenings – and just staring at that empty till next to me, I'm starting to get worried. So is Juliette. He hasn't called her at all. By the end of the third shift with no sign of Tree, my stomach is gurgling, my fingers twitching, and all the while my eyes won't stop switching between the till and the supermarket doors. Just hoping, hoping he'll walk through them. But he doesn't.

That's it, Tristan. I'm calling you. I don't care. I don't care if you get angry, I don't even care if you don't want to talk to me, I just want to know you're okay. That you haven't left. That you haven't quit on me, because that's not fair. That's not bloody fair. You promised.

'Hello?'

A gasp of breath leaves my mouth as I grip my phone. I can't reply. Although I rang him, I wasn't expecting him to answer – I truly believed I was going to have to listen to his answerphone. I didn't know if I'd hear his voice again. But I am. It's okay. He's still with me.

'Zoe, where are you?'

My stomach drops. That's not Tristan's voice.

'Luke?'

I don't understand. Why is Luke on Tristan's phone? Why didn't Tristan answer?

'Zoe, are you with Tristan?'

'No ... why?'

'Do you know where he is, Zoe?'

'Why? Is he okay? What's happened?'

'Now not's the time.'

'No, Luke – wait!'

'I have to go.'

'Luke. Just wait. Please. I just want to ask you something—'

He hangs up on me.

I stare at my phone; it's trembling in my shaking hand. I try to contain my breathing, which is coming out in ragged gasps.

'Just wait,' I hear myself saying as I stare at Tristan's number on my phone screen. 'Please, just wait.'

Chapter 46

Zoe

'Want a beer?' Luke says, walking into the living room with a six pack in his hand. I look around the room, taking in the many empty cans. Sally hasn't been today, then. I see a tray of food on the side, with a Post-it note on it. It must be from her, I've noticed she does that for the boys when she's not going to be around for a couple of days. Misha hops over to me as I sit down, his tongue hanging out of his mouth. I pull him up on to the sofa with me, and stroke his belly, then realise Luke is still waiting for an answer. I look up and shake my head.

'All right,' he says, slumping back down on to the sofa opposite me. He opens the beer and presses the bottle to his pale cracked lips, before roughly plonking it on to the table. He looks at me through squinted, bloodshot eyes, as his head starts to shake from side to side. It looks like a tremor.

Luke doesn't look good. In fact, he looks a mess. And as

bad as this is going to sound, from this angle I can finally see the similarities between him and Tristan. The deep-set bags that rest under Luke's eyes, his messy frazzled hair, the sad eyes and furrowed brow. They have the same miserable qualities. 'Shouldn't you be at university, or work – or something?' Luke is slurring slightly. How much beer has he had?

My mouth twitches. 'Shouldn't you be at work?'

Luke chuckles, and grabs his beer again. 'Should be – but Tree took my car.'

'Oh ... and he left his phone here?'

'Yep,' he replies, taking a swig from the bottle. He doesn't sound panicked now, like he did on the phone. Just tired. What's going on?

'So ... was it you reading my texts?'

Luke frowns at me questioningly.

'My phone was saying someone was reading the messages I sent.'

'When did you text him?'

'Last couple of days.'

'It probably was Tristan reading them, then.' Luke takes another swig. 'He left last night.'

I let go of Misha and sit forward. 'What do you mean he left last night?'

'He just left. With no warning, he just took my car and hasn't come back.'

I feel my heart starting to beat faster. 'But ... he hasn't been at work for the last three days.'

Luke leans forward. 'He hasn't?'

'No. Did you notice anything off with him before he left?' I try to keep my voice calm, but my heart is racing.

'Zoe. Tristan is always off.'

'Well what was he doing if he wasn't at work?'

'I don't know. I thought he *was* going. He was leaving in the morning and coming home in the evening.'

'Weren't you checking up on him using the thing you have on his phone?'

'No, I promised him I'd disable it. And I can't switch it back on now.'

'This makes no sense. Did you guys have an argument?'

'Don't blame this on me, Zoe.'

'I'm just trying to work it out.'

'Obviously we had an argument, we always have arguments.'

'About anything different to usual?'

Luke rubs his forehead. 'Do you want to know what I had for breakfast, too?'

I feel my mouth pulling down at the corners. Isn't this stressing him out? Does he not care? Luke's eyes catch mine and he sighs. 'We argued about smoking, but I don't see why that would have made him bugger off. He kept smoking in the house. And we had a pretty big "disagreement" over that. I thought he had stopped.'

'Me too,' I say, though it doesn't surprise me that's he started again. That's probably because of me as well. I shuffle in my seat. Why are we just sitting here? Why aren't we looking for him now? 'Have you called the police?'

Luke looks at me before lowering his eyes, then shaking his head. 'I don't know what to do,' he mumbles.

'Call the police, Luke.'

'I can't go to the police until it's been over twenty-four hours. Because he's an adult they won't take it seriously.'

'But if he has a history of mental—'

'It's my fault, you know.'

Luke lifts his face to me, his eyes starting to gloss over.

'How is it your fault, Luke?' I ask.

'There will be a day when he *is* going to leave me and he won't come back that time.'

I feel my stomach jolt. By leaving him, he doesn't mean Tristan moving house or something. He means actually leave. 'So ... you think Tree is going to come back this time?'

'I don't know.' His voice is starting to shake. 'I struggle, Zoe.'

I look around. No shit.

'I know I'm the oldest so I shouldn't, but I do. I struggle to be the big brother, while being the parent, while being the therapist, while trying to have a job, while trying to have a social life, while trying to sort out my own problems. I still grieve over Dad, you know. I know it's been nearly two years but I need to man up. How can Tristan ever think things will be all right if he sees me like this?'

'Luke, I don't think—'

'I mute my feelings with alcohol and sex. I know that.'

Jesus Christ. How drunk is Luke? Drunk enough to

304

be this open with me. I look back up at him, as he runs a hand through his hair and fixes his eyes on the floor again. I'm starting to feel sorry for him. I forget that he lost his dad too. That he had to be in charge while grieving, and to deal with his brother going to hospital. He had to deal with being completely alone for six months. I couldn't have done that.

'It's not your fault, Luke,' I say. My mouth suddenly feels very dry. 'I think it's mine this time.'

'No, it'll be my fault,' he says, eyes downcast still. 'I don't know what to do any more, apart from wait. Just sit here, drink beer and wait.'

'Wait ... for what?'

'Wait to see if he comes home, or if I get a phone call like last time.'

There's a buzzing in my ears and I start stroking Misha mechanically again. My eyes have settled on an ash tray on the table. Why did Tree have to keep smoking in the house when he knew it would annoy his brother? Couldn't he have just smoked somewhere outside, like any normal person?

Oh, shit. Wait.

I snap my head around to Luke, feeling my heart pound. 'Luke,' I say, standing up, 'call a taxi.'

Chapter 47

Zoe

This taxi is going annoyingly slowly. Luke sits beside me, his leg dancing up and down against the car door.

'Why do you call him Tree, Zoe?' He turns to me suddenly.

I look back at him carefully. 'I think it suits him.'

'It's a bit of a weird one, though, isn't it?'

I nod my head. Luke turns back to the window.

'Luke, why don't you like Tree driving your car?' Luke doesn't reply, so I carry on. 'I just think it's strange. He's got a licence, and he's a good driver. He always takes care of your car.'

Luke frowns at me as if I'm talking rubbish. 'No, Zoe. It's not just my car – he's not allowed to drive full stop. If he gets caught driving, he can get in real trouble with the police.'

I'm the one who looks confused now. 'What? Why?'

Luke suddenly looks uncomfortable. 'The last time Tree drove, before ... the hospital, it wasn't great. Something happened.'

'What do you mean?'

'He got ... upset, very upset. And he purposely drove himself into the river. My car was destroyed. But Tristan was fine. Well ... he was as okay as he is ever going to be.'

I turn away from Luke, looking through the window but focusing on nothing as I feel my heart pound.

I stay silent for the rest of the journey.

Chapter 48

Zoe

Once we reach the rooftop, I deflate. Tristan isn't here. It's just empty concrete leading on to the vast view. It doesn't look so beautiful today, even if the sun is starting to set.

I slump down on to the concrete. 'I'm sorry, I thought he would be here.'

Luke sits down beside me. 'At least he's not lying on the floor beneath us.' I shoot my eyes to him. I thought the same thing, but at least I don't go around saying it aloud. 'It doesn't mean he hasn't done something stupid some-where else, though,' Luke goes on.

The sky is overcast today, throwing shadows over the grey buildings of the town in the distance, which nestle together beneath a heavy fog.

I wonder how Luke can sound so relaxed, but then I realise he's actually resigned. He knows there is nothing he can do. And even if he does do something now, manages to find Tristan and bring him back, there will be another time, and a time after that, until it eventually happens. And that's that.

The ugly truth is that there is no escape from your mind. No escape for Tristan.

'So, this is where you guys always go then?'

'We've been up here a few times, yeah.'

'Strange place to take him, considering.'

'I know. Sorry.'

'Stop apologising, Zoe.'

I have to stop myself from saying sorry again. 'I just don't know what to do.'

'I know,' Luke sighs, as his hand starts tracing marks in the concrete. 'I'm going to call the police when I get home.' But he doesn't get up to leave. I move a little closer towards him, and I can see his chest rising and falling, as he flicks tiny little stones along the ground. 'I remember Mum a bit, but Tristan doesn't, obviously. It was just us, Dad and Grandad. Then our grandad died. Lung cancer. He smoked fifty a day, never could beat the habit. Until the day he found out he was dying. That's when he stopped smoking. As if he thought that would make a difference.' Luke looks at me, his tired eyes red and squinting. 'Seeing the life slowly and brutally sucked from someone you love, day by day, until they can't function any more. It ain't right. Fuck cancer.'

I stay silent. How is that fair? How can one family experience so much death and heartbreak? Both sets of my grandparents are alive, and both my parents, too.

I don't know what to say. I don't know what to do. So I just keep breathing, ignoring my heart rattling against my chest, and listen to Luke. As painful as it is, I just listen.

'Then Dad died,' Luke goes on, lowering his head still further. 'Dad died and I felt more pain than anyone could imagine. I thought I could handle it, after seeing Grandad die, but it was just so sudden. Just like that, my dad was dead. I didn't make the most of my time with him.' Luke finally brings his eyes towards mine. 'You know what the last words I said to him were?'

I very slowly shrug my shoulders.

He looks down. *Fuck you, Dad.*

'Oh.'

'We'd had an argument about my drunk driving. I was pissed off, so I shouted at him, and left for the night. When I got back the next morning he wasn't there. Everyone always says my dad knew I loved him, but I don't think he did. I never really let him know.' Luke pauses. 'Always tell your parents you love them, Zoe.'

I'm always storming off after saying crap to my parents, but what if that was it? The end. What was the last thing I said to Jerry today? To Paul? To Leia?

'He died driving to work,' Luke says. 'Nearly two years ago now. A lorry driver was on his phone and hit his car. It didn't feel real when it happened. We got a lot of insurance money. And we got the mortgage paid off. But money didn't make my dad come back, money can't make my little brother himself again. Money does shit all.'

There's a silence. Luke pauses and looks up, taking a deep breath in, before looking back to me again. 'Now with Tristan, it's like a combination of what happened to Grandad and to Dad. I'm slowly having to see someone I love have the life drawn out of him, gradually and painfully – killing himself slowly – but I also have to deal with the fact that one day I might wake up and it's going to just be me that's left. I don't want to be alone.'

My heart aches for Luke. All this time I thought he was a drunk, a jerk who sleeps around. Not that he isn't those things, but he's also a person, and he's in pain too. He's trying to deal with it, but he doesn't know how. How could he? No one teaches us how to deal with life. There's no guide, no cheat sheet. So how do we deal with it? How does it work, when humans are so fragile?

I need to leave.

I wipe my eyes, stand up and start walking towards the stairs. As I walk, something rolls beneath my foot and gets stuck to my shoe. I pause and lift my foot up to see a squashed cigarette butt stuck to the bottom of my sole. My eyes scan the ground and I see more cigarette butts on the concrete.

They're Tristan's. I look over at the array of smiley faces I have planted on the ground over time. One single face catches my attention. It's in the corner, partially hidden by the cigarette butts. One wobbly face, with a slightly wonky eye and overly curved mouth. This face is drawn in a red marker.

'Tree was here.'

'What?' I hear Luke behind me.

I turn towards him with a slight smile on my face. 'Tree was here.'

Chapter 49

Zoe

'I can get the bus home,' I say, clambering out of the taxi and following the Luke to the door.

'I'd rather you didn't get the bus. Just get your bag quick, the taxi won't wait for ever.'

I hurry through the door behind Luke but as soon as he's inside he comes to a standstill, blocking my entry. I try squeezing myself past him, then suddenly stop.

'Tree?' I stare at him sitting on the sofa on the opposite side of the room. Tristan looks up at me, his mouth curved into a small smile. 'You're ... okay.' It's barely more than a whisper.

'Of course I'm okay.'

'I ... We thought you had ...'

'Where's the car?' Luke is staring at Tristan, his eyes narrowed. I can't read his expression, is he happy? Angry?

'I'm sorry I took it, Luke.'

'Where is it? It's not in the drive.'

'Some idiot parked in front of our drive. I parked round the corner.'

Luke seems satisfied with that answer. He plonks himself down on the sofa with a sigh.

Luke grabs a beer. 'Jesus Christ, Tristan ... you do take years off me.' He opens a can and brings it to his mouth. I can't believe how calm he's acting. Is he really so used to this?

'You scared us,' I say forcefully, not allowing my eyes to leave him.

'Sorry,' Tristan says, leaning over the table and taking a can, 'I was ... just getting beer.' He moves his eyes to mine, and smiles again. It's a weak smile – pleading and forced. 'You want one?'

I move my eyes down to his hand as he holds a can of beer to me. I take the can, which is cool against my skin.

Tristan gets up and pulls me away from where Luke is sitting on the sofa. The smile drops. 'I really am sorry,' he says quietly, and for once his eyes hold mine.

'It's fine ... ' I say, though it's not. 'I was just so worried.'

And then without saying another word he wraps his arms around me. My head falls on his chest as he holds me tightly. He doesn't let go.

Chapter 50

Tristan

I went to that rooftop three times, and each time I had the intention of jumping. The last day, I knew I was going to do it. I couldn't stop hurting people. Not only had I already hurt Zoe's friend Jack, I could have hurt Zoe. That's the person I am, and the person I am always going to be. I didn't want to live with that any more.

When I got back from the rooftop on the second day, after just standing up there in a haze as I tried to work out my feelings, I had the usual argument with Luke and I just snapped. I took his car and drove right back to the rooftop. I felt so sure this would be it. No returning this time. No backing out. I ended up spending all night up there, looking at the stars, saying goodbye to each individual light. This was it. I could feel it. It felt good. Then the morning came and I looked at the sunrise, my last sunrise, while smoking my last cigarette. I lay back down on the concrete, tracing my fingers along the smiling faces Zoe had tattooed on the ground, and I found myself thinking about her.

About the times she made me smile. About the times we had talked. The times I was able to open up to her. As the end of the cigarette started burning my fingers, I also thought about the time I could have hit her. Then I dropped the cigarette butt, stood up and walked towards the edge. I closed my eyes, and I just breathed.

Then I forgot how to breathe. I panicked, opened my eyes, and I stared down to the drop beneath me.

I realised for the first time in my life that I was uncertain. I'd never felt that before, but I was truly scared. I was thinking about her, Zoe. I was thinking about Luke, about Misha. Suddenly, I didn't know if I wanted to do it. I stumbled back, further away from the edge, but that didn't seem far enough, I could still fall from there, so I took more steps back until I tripped on my own feet and fell back on to the concrete. I lay there, looking up at the clouds as I gasped for breath, my chest compressing, head pulsing. I felt like I was dying, and had to take a second to work out if I'd fallen after all.

That's when I realised I didn't want to die.

This is my life and, as crap as it is, I don't want to leave it. Not when there are people in my life who I love. I can't do that. I don't want to do that.

After I managed to calm myself down, I sat up and

stayed there for ... I don't know how long. I drew a smiley face on the concrete next to Zoe's, and left.

I felt calm.

I sit on my bed with Misha. I carried him up here, because as well as he is getting on with his three legs, he can't climb up the stairs like he used to. On the bright side that means I won't be woken up by his slobbery breath any more. Misha nestles his head into me and I almost well up. I'm so lucky, not only that he survived, but that he's the same stupid mutt. The mutt I love. I push my phone up to my ear as I continue to give Misha attention.

'Hey, Tree.'

I can't help but smile at the sound of her voice. 'Hey, Zoe.'

'You all right?'

'I'm pretty good.'

There's a pause. An awkward pause. Great way to start off a phone call. I rush to fill it.

'Listen, I wanted to explain again how sorry I am – about what I said,' I pause and swallow, 'and that I nearly hurt—'

'Tree, it's fine.'

'No, it's not. I was a dick. I was—'

'It's fine.'

'But ... what I could have done ...'

'But you didn't.'

There's a pause again.

'I ended things with Alice. For good this time,' I say.

Zoe is quiet for a couple of seconds.

'You were right,' I continue. 'I was acting that way because I was avoiding facing up to some other things.'

I think we both know what I was avoiding, though I don't say it. But I don't want to avoid it any more.

'Well ... at least you're facing it now.'

'And I'm sorry about not replying to you, not letting you know I was fine when I didn't come into work for those couple of days – and for going away in the first place, because that was a shitty move. But ... I think I needed it.'

'Well, I'm glad you're sorry – because you should be – but I forgive you,' she says quickly, but I can almost hear the smile in her voice. I want to see her, right now.

'You know I care about you, Zoe.'

'I think I do know that ... now.'

'I want to see you.'

'Turn up to work tomorrow and you can. I'm sure Juliette has something to say to you.'

'I've already spoken to her, she's was fine with me.' I pause, and then add, 'She's nice to me because I'm crazy.'

I hear Zoe laugh. 'I think she's nice to you for another reason.'

Another pause. 'I want to see you now,' I say.

'Okay,' Zoe replies. 'Let's go to Laser Quest.'

318

'Very funny, Zoe.'

'No, I'm being serious, Tree, it'll be open, and I'm not doing anything today.'

'But ...'

'You were right about some things – I am a hypocrite. I'm not really living my life to the full. I'm not doing everything I want to do. But today I want to go to Laser Quest, so if you're up for it ...?'

'I'm up for it.'

'Okay, let's do it.'

Chapter 51

Tristan

We did it all.

Over the next few weeks we found time to go to Laser Quest, go paintballing, go-karting, bowling – Zoe even took me running at the tracks where she used to train. Jesus, she is quick. We decided to live by the 'fuck it' mentality. If we got to the end of the day and there was something we still wanted to do, even if it was too expensive, or we weren't 100% on it, we said, 'Fuck it. Let's just do it.'

And we did.

Zoe has nearly finished her dissertation, too – I've been making her spend a good hour on it before she spends time with me. God knows if I'm any help, but the amount of work she's doing, she deserves to do well.

Today, we planned to go trampolining. Zoe said she's always wanted to. I went along with it, though in my opinion I didn't see trampolining as much of a 'fuck it' thing to do – Zoe has a bloody trampoline in her garden.

But you see, when Zoe said 'let's go trampolining', she didn't mean let's bounce on a small circular trampoline like I have in my garden. She meant let's go to a trampoline park. A warehouse filled with lots and lots of deep, bouncy trampolines from wall to wall. Even *on* the walls. It was what I imagine to be Zoe's idea of heaven.

An extremely tiring heaven. Bouncing on these trampolines doesn't look like much, but God it takes it out of you. It feels like I've done more exercise than I ever have before in my life.

I step off a trampoline, legs shaking, and lean on the railing while I get my breath back.

'You tired?'

I turn around to see a red-faced Zoe, also panting, her chest maybe even heaving more than mine. 'Just a tad,' I say, but even that takes effort.

Zoe grins and opens her hand out to me. 'Let's go to the foam pit.'

Seriously? My legs are begging for a break but I take hold of her hand. 'All right,' I say with a sigh, still trying to get my breath back. 'As long as there is no more bouncing.'

Once we get to the foam pit, I understand why Zoe suggested it. I've not only learnt how fast Zoe is over these last few weeks – nobody could catch her when we were paintballing – but I've also learnt that she has the upper body strength of Conor McGregor. She suggested a competition: Who can hold on to the pull-up bars for the longest? And my arms are dying.

'Is this going to be like the go-karting?' Zoe says smugly, her face as relaxed as someone doing yoga.

'No,' I reply through gritted teeth. I am not letting her beat me again.

'And Laser Quest, don't forget that, too?' she says, poking her tongue out at me.

'It won't,' I struggle to say.

'Let's face it, I always win,' Zoe says as she starts doing pull-ups. How? Aren't her arms on fire? Isn't she feeling a burn travelling all through her body, right to her fingertips? Can't she feel the temptation to let go?

Oh. My arms have decided to give up, and I'm falling, falling, falling and in I go. Once I hit the foam I'm surprised by the lightness of the fall. It's comfortable, almost like floating. I look up to see Zoe, still hanging there with a smug smile, hair tumbling down as she grins at me.

'Watch out, Tree!'

I hear her shortly before I feel the force of her landing on me. 'Shit,' Zoe says. She is lying on top of me, scrambling to turn to face me and causing me to slowly sink into this pit of giant marshmallows. Soon I'm going to be swallowed up. Buried alive. Drowned in foam. But she stays there, on me. Then she lifts her head up, her red, sweaty face looking down at me. She smiles. 'Sorry, I didn't mean to land on you—'

I push my mouth on hers.

I'm kissing her. I'm kissing Zoe, and it feels good. She tastes good. A moment passes before I feel her mouth push against my lips, then she's kissing me back. It feels better than anything I've ever felt before, and I don't want this to end – even if I am aware this is not the most comfortable place to be kissing, and there are definitely a few kids watching us. I just want to concentrate on the feeling of her lips on mine – how soft they are, how gentle, how they . . .

How they have left my mouth. I open my eyes.

Zoe bites her lip, before she smiles at me again. 'I guess . . . I should get off you now,' she says, her breathing heavy.

Or we can stay here. 'Yeah, okay.'

'Do you want to go get food?'

Now I'm the one smiling. 'Food would be good.'

Chapter 52

Zoe

He kissed me. I don't understand it, but he kissed me.

I feel dizzy, out of breath. I feel faint. I feel sick with shock.

He kissed me. My heart is beating hard – properly pounding. I don't know what happens now. But what I do know is Tristan is a bloody good kisser. I felt the spark.

I press my hands on the cool table as I try to centre my vision. I really am feeling dizzy. Either it was the trampolining or the kiss, but something took it out of me. Nothing a bit of food can't solve. Once I manage to blink away the stars in my eyes, Tristan comes back into focus, and he's frowning at me.

'You okay?'

'I'm great,' I say through a smile. 'What about you?'

'Worn out and hungry,' he says, but the corners of his mouth turn up.

'Me too.' I'm even getting a headache. But that doesn't matter because – I don't know if I mentioned it – Tree kissed me.

The waitress comes over, and smiles at us both. 'You ready to order?'

Tristan looks at me. 'Zoe?'

'You first.'

His eyes flick to his menu. I don't think he's even looked at it yet, I know I haven't. I've mainly just been staring at him since we got here, and probably smiling like a lunatic. Glancing down at the menu, I realise I don't even know what this place really serves – after leaving the trampoline centre we wandered straight into the first restaurant we saw. I don't think it was the most important thing on our minds. Well, I know it wasn't for me.

'Erm, I'll have the pizza and a coke please,' Tristan says.

'I'll have the same.' I feel Tristan's eyes on me.

Once the waiter leaves, Tristan raises his eyebrows at me. 'No salad and water?'

I can't help but smile. 'Not this time.'

Tree leans forward, mirroring my stupid grin. 'So . . . ' he says.

'So.'

'I have decided I like the name Tree.'

I smile. 'You do?'

'I think it suits me.'

'It does.'

He chuckles, leaning back in his chair.

'What do you think Tristan means?' I ask him.

'Why would it mean anything?'

'Everyone's name means something. I have a thing about names, don't I? I believe I was called Zoe and you were called Tristan for a reason.'

'You don't think our parents just randomly chose them because they liked them?'

'Maybe they did, but I think they liked them for a reason that they didn't even know themselves. I think our names define who we are in life, who we will be. That's why I want to know what Tristan means and how different it is from Tree. Don't you think it'll be interesting?'

'Not really.'

'I do, I'm going to look it up as soon as I get home.'

'Okay, you do that.'

'Right after this meal, right when I walk through the door.'

'Okay, I trust you will.'

I smile sleepily at him and he smiles back. I'm thinking how nice it is to see him like this, relaxed and content, when his smile starts to disappear from his face. I feel my own expression change. Is he thinking about the kiss?

What if he regrets it?

He probably thinks things will be weird now. Or maybe he's thinking I'm going to make more out of it than what he meant from it.

He probably meant nothing.

He's probably not even thinking about me at all.

Chapter 53

Tristan

I'm going to walk this girl home tonight, and then I'm going to kiss her again.

And again.

If she'll let me – I still don't really know if she liked the kiss. She was the one that pulled away. I know I liked it.

Zoe looks at me questioningly. 'Am I still red?' she says, placing a hand to her cheeks. I shake my head. Because she's not red at all; in fact, she looks quite pale. I notice her chest is still heaving a little. I'm glad I'm not the only one still tired from that brutal trampolining.

'Am *I* red?' I ask.

Zoe chuckles. 'Yeah. Trampolining took it out of you, huh?'

'Sorry, Zoe, not all of us are as fit as you,' I say with a warm smile, nudging her under the table.

'You just need some training, that's all,' she says. The

waiter comes over and gives us our Cokes. Zoe immediately starts gulping it down. Once she's quenched her thirst she cocks her head at me. 'I can train you if you want.'

'All right.'

'Yeah?'

'Yeah, but I'm holding that to you, Zoe.'

'No, but I totally will. We can play badminton. Or do circuit training.'

'Promise?'

'Promise, and I always keep my promises,' she says confidently. 'Maybe we could even train for a colour run.'

I think about that, imagining myself running for fun, and chuckle. I think about how much has changed since Zoe first told me about colour runs, and I see now how Zoe's obsession with the idea makes sense.

As she dives back into her drink, something starts to dawn on me.

I like Zoe. And not only that, I think I have done for a lot longer than I realised. I just needed to get out of my own head to notice it. I was using Alice as an excuse, I was trying to stop from getting too close to Zoe. I thought I would hurt Zoe the way I've hurt myself. But maybe I won't, she gets me more than anyone else. She makes me feel different. I think this will be different.

It won't be awkward that I kissed her, will it? Does she feel the same? Will it be awkward now that I've realised . . . I've realised I . . .

I realise how much of a daydream I've been in when I

328

feel a sharp pressure on my hand and look down to see Zoe slowly and carefully drawing a smiley face on my hand. As she moves towards the mouth it's more wobbly and uneven than normal. 'Smile, Tristan,' she says.

As she brings her hand away, I notice how much it's shaking, in fact both her hands are.

'Are you cold?' I'm still hot from the exercise, and it's stuffy in here, too. There's a pause as Zoe looks down at her hands, staring at them in complete silence. 'Earth to Zoe?'

'No,' she says, looking up at me with wide, expression-less eyes. 'I'm not cold.'

'Oh, well, it's the Coke then. You're not that used to all that sugar. Zoe's got a sugar rush.'

But Zoe doesn't respond. Her smile has fallen and her face is serious. Once she finally moves her eyes away from her hands she lifts her Coke to her mouth, but then pauses as if she's forgotten what she was doing. She stares at it, eyes sunken.

'Excuse me,' she calls out to a passing waiter. She's breathing heavily, resting a hand on her chest. 'Can we have some water please?'

'No problem,' the waiter replies.

Zoe looks like she's concentrating as she places both of her palms on the table, almost as if she's steadying her-self. 'Zoe?'

I don't know if she hears me.

'Hey, Zoe.'

She looks up towards me and forces out a small smile. She looks even more pale now. Maybe it's not just the sugar. 'Are you okay?'

She nods her head, as she brings her hand towards her chest and starts rubbing it. What the hell is she doing?

'Are you sure?

'Yeah, it's just quite ...' She stops to take a heavy breath, then suddenly stands up. 'I'll be right back ... I'm just going to ... I'm just going to go to ...' She breaks off, then tries again, 'I need the toilet ... so I'll be ...'

'Zoe.'

She looks at me. A glint of colour appears on her face, a slow drop of ruby red above her lip, followed by another drop.

'Your ... Zoe, your nose is bleeding.'

She slowly moves her fingers up to her nose where it's coming out faster now, dripping on to her mouth, her chin, her top. 'Oh,' she says.

I quickly pass my napkin to her. She doesn't take it. Her glassy eyes move from her fingers to me.

Then she falls to the floor.

'Zoe!'

I don't think I've ever moved faster as I run over to pick her up from the floor, but her body just flops in my arms. 'Zoe? Zoe, speak to me.' I turn her towards me and her emotionless eyes roll back as her nose continues to bleed, and she lies heavy in my arms. 'Zoe.' I'm shaking her a little, I'm tapping on her face. I don't know what to do.

I cradle her close to me, as I look around the restaurant, people already starting to crowd round. 'Someone help me,' I shout, keeping her close to me. I can't feel her heart beating on my chest. I can't feel her heart. I can't feel it. 'Someone fucking help me. Please. Help me.'

Chapter 54

Tristan

'Can you tell us your name?'

I stare at Zoe as I sit in the ambulance. They are doing all these things to her, putting a mask on, checking her pulse, checking her eyes. Using words I don't understand, putting something around her neck. Strapping her on to the stretcher.

I feel a hand on my shoulder. I quickly shrug it off, turning to face the other paramedic. 'What's your name?' she asks me again. I turn my head back to Zoe. 'Hey, it's okay, hon,' she says. I feel her hand return to my shoulder.

'Tree. My name is Tree.'

'Okay, Dree, has Zoe taken any medication or drugs that you know of?'

She's not moving. Is she breathing? A paramedic is doing something with tubes, as he holds a mask over her mouth.

He's talking to her like she can hear him. 'Zoe, stay with us. Stay with us,' he says.

'Why is he saying that?' I whisper, my eyes not leaving Zoe.

'Dree? Did she take any drugs?'

I'm still staring at Zoe, my eyes fixed on her. 'No.'

'Any painkillers? Paracetamol? Ibuprofen?'

'I don't . . . I don't know.'

'Dree, does Zoe have any medical conditions that you know of?'

I try to think. Has she ever mentioned anything? Diabetes, something like that? But there's nothing I can think of. She's one of the healthiest people I know. 'No. What's wrong with her?'

'Can you tell me the names of her parents?'

'Umm . . . Miller. Jerry and Patrick Miller, I think. No – Paul. It might be Paul. I don't know, I've only met them a few times. Is she going to be okay?'

Before I know it, we've reached the hospital and doctors are pushing her along the corridor, exchanging more terms and words that I still don't understand. They are going fast, and I'm following them fast, until they shut a door in my face. I go to open it but I feel a hand on my shoulder. I turn to see a nurse I haven't seen before.

'It's Dree, isn't it? I'm afraid you can't go in there,' she says.

'What?'

'Hospital personnel only.'

'But I need to be there. You have to let me . . . ' My voice is shaking now.

'If you take a seat, I can get you something to drink.'

I put my hand up against the glass, trying to work out what they are doing in there.

'Dree? Is there any one we can contact?'

She's going to be okay. She's got to be. I put my head on the glass. Please be okay, Zoe.

I said I wasn't going to leave; that means she can't either. Because that's not fair.

Chapter 55

Zoe

'Zoe? Zoe, can you hear me?'

That's Tree. Where is he? I am here. I'm sinking. I'm heavy. Everything is clouding over. Are we still at the restaurant? The last thing I can remember is standing up to go to the toilet. I can't quite ... I can't ... I can't ...

Everything feels so hard. It's so heavy.

'Zoe. Zoe, speak to me. Zoe, speak.'

I can't. I can't, Tree.

'Zoe, honey, can you hear me? My name's Dr Steele. Try and stay with us, Zoe.'

Am I at hospital? I try to open my eyes, but I can't. There's just darkness, a limp heavy darkness.

'Let's carry on with the IV fluids please.'

Come on. You're not some weakling. You're Zoe Miller. Make some noise. Open your mouth. Do something. Say something.

There's a moan. Did it come from me?

'She's responsive. Zoe, stay with us. It's okay, darling. It's okay,' the doctor says, his voice soothing. He seems like a nice guy. I just wish I could see him. 'It's okay,' he says again.

I believe him, but I'm not feeling very okay. In fact, the more I try to respond, the more I realise I can't.

'Can I have a 12-lead ECG please?'

What the hell is that? What's happening? I don't want them to do something they shouldn't. I'm here. I'm here, guys. I push as hard as I can to open my eyes, and that's when the pain hits me. All over my body, chest compressed, arms aching, eyes burning. But wait, my eyes. They are opening. I see a soft blur of blinding white light in front of me.

'Let's get a heart echo, please?'

I think I pushed myself too far. My body is an elastic band that has been pulled too tight, it flings back. And I feel it all in one rush. One final rush as I sink. Not just sink, but fall. 'Can you hear me, Zoe?'

His voice is getting quieter. It's muffled, fuzzy. Where's he going? I want him to stay here.

There is a beeping noise now, but I don't care about that. I'm getting further and further away from it.

'She's in VT.'

'I can't feel a pulse, Doctor.'

'Okay, let's start with compressions, please.'

This isn't like sleep.

'Get the bag and mask on, please.'

I can't feel anything.

'Zoe, I'm with you, okay? I'm here. Stay with me. Come on, Zoe.'

I don't think I can.

' ... 27. 28. 29. 30.'

'Still no pulse, doctor.'

'Okay, let's shock her then, please.'

'Charging.'

'All clear?'

'Clear.'

'Shocking.'

I understand what happened, but I don't remember it. I don't remember collapsing. I don't remember the ambulance. I don't remember the feeling of getting shocked. I don't even remember waking up. Isn't that weird? I don't remember waking up. It's not like the movies where your eyes slowly open to the worried faces surrounding your bed. Instead, one minute you're not there, and the next you are. With this big hole in your memory, and you don't know what happened.

One thing I do know is that I hurt. All over. I can barely

move because it feels like someone is sitting on my chest, cracking my ribs. I have these tiny oxygen tubes sitting in my nostrils and I don't like it. I'm bruised. Achey. I feel light-headed, dizzy. I have needles in both arms, and who knows what the IVs are doing. I feel pathetic.

I hate moaning, it isn't my style. I just hate feeling like this. I hate feeling weak. I hate being weak. I hate not feeling in control. I look across the room to where Jerry and Paul are talking to each other, and Jerry catches my eye and smiles. 'We're just going to get a coffee, all right, sweetheart?'

'Do you want anything?' Paul adds.

I shake my head slowly and carefully. They glance at Dr Steele, before quietly leaving the room. Dr Steele has been hovering over me. 'Okay, well it's all sounding good,' he says, a clipboard in hand.

'I wish I felt good,' I mumble.

I feel Dr Steele's serious eyes on me. 'Are you feeling bad, Zoe?'

I bring my arms into my lap, but even that hurts as my IV pulls on my veins. 'I'm just being dramatic.'

'No, you're not,' he almost chuckles. 'I can arrange to get more painkillers if you'd like?'

'I'm fine.' The last thing I want is more drugs. 'I'm just not feeling very strong at the moment.' My voice cracks. 'I feel ...'

'Scared? You don't have to be strong all the time. You've been so strong for the last few days.'

My lip starts to quiver. 'I could have died … I was nearly dead.'

'You didn't die, Zoe. You got close, but the important thing is you're still here.'

I can feel my nose start to burn. Not this again. I burst into tears when I found out what happened. I never usually cry, what is happening to me? I've been trying to keep it together for Paul and Jerry, but now they're out of the room, I just feel weak. 'I know it's just … I still have a lot more living to do yet. I don't … I don't want to die. Not yet. I still have more to do.'

Dr Steele rests a hand on my shoulder, his blue eyes looking into mine. He has kind eyes. 'And I believe you're going to do that living,' he says, his voice so calm and gentle. 'Your obs are all normal, your heart has regulated. You just need a couple of days and you'll be back to yourself. You're okay, Zoe.'

I take a huge sniff, dabbing at my eyes weakly as I nod my head.

He's right. I'm okay. And even if that had been my time, and I died there in the restaurant, at least I've had a good life. I know I lived every minute of it. I've loved every minute of it, so it wouldn't have been a life wasted. It just would have been a dog's life – by which I mean short but valued. Not so bad, hey? Whatever the doctors say, I'm going to keep living the way I have these past few weeks – the way I used to. I'm going to enjoy my life, do the things I want to do. I'm going to live a good life.

'One of the nurses will be with you shortly,' Dr Steele says, standing up and gently squeezing my arm.

Leaning my head back on to my pillow, I close my eyes. I'm so tired I could fall asleep for years. I hear the door close as Dr Steele leaves. You know what? I might try to get some sleep. I hear the door open again, but I don't open my eyes. It's probably Dr Steele coming back for something he forgot.

Someone touches my hand. What are they doing to me now? I assume it's the nurse, but they don't move. In fact, they wrap their hand around mine and hold on to it tightly.

I open my eyes to see Tristan.

'Tree?' And there I go again – my eyes well up and my mouth starts to tremble.

'Zoe,' he says with an exhale. He is clutching on to my hand with both of his, not letting go and not letting his eyes leave mine. His tired, sunken, shining eyes.

'You look rough, Tree.'

He lets out a small chuckle. 'You don't look so great yourself.'

'I didn't know you were here.'

'I've been visiting every day, but they wouldn't let me in until now.'

I don't really know how many days it's been since I collapsed – all I know is I've been in and out of consciousness and am too tired to work out how much time has passed. Why didn't they let him in sooner? I bet that was Jerry, being his bloody over-protective self.

Tree is still talking, still clutching my hand. 'I . . . I didn't know if you were okay, or ... I didn't know anything. No one was telling me anything. I was worried.'

'You don't need to be. I'm okay, Tree. I'm fine now.'

He brings one hand through his hair. 'I don't understand what happened.'

My heart sinks. So he doesn't know. Do I tell him? If I do, will that change things? How will he feel about me lying to him? Will that mean things will never go back to normal? 'I guess I just passed out, Tree.'

'But your nose was bleeding.'

'That must have been a ...' A side effect of my medication? Or maybe it was my blood pressure. I look up at Tree. I'll tell him. I'll tell him when I get home. It's not that big of a deal anyway. Like the doctor said, I'm okay.

'It must have been a what?' Tree asks.

'I don't know. I guess when I fainted it was more dramatic than I thought.'

His eyes gloss over. 'I think you're lying to me. No one would let me in till now, everyone seemed so worried. People don't "faint" like that.'

I stare at him sadly. I can't keep hiding it.

'You're lying, aren't you?' He watches me carefully, his eyes shining.

I nod my head sadly. 'Tree ... it's a long story ... but I promise I'll tell you ... I'll tell you when we are home, if that's okay? I'm sorry.'

His eyes widen, he immediately moves even closer to me. 'What does that mean? Are you—'

'I'm going to be okay, that's the important thing. I'm going to be fine, I will tell you. But not now, Tree. I'm so tired.'

His forehead is wrinkled in frustration, but he knows he can't argue. 'You promise you're okay?'

'Yeah, I'm dandy.' I offer a weak smile.

Tree exhales a heavy sigh, resigned. He wipes a hand across his face. 'I thought ... I thought ... I don't know.'

'What?'

'Well, I thought you were going to die.'

My mouth curves at the ends. 'Tree, you're not getting away from me that easy.'

'I freaked out. I don't want you leave me, Zoe.'

'Why would I? What would be the fun in that?' Tree makes a sound that's half sniff, half laugh. He looks at me with his confused beautiful face. 'Anyway, you're okay for now, because I don't get bored too easily.'

Tree raises an eyebrow. 'I thought you *did* get bored easily.'

I hook my eyes on to his. 'Something made me change my mind.'

Tree lowers his eyes towards my hand. He lets go. I feel the absence of it. I like him holding my hand. He gets out a pen, God knows from where, and starts delicately drawing on my skin. He's soft and gentle and it almost tickles. I like it but I'm not so sure the nurses will be too pleased. Once he's done he puts the pen away and grins at me proudly. I look down to see two dots and a curved line. A smiley face.

I want to say something. The words start to choke their way up, but get lodged in my throat and stay there. There's a knock from the door and one of nurses from earlier enters, a short stocky type with black curly hair that spews out in all directions. 'Zoe's going to need some rest.'

'I'm fine,' I say weakly, as she trots into the room.

'Sorry, honey, but no visitors for the minute.' She addresses Tree, taking the decision out of my hands.

'It's okay.' Tree nods, standing up. 'I'll just be out there, Zoe.'

'Tree, you're allowed to go home, get some sleep.'

He smiles at me. 'I don't want to. I'm staying out there.'

As he walks to the door I feel an urge run through me, like a fire burning in my chest. I've got to say it. I've got to push those words out of my throat and say it.

'Tree!'

He pauses by the door. 'Yeah?'

'I ... I ... Thank you, Tree. For looking after me.' Tree smiles, and then he leaves, closing the door after him.

Those weren't the right three words. I look at my hand, staring at the wonky smiling face, as I let out a heavy tired sigh. I'll tell him. I'll tell him when I get home.

I'll tell him everything.

Chapter 56

Tristan

My foot loses balance and knocks a small stone. It rolls off the edge and falls. It falls down, and keeps falling until it hits the ground five storeys below. I feel my stomach drop as I shuffle closer. This is it. My feet are hanging over the edge. I'm ready.

'Tristan?'

A gasp sticks in my throat. It's Luke.

I don't turn around.

'Tristan?' His voice is quiet.

'What are you doing here?' I manage to ask, eyes still facing forward.

'Stopping you.'

'You can't.'

'Tristan,' his voice cracks this time as he says my name. 'Don't be stupid, please.' I can hear the desperation in his voice.

'How did you know I was here?'

'I came up here with Zoe once, when we were looking for you. She showed me this place.'

Zoe.

My mouth begins to tremble, and my vision is starting to blur. I'm finding it hard to see. Has the sun set yet, the gloomy colours spreading across the sky, ready for the darkness to take over? I barely know. My whole body is tense, my arms, my legs, my torso, all statue still. It feels like any type of movement will make me fall. And I don't want to fall when I'm not ready – I need to be ready. I look down for the briefest of moments and my stomach drops again. 'It's high,' I hear myself say. I can't remember it being this high last time I stood here. I can't remember it being this high when I was here with her ...

'Tristan, just step down, we can talk.'

The wind is blowing right at me, through my hair, pushing against my body, making it difficult for me to keep my balance. 'Zoe's dead, Luke.'

There's a pause. 'I know, Tristan. I know and it's— It's crap.'

'Fucking awful, it's more than that.'

'It is.'

Zoe died at six forty-seven this morning. Four hours and thirty-two minutes ago. Twelve hours since I saw her last.

She was three weeks away from turning twenty-one. Four months away from graduating. Two weeks away from handing in her stupid dissertation.

345

Her heart gave up on her.

Zoe had something called Hypertrophic Cardiomyopathy. Or HCM, for short. Like it has a bloody nickname. How can something I've never even heard of kill Zoe? According to Zoe's parents – and to Google – it's when your heart muscle is thickened, making the heart stiff. This means it struggles to pump blood around your body. We were never taught about HCM at school. I was taught about cancer, about AIDS and HIV. I know about cystic fibrosis, I know about STIs, I know about diabetes, I even know about lupus, for fuck's sake. Why didn't I know about HCM?

Why didn't she tell me she had it?

It turns out, when I first met Zoe in hospital she wasn't visiting her gran after all. She was having an appointment about getting a pacemaker fitted. All the other times she was 'seeing her gran' were fake as well. She was having check-ups and appointments instead. It turns out they didn't arrange to have the pacemaker fitted quick enough.

And now Zoe is dead.

I wipe a tear from my cheek, looking down again. I'm starting to feel wobbly, like someone has dropped a brick into water and the ripples are running through me. I still haven't turned to look at Luke. What is he doing right now? How close is he?

How long will it take to fall?

Will I feel it?

'It's not fair, Luke. She was so good.'

'I know she was, Tristan.' By the sound of the voice he's making his way towards me, but slowly. Carefully.

'No, not just that. She loved life, she bloody loved it. It's not fair that she died. She didn't deserve to.'

'No, she didn't, but you don't either, Tristan. You don't.'

'I do.' The sun has disappeared now and it's cold up here. I'm trembling and I'm starting to feel dizzy, too, like my body is getting impatient now. 'I'm the one who doesn't even like being alive, it should have been me. It should have been—'

'Tristan, stop it.' Luke's voice is firm now, and closer still, but I can hear the trembling beneath it.

I'm heaving, great big gulps of air. 'I'm the one who wanted to ... I'm the one who wants to die.'

'Tristan ...'

'She was going to do so much. Why did that get taken away from her?'

'I don't know, Tristan, but please just come down, we can talk when you are down here—'

'Why does everyone in our life die?'

There's a pause. The wind has dropped and it's so quiet; I don't even know if Luke's still here. But then quietly he says, 'We always choose the best things.'

'What?' I finally turn my head to look back at Luke. He's a careful distance behind me, standing attentively, almost as if he's the one on the edge.

'We ... we always choose the best things, Tristan.'

Facing forwards again, and holding my hands out either side of me for balance, I quickly shoot one hand up to my face and wipe my cheeks. 'You're not making sense,' I mumble.

'It's like flowers. We always pick the nicest flower, even though we know that once it's picked it'll eventually die.'

I look down at the ground again. It's so far down.

'I think the earth has its pick, too. It chooses the prettiest flowers,' Luke says. 'She was the best of the bunch, you can't deny that, Tristan.'

It sounds like something Zoe would have said. The tears blurring my eyes are too stubborn now for me to blink away.

'Please just come down, Tristan.'

'It hurts,' I whisper. 'It hurts so much.'

'I know.'

I look up. I can see the town lit up in the distance – houses, shops, cars, even tiny people. I can see them all from here. Can they see me? Do any of them feel this way or is it just me?

'I want it to stop.'

'It can. You just need to step down, Tristan.'

'I can't.'

'You can.'

I lick my lips, tasting the saltiness of the tears that by now are covering my face.

'I want to go, Luke.'

'But Tristan, I don't want you to.'

'I can't live feeling like this all day, every day.'

'But if you ...' Luke's voice cracks. 'I don't know what I'm going to do without you.'

Very carefully, I turn around so that I'm still standing on the edge but facing Luke now.

'Please, Tristan,' Luke says, his eyes creasing.

A numbness creeps through my whole body. My feet shake as they try to maintain my balance on the edge.

'You're my brother, Tristan. I can't lose you as well.'

'But I just make things worse for you.'

'No. No. No, you don't, Tristan. We're fucked up. Fucked up together, we can get help. Both of us. We can both get help. But without you, I ... I don't know what ... what ...' Luke pauses and brings his hand up to his face, before quickly bringing it back down. He then holds his hand out to me. 'Please, Tristan.'

I stare at his hand, my fingers itching to reach out and take it. But it's not that easy. Taking his hand doesn't mean I'll get better, that I'm not still mentally ill. It doesn't mean Zoe's not dead. It doesn't mean I know what I'm doing with my life.

'It's you and me.'

I look at Luke's hand again and I feel myself nodding. I take a slow, careful shuffle forward, then another step, holding out my hand to him.

And that's when I slip. My foot catches on the ledge and my heart jumps, as my body collapses down. And I know that I'm going to fall.

But then I feel a hand grab on to me and heave my limp body forwards. Luke keeps a strong grasp of me, pulling me roughly back up towards him and then dragging me into the centre of the rooftop. Once there, he stays holding on to me, resting a heavy hand on my shoulder. 'Tristan?' he says, looking me in the eyes. 'Are you okay?'

I look up to him, and start nodding, but then my nodding starts to sway, and now I'm shaking my head. And I hold on to Luke, and I don't let go.

Chapter 57

Tristan

Life just keeps going.

I go back to work, and it hurts. It's hard to see Ree and Anna chatting in the corridor and not see Zoe there with them, trying to keep up with their gossip. It's hard to see everyone getting on with living their lives, when she's not any more.

It's hard to understand that she will never come back. That I will never see her again.

On my first day back there was someone else on her till, which felt worse than if it had been left empty. You can't act like it hasn't happened, you can't just replace her. There's a tiny indentation of a smile that she etched into the side of the till, and it stares at me, every single day, like a reminder.

No. I will not fucking smile. The only time I've temporarily forgotten the pain has been when I've been

351

wasted, rinsing this feeling out of my head with alcohol, drinking until I can't remember who I am any more, or what's missing.

I go out on walks with Misha in the hope that I might just bump into her, that I might see her walking towards me, no shoes on her feet, hair drenched wet. That she'll come back to mine and get changed. That we can start again.

Sometimes I nearly text her. Even though I never texted her that much in the first place, I was always crap at replying. I should have texted her more.

I place a hot chocolate and an espresso down on the table. Leia looks up at me as she takes her hot chocolate, mixing the whipped cream into her drink. 'Thanks,' she mumbles.

I nervously take a sip of my espresso, hoping it will dull my thumping headache. I think I might still be a little bit drunk from last night.

'So, how are you, Leia?' She just glares at me, as she continues to stir her drink. 'Sorry ... stupid question.' I start getting panicked and fumble my words. 'Are ... Are your parents all right?'

She shrugs her shoulders. 'They're dealing.'

The last time I saw Leia was at the funeral six weeks ago. I remember her, dressed in that pink and yellow dress, a silent tear rolling down her face as the upbeat music echoed around the room. It turned out Zoe had left specific instructions for what she wanted to happen at her funeral, and black was banned – just like she told me it would be. Leia hadn't said one word to me.

I take a deep breath. There's so many things I want to ask. 'Did you know it was coming?'

Leia lowers her eyebrows. 'No, Tree, no one saw it coming.'

Tree.

'It's just, I thought because you guys knew she had HCM . . . '

'That didn't mean she was dying, Tree. It just meant she had to be careful. She understood her life might not be as long as yours or mine, and that's why she loved life so much, why she didn't take it for granted.'

I think about the times I complained about my life to her, about how I wanted to leave everything behind, about how hard I was finding it, about how she didn't understand me – and then there was Zoe with her life-threatening heart condition. 'But that didn't mean she was dying, Tree. People with HCM can live normal, healthy, long lives.'

'But Zoe didn't.'

Leia just stares at me, before sighing. 'Did you want to see me because you want closure, Tree?'

I nod my head. 'I suppose I . . . '

Leia sighs. 'Ask me what you came here to ask.'

'How long had she had it for?'

'She was born with it. But we only found out last summer. We never knew she had HCM until she collapsed after the British Athletics Championships. It didn't make sense, she was one of the healthiest people ever. She nearly died then, Tree.'

'So when did ... how did they ...'

'She had some tests. After an ECG and an MRI they diagnosed her with it. The doctor told her they were going to follow up with tests for medication to control her blood pressure and abnormal heart rhythms. But they told her she would have to have a part in this as well, that she'd need to make some lifestyle changes.'

I rub my hand through my hair uncomfortably. 'She had to give up sport.' It comes out as barely a whisper.

'Yeah, she had to give up competitive sports, athletics training, all of it. She was allowed to do light exercise but nothing that would strain her heart. But for Zoe there was no such thing as light exercise. So that was it, she decided to cut it all out – give up on her dreams, effectively. She even stopped seeing some of her friends – I think they reminded her of what she would never be able to do. I knew it made her angry to see them carrying on with their lives, and that just wasn't Zoe – so she avoided them, deleted their numbers, took them off Facebook.'

'I think we might have seen one of her old friends at a restaurant once.'

'Probably. After she stopped seeing them, she seemed to make a fresh start for herself – to keep her busy more than anything. She got a job at the supermarket, and it helped her to find new friends who didn't know what had happened. She just wanted to keep her head down and start a new life, and I know she didn't want us to worry about her. But I knew she was truly heartbroken. It was like, in giving up sport, she'd broken up with someone, and tried to erase them from her life, but instead she had to see them every day and was reminded of that heartbreak all the time.'

It makes so much sense that I can't believe I didn't work it all out before. I look up to Leia, and take a deep breath. It's all my fault. 'You know, we did loads of activities before she collapsed. I didn't stop her, I encouraged her—'

'It was Zoe's decision to live the way she did, Tristan.'

'But I should have worked it out. I should have stopped her . . .' My head starts to pound as I piece it all together, but Leia raises a hand.

'Stop. You can't blame yourself. That's something I've had to learn. If anything, she was grateful that you reminded her how to live. She was happier in those last few weeks than I'd seen her since . . . ever. How someone so sad helped my sister learn to be happy again baffles me. But that's what you did.

'Zoe was her own person with her own choices. Not long before she died, she sat us down and told us she was going to change the way she was living – her exact words were she "wanted to start living again". She made those choices, knowing the possible consequences. The doctors still don't know exactly what caused her to die when she did, they told us she was stable. As a precaution, they'd brought forward her pacemaker operation to the very next week, just in case she collapsed again, and then the next thing we know her heart has stopped. Stopped for good this time.'

'I don't understand how it could have just happened like that, though.' I don't want to make Leia go over it all again, but I need answers.

'They think she was having symptoms but not telling anyone. But that was just Zoe, she shrugged everything off, she was dramatic in some senses, but then in others not at all.'

'Why didn't she just tell me? I would have treated her differently. I would have made her be more careful.'

'Exactly. She had a condition, Tree, she wasn't *the* condition. HCM didn't make her who she was, it wasn't her whole life, it was just something she dealt with.'

I shove my now shaking hands into my lap. 'I miss her so much, I don't know what to do with myself.'

'Tree, if there's one thing I'm learning, it's that we need to say goodbye.'

I lift my eyes slowly to Leia's face. She's looking straight at me, eyes unblinking, mouth set in a serious line. 'I can't just say goodbye and live my life while she isn't living hers.'

'But that is exactly what you have to do. Zoe had her life and she lived it – it might have been short, but it doesn't mean it wasn't a good one. Because it was, she lived her life to the full, she lived it till the very end. If you could ask her now, she'd say she had a . . .'

'A dog's life,' I mumble.

Leia's face softens. 'Just because Zoe isn't living her life any more, doesn't mean you can't. She wouldn't want that.' There's a pause, then Leia seems to suddenly remember something, because she flicks her eyes down to the floor, picks up her bag and start rummaging through it. 'We developed her last disposable cameras, and we think it's probably better for you to have them.' She passes an envelope to me. 'I mean, they are mainly of you.'

I stare at it in her hand. 'I don't want them.'

Leia rolls her eyes at me. 'Just take the pictures.'

I slowly move my hand forward and take the envelope from Leia. I hold it nervously in my shaking hand while Leia continues to root through her bag. 'I've got something else for you.' She shoves some grey clothes into my hands. 'I assume they're yours?'

They are mine. I'd forgotten about them – my tracksuit bottoms and my top. Without thinking I bring the clothes up to my face. They smell of her, and it makes me smile.

'I loved your sister,' I say through trembling lips. 'It took me a while to work it out, but I loved her. I'm sorry she never knew that.'

I feel a hand on my shoulder. 'I think she did know. But even if she didn't, she loved you anyway.'

Chapter 58

Tristan

Luke drives me back from meeting Leia in town. It's dark out and the rain is pattering against the window. I pick up the envelope of photos again. I just hold it in my hands, staring. Staring and breathing. Breathing and staring. And then I open it, take out the pictures and look down. A gasp gets stuck in my throat as I look at the first picture – a close-up that Zoe somehow managed to take of herself the night of the party. It hurts to see, I don't know why it does. At the end of the day they're only pictures, pictures of Zoe, pictures of me, pictures I didn't even know she took, pictures where she looks even more beautiful than I remember.

It's the last one I gaze at for the longest. I can feel Luke shifting his eyes between me and the road, but he stays quiet. He's letting me have my moment. It's not the last photo we took together, but to look at it feels like a physical slash across the chest. In the photo, I'm at her house. It's clear from my dazed eyes, looking somewhere off camera, that I wasn't ready, but that's not what hurts about this. What hurts is that just before she took the photo, she had turned and kissed me on the cheek. I remember how confused I had been in the moment, even a bit annoyed at Zoe's constant weirdness and unpredictability. But now, all I want is for her to kiss me again.

It happens like a switch. A broken one at that. As memories of Zoe crowd into my head, things start to get dark. It's like my light won't turn back on, it refuses to. It doesn't want to light the room, it wants it to be swallowed up with the engulfing darkness of the night sky. It won't switch back on.

I move my hand up to my throat. It feels like something has tied itself around my neck. But nothing's there, so why does my throat feel so— So tight. I don't think I'm breathing. I can't breathe. I quickly unplug my seat belt, and twist myself free from the strap, but that doesn't help. I can feel Luke's eyes on me. I seem to be panting for air, gasping, so why doesn't it feel like I'm breathing? Am I choking?

'Tristan? You okay?'

'It's too hot in here. It's too hot.' I run down the window and feel cold air and rain hit my face. It's not doing anything. I still can't breathe. But I can feel the wind, I can feel the water, so this horrible nightmare is real. This is happening.

Am I dying? Is this what it feels like? Is this what Zoe felt?

'Tristan?'

I start shaking my head, still gasping. I try to slow my breathing down, but it just gets quicker and quicker. I'm gasping so much now that it feels like I'm gagging.

'Shall I pull over?' Luke's voice is distant in my ears.

My chest feels like it's crushing in. It's crushing me.

'Are you going to be sick?' Luke says.

I nod my head. That's it. I'm going to throw up. My stomach is clenching, the pressure building, and I'm going to be sick. I think we've stopped moving now, but I can't seem to move my body.

'Tristan, talk to me.' I feel Luke touch my shoulder. I instantly shrug it off, wrench the door open and run outside, despite the rain slapping my face. It's not helping but I keep running. I want to run until this feeling stops. I want to run out of my body, I want to run out of myself. I want to leave.

'Tristan!'

My legs stagger and force me to stop, crouching over on myself, my eyes on the floor.

'Stay ... stay ... Don't come close,' I manage to gasp.

There's rain falling on my head, but I can't feel it. Was I poisoned? Am I having a heart attack? It seems impossible that I've lasted this long without breathing. I see Luke's feet in my vision, he's standing opposite me.

'I can't ... I can't ... I'm not ... I'm not breathing, Luke.'

'Tristan, you are breathing.' I shoot my eyes to look up at him, getting gradually wetter in the rain. I shake my head. 'Tristan, you *are* breathing. It's okay. I think you're having a panic attack. You just need to slow it down, breathe with me, it's okay.' Luke takes a deep breath in, and then slowly releases. 'Come on, Tristan, do it with me.'

I try to copy him, and take a deep breath, hold it, and then exhale. We do it again, and then again, and by the fifth time, I'm able to straighten up, and feel the oxygen hitting my lungs. And I can walk. I can breathe. I can function.

Whatever it was, I've never felt that in my life. I've been to the bottom and back, but I've never felt that. Not when Dad died. Not when I lost it at work. Not when I quit uni. Not when I drove myself into the river. Not when I got sectioned. I look at Luke standing opposite me, keeping careful distance. I feel like I could collapse at any moment, but I'm breathing. He is utterly soaked, his shirt almost see-through, his hair flat, and the tip of his nose collecting rain drops. 'Are you all right now?'

I shake my head.

'Luke,' I mumble. My teeth are chattering. I'm not so hot any more. 'I'm not okay, Luke. I think ... I think I need help.'

'Help?'

I nod my head.

Luke nods his head in return. 'Yeah, we can do that. It's okay. We can do that.'

'I need help.'

'We'll get you help.'

Chapter 59

Tristan

beep
  beep
  beep
  beep

I ignore my alarm until it goes off again at 6.20 a.m., when Luke takes my duvet and throws it down the stairs. I slump into the kitchen to be greeted by a breakfast of orange juice, fruit and porridge. I sit at the table across from Luke.

It's been six months since Zoe.

I struggled. Even after meeting with Leia, I was finding it hard to accept things, and get on with life. I found myself questioning everything. Work: what was the point? Going out: why should I get to have fun? Life: why do I get to create memories when Zoe never will?

I went back to hospital again, it was voluntary this time. There was no screaming and kicking, no sedation, just me signing the papers, walking in, and walking out two weeks later. I needed it. It helped me because I wanted to be helped this time. And I'm well now – I'm back on antidepressants, and I'm taking them this time. I talked to the doctor about how they made me feel, the side effects, the thoughts in my brain, and he prescribed some different ones, ones that should help me, not hurt me. I don't know how to explain it, but these ones make things easier, without taking me away. I'm still Tree.

It doesn't mean that I'm not depressed any more. I have my good days – a lot more than I used to, in fact – but there are bad days, too. I still believe my depression is always going to be a part of me, but I accept that now. I'm learning to cope. When I'm going through a rough patch, people often tell me to take it one day at a time – but they don't realise how long a day actually is. It's twenty-four hours, 1440 minutes, 86,400 seconds. So taking it day by day is hard. Instead, I focus on getting through the next twenty minutes. That's how long an episode of *Rick and Morty* is. That's how long it takes to take Misha around the park. And then once I get through those twenty minutes, I focus on another twenty minutes, because that isn't so long. I keep doing twenty minutes by twenty minutes and before I know it I've gone through an hour, half a day, a whole day, and it's all right, it's okay, it works.

'This is for you.' Luke slides an envelope across the table.

I open it, butterflies rising in my tummy.

It's from the University of Surrey. My old uni. Zoe's uni. I applied to retake my last year, and this letter has just confirmed I will be returning. I close my eyes, silently absorbing this moment and look to Luke.

'Next year is a-go?' he asks.

I nod my head. I can feel my leg already lifting up and down with nerves. This seems to entertain Luke as he scoffs a laugh in between a mouthful of porridge. Then he says, 'Sally is coming today, by the way.'

Sally's still putting up with us. God knows how, but I feel a lot better knowing she's going to be there today. I look at Luke and smile slightly in acknowledgement. Me and Luke, well … we're still me and Luke, so we do still have arguments. I have my problems, he still has his. I still smoke, and get angry; he still drinks more than he should. But we're getting better. Better doesn't mean straight back to how it was before Dad died, or back to normal. Better means improvement, and that's what is important. We're improving.

He's been taking me to the gym, started training me up. And exercise has helped me a lot, not just physically but emotionally. It's my way of clearing my thoughts. I know now why Luke has such a love for it. And Zoe, too.

Luke scrapes back his chair. 'We better get going, it's an hour's drive.'

After a two-hour journey (Luke lied) we get there. There are loads of other people dressed in white, like we're at Wimbledon. I look down at my own white T-shirt and white shorts. I suddenly don't feel so stupid any more. I move over to the desk where people are signing in, a short lady smiles at me and looks down at the list of names. 'What's your name, my dear?'

I look down and see my name bang in the middle of the paper. I place my finger on it and the lady follows with her eyes. 'Tree?' she says questioningly.

'Yeah ... that's me,' I say. I look over my shoulder to check Luke hasn't abandoned me to talk to one of the groups of girls doing stretches. No. He's still here.

'Okay, here is your pack.' She hands me a paper number, which I pin to my top. 'Go join the others, we'll be starting shortly.' I give her a short nod. 'And I love your name!'

I feel my eyes move to the floor. 'Thanks,' I mumble.

Once Zoe died, I found myself thinking a lot about what she used to say, the things she did. I thought about what she said about names, and I think I agree with her. I think our names can have meanings. Maybe we are sometimes set out to be a certain person from birth, maybe it is fate. I don't know if it's true. I've just had a lot of thinking space recently.

I looked up Zoe's name. It means 'alive', or 'life'. Zoe, the girl whose own heart killed her, had a name that meant *life*. When I read that, I felt so angry. Was the world taking the piss?

But then I came back to it a couple of weeks later, and I realised her name couldn't have been more perfect for her. Because Zoe made life worth living. She made me and everyone she knew *feel* alive. I know that was special. She showed me to how to live.

I often wonder what Tristan means. But I'm not going to look it up, because I'm not Tristan any more. I'm Tree. I'm going to be the person Zoe saw in me. Like Zoe said, trees are good things on earth, helping us live, helping us to breathe, and making the world a more beautiful place. That's what Zoe did. I want to be the person she was, to affect people the way she affected me.

'Do some stretches, Tristan!'

I look up at Luke and shake my head. He has his number on now, and is jogging on the spot looking like an absolute tool. Then I spot Sally weaving through the crowd and making her way up to him. He leans down to give her a hug. As I reach them Sally sees me and immediately wraps her arms around me, before pulling back and looking straight at me, a proud smile on her face. 'Have fun, sweet,' she says with a smile.

'I'll try,' I say nodding my head. Then, over her shoulder, I see a brown tuft of curly hair walking towards me. It's Joe. We've resumed our weekly trips to the pub recently, and when I told him about today he said he'd come along – not that I thought he actually would. He walks up to me, embracing me in a big hug, and for what feels like the first time since I got this illness in my head, it's like old times.

'You came,' I mumble, a little awkward.

'I keep my promises, dude.' Joe's eyes crinkle.

I pull back, his words stirring the butterflies in my stomach. Well, this is my promise. There's an announcement over a tannoy and I look around as everyone starts heading towards the starting line.

I feel so nervous. But this is for her. This is for Zoe.

We had a story, short, but not a simple one. I wouldn't be able to stay here and explain it all to you. I wasn't the nicest to her. And it pains me to think that her last couple of months were some of the times where I hurt her the most, but I was unhappy because I was unwell – and being unwell is what took me to the hospital, and maybe if I never was in the hospital I wouldn't have met Zoe in the first place. She called it fate. I call it my time with Zoe. The girl whose heart didn't work taught mine how to. I'm glad I didn't give up. My heart's beating because of Zoe, so it's only fair that I keep it beating on for her.

Everyone starts running, I didn't hear the call to go, maybe I was too distracted. So I quickly start moving my feet, glancing round to check that Luke is by my side. He is, he's here. He flashes me a smile as if running is easy. I already feel out of breath. That's smoking lungs for you. I hear some shouts and whoops of happiness from the group in front, and my stomach flips. Zoe was always so loud, so happy, so bright. Is that something you're born with? Or something you create?

I'm not sure. What I do know is that she was a strange one, but all the best people are.

I feel my first hit of colour. Someone throws powdered paint and it hits me right in the face, goes in my mouth, my hair, across my arms and legs, but I keep running. I hear Luke laughing next to me. I think he's been hit too. I look down to see how much paint is on me, and I feel myself smile. It's my favourite colour.

Acknowledgements

I want to start with all my family. Big thank you to Mum and Dad for your support. Mum, your words 'Your time will come eventually' have pushed me through rejection after rejection. Thank you to my brother, Henry, for taking my author picture and letting me blast my writing playlist day after day. Thank you to my sister Grace for allowing me the weeks when I should be working on our channel to transport myself back to Tree and Zoe's world. You have a lot of support for me. Thank you to both Nan and Gran, who always showed interest in my writing, and both cried on the phone when I told them about my book deal. A big thank you to my Auntie Lucie, who spent month after month reading my first novel, editing it, and helping me. It meant so much.

I want to say thank you to Julia Sanderson, who also took so much time to read the second novel I wrote, and I will always appreciate it. I don't believe I would have got here without your help.

I want to thank my lovely big group of friends, who dealt with my constant book update messages, and all my book questions. You were always quick to give helpful advice on this writing journey. I feel a lot of love from you all, and hope Tree can have friends only a fraction like you one day.

I want to thank my old management, for putting in the effort and time to contact publishers. Thank you, Juliette, for getting me to the meeting, for editing my submissions, for being one of the few people to read my work, I believe Little, Brown wouldn't have known about my novel without your help.

Thank you, Manpreet, even though you were only my editor at Little, Brown for a short time. I valued it a lot, and respect that you were the one who took the chance on me. You brought *Every Colour Of You* to life – quite literally, as the beautiful title is your work. Thank you.

Thank you, Abby, for being the most amazing and cool editor I could ever ask for. You are just as connected to Tree and Zoe and the rest of the characters as I am. You have helped me transform *Every Colour Of You* into the story I want it to be. Thank you for dealing with my constant silly questions, and numerous spelling mistakes, again and again. I have loved our process of writing this book. It's been amazing!

Thank you also to Amy, Stephanie, Thalia and Cath, and the rest of Little, Brown, for all the work you've done on my book, and letting it be part of the Little, Brown team, spreading my little story out there in the world.

Thank you to Green Day for letting Tree be totally inspired by you, or at least in Zoe's eyes.

Thanks to my boyfriend Pete, someone who is always quick to praise my achievements to me and other people. You believe in every aspect of my writing, allowing me to spend many evenings typing away at your house and always encouraging me to fuel my creativity. You are very important.

And I can't finish this without saying thank you to my viewers, for following and encouraging me year after year. I appreciate that ongoing support from you.